EVOCATUS

EVOCATUS

a novel

BURKE SPEED

Ambassador International
GREENVILLE, SOUTH CAROLINA & BELFAST, NORTHERN IRELAND

www.ambassador-international.com

Evocatus: A Novel

©2020 by Burke Speed
All rights reserved

ISBN: 978-1-62020-730-7
eISBN: 978-1-62020-749-9
Library of Congress Control Number: 2020938641

Cover Design and Interior Typesetting by Hannah Nichols

This is a work of fiction. Names, characters, and incidents are all products of the author's imagination or are used for fictional purposes. Any resemblance to actual events or persons, living or dead, is entirely coincidental. Any mentioned brand names, places, and trademarks remain the property of their respective owners, bear no association with the author or the publisher, and are used for fictional purposes only.

THE HOLY BIBLE, NEW INTERNATIONAL VERSION®, NIV® Copyright © 1973, 1978, 1984, 2011 by Biblica, Inc.® Used by permission. All rights reserved worldwide.

AMBASSADOR INTERNATIONAL
Emerald House
411 University Ridge, Suite B14
Greenville, SC 29601, USA
www.ambassador-international.com

AMBASSADOR BOOKS
The Mount
2 Woodstock Link
Belfast, BT6 8DD, Northern Ireland, UK
www.ambassadormedia.co.uk

The colophon is a trademark of Ambassador, a Christian publishing house.

For Pap-Pap, A-ma, and the twins . . . we can't wait to see you on the other side.

Evocatus

1: a soldier in the Roman army who has served out his time and obtained a discharge but has voluntarily enlisted again at the invitation of the commander

2: a veteran called again to service

PART I
DREAMS

CHAPTER 1

When I left home my mom told me there'd be difficult days, but she never told me there'd be days like this. Honestly, we probably would've had her medicated if she had. It just goes to show that there's more to this life than meets the eye.

* * *

The little bell tinkled as I stepped into the gas station's mini-mart. I stood motionless and looked around the place, my head full of fuzz and my nerves tingling the way they used to, you know, before.

Why am I here?

A small light flickered in the dim recesses of my mind.

Hmm. I'm . . . here to get something. No, that's not right. I'm here for . . . some-*one*?

I shook my head, trying to clear it.

Yeah, Jamie. That's not weird at all. Going "person shopping" now? Why would I possibly need to look for somebody in a mini-mart?

And yet I settled in place, stock-still, heart bumping an insistent beat. I kept watch, carefully scanning the store over the rows of products. I numbly registered that they had everything from motor oil to Milky Ways, two-day-old burritos to bubble gum. Everything except . . .

Why wouldn't it come to me?

The cashier and the store's patrons paid me no mind. In fact, no one had looked up since I strolled in. It was almost like I wasn't even there.

Whatever.

I exhaled a long breath and waited.

Even at five foot nine, I had no problem seeing over the tops of the rows of gas cans and air fresheners. There weren't that many people in the store, which allowed me to carefully inspect each face.

That seems an odd thing to do, right? But that was my move when I was spooked, and for some reason my senses were on high alert. In my previous job, I'd spent a lot of time reading people. One of the first indicators of something wrong wasn't what people did, or even what they said . . . it was their eyes.

The nearest person, a four-and-a-half-foot-tall geriatric lady with blue hair and thick glasses, studiously consulted the back of a container of antacids. Her lips were moving slightly as she read the instructions, her age-spotted hands trembling slightly. She reminded me a bit of my grandmother's friends, and her crinkled, kind eyes told me she wasn't the one I was looking for.

A young couple shopped two rows over from where I stood. The guy looked like he had stepped out of an Abercrombie & Fitch advertisement, and the girl was similarly dressed. Their full attention was devoted to the magazine rack and the rows of beautiful people staring back at them from the covers of the magazines. Neither of them looked up from their evaluation of *L.A. Style*. Both seemed oblivious to their less-than-glamorous surroundings, and their eyes were bored. I moved on.

The one other customer in the store stood in the back by the beverage cooler. Though he was about the same height as me and appeared to be in his twenties, it was difficult to be sure. He was dressed in blue jeans, dull tennis shoes, and a dark T-shirt, and his persona was, well, unremarkable.

His hair was short, as black as his T-shirt, and he had a small, angular face to go with it. He acted as if he was carefully considering what type of potato chip to buy. He had his hand to his chin and was studying them like a selection of precious diamonds.

As if.

I mean, really. How tough can it be to choose between onion-flavored and spicy?

For no conscious reason, my heart began to bang like an artillery piece, and my hands involuntarily clenched into fists. My stare burned into him for a moment longer, and when he looked up, our eyes met.

We have a winner.

He gazed back at me, and in a fraction of a second his demeanor morphed from one of passive indifference . . . to something terrible.

His black eyes locked onto mine with an intense hate that felt endless.

Then he smiled. Well, I guess you could call it a smile, but it was actually somewhere between a smirk and vicious grin. Whatever you call it, my blood ran cold.

As he kept his gaze fixed on me, he tilted his head forward, then turned it slightly left and right. I felt like prey being appraised by a predator. He calmly stepped from behind the shelves. What I saw next froze me in place.

He held a dark, three-foot-long sword.

Okay, I admit that it was weird enough to see a dude carrying a sword in a mini-mart, looking like a lost child of the Manson family. But the sword itself was morbidly fascinating. It was black. I mean, really black, from tip to hilt to handle, so much so that it kept disappearing in the shadows.

He swung it back and forth, nicking the floor and spewing sparks.

"You're a pathetic joke!" he boomed in a voice much bigger than his body.

It's embarrassing, but I honestly did one of those quick look-behind-you-for-someone-else things to see who he was talking to. Yep, there was no one behind, or anywhere near me, and my awkward glance just made him laugh. At least I think it was a laugh. It came out as a deep, sinister noise that made the hair on the back of my sweaty neck stand on end.

"You shouldn't have come here. I guess I'll kill you," he said very matter-of-factly.

Wow. Right to the point.

The mocking grin still on his face, he took a step closer to me, swinging the sword back and forth. It was mesmerizing in its own dreadful way.

Congrats, Jamie. You found what you were looking for. Now what?

Eyes darting, brain on hyperdrive, I quickly glanced around the store. Lady Blue Hair and the Abercrombie Twins didn't seem to notice what was going down. In fact, it was clear that they neither heard nor cared what was going on between Lord Dark Sword and me.

With the old lady, I could understand if her vision and hearing weren't what they used to be. But I was at a loss to explain the rest of the group's collective lack of reaction.

We've got bystander laws here, people! Sheesh.

Well, if they weren't friends of mine, hopefully they weren't enemies, either.

A detached part of my brain tried to process the whole thing. Why *was* I looking for this guy in the first place, and why did he want to kill me? And what is up with the sword?

To complicate things, I began to feel angry. Really angry. Not a someone-stole-my-parking-spot-at-Walmart kind of anger, though. A righteous fury coursed through my body like I was full of some sort of primal, crackling energy.

Though I had every reason to feel fear, I was confident and kept my gaze steady on his soulless eyes. My stare-down did not impress Dark Sword. In fact, he laughed again.

He looked me up and down with hunter's eyes and slowly shook his head. He even made a guttural noise that sounded like a "tsk, tsk." Suddenly, he drew a deep, raspy breath and set his lips in a snarl.

He ran straight at me.

He covered half the distance before I could register what was happening. Dark Sword was a blur of motion, his blade twirling above his head, a grotesque noise escaping his lips. He covered the remaining steps and swung his sword at my head.

In that half-second, I did something really ridiculous. I smiled.

No, that isn't right. I grinned. I grinned the way you do when you are about to level a guy on a football field and he doesn't see it coming.

He brought his blade down in a screaming arc, that sick, snarling grin still on his face. He swung the sword like an axe, using every bit of his weight to try and kill me. You could say he was enthusiastic.

I moved, but all it took was a slight lean to the left.

His blade swept an inch away from my right cheek. I could feel the frostbite-like cold of his blade and hear small *snaps* of some of my stray hairs being cut. My barber might not be happy, but otherwise the blade passed harmlessly off my right side.

Aided by a foot I left in his way, he tripped as he flew past.

The result was a sidelong crash into the ice cream machine, which scattered sets of cups and rows of bubble gum. His unstoppable momentum flipped him over the counter headfirst, and he landed in an ungraceful tangle of arms, legs, foul language, and vanilla ice sprinkles.

Even though the guy almost caught a sword tip in the chin, all of this went unnoticed by the cashier, who was less than two feet away. So strange. I didn't have time to ponder, though.

Dark Sword wasn't done.

Hands tingling, eyes padlocked, I took a few steps away.

He rose from behind the counter, then slowly crawled over the ledge. He looked really unhappy. He also looked a little different, at least for a moment, and not in a good way.

If I didn't know better, it was almost as if his face flickered a couple of times. His features jumped back and forth between somewhat normal ones and another face that looked, well, grotesque.

His mug had not been much to look at in the first place, but the face I thought I saw looked drastically worse. It was like the skin on his face had melted and then refrozen, and each of his teeth grew half an inch into sharpened points. His eyes turned soot black, as if filled with death.

My brain had barely registered the sight when he flickered back to normal. The change froze me for a moment.

"Dude! Seriously?" I said in disgusted wonder.

Not helpful.

His body tremored in anger and he snarled at me. His chest heaved and I could see a pulse pounding in the side of his head. At least it wasn't the melted-face version. Nasty.

Then something else changed. His body tensed and his eyes flashed.

He stared at me but not my face. He gawked at my right hand.

At first I thought, No, you're not going to get me with the whole, I'm-looking-at-something-so-you'll-look-away-and-be-an-idiot thing . . . but he kept staring.

I knew better than to look away, but his eyes were locked by my side, and his expression gave traces of . . . what? Fear?

I couldn't help it. I stole a quick glace down by my side.

There, in my right hand, was a sword.

Not just any sword, but a gold-handled, silver-bladed beauty that actually gave off a pale white light. I had no idea where it came from or how it got to my hand. It felt perfectly balanced and almost hummed with its own energy. It shouldn't have, but it seemed familiar and comforting.

I looked back at Dark Sword and shrugged. "Them's the breaks, dude."

I was surprised that I wasn't surprised by a sword showing up in my hand, if that makes any sense at all. It just seemed right.

I don't know what was going through his mind, but his body's tremors heightened into a quake and his growl turned into a scream. For a brief moment, he was melted-face-sharp-tooth guy, and then not. Despite the flash of fear in Dark Sword's eyes, he rushed me again.

He was more careful this time. He wound up like he was going to go all lumberjack with his sword again. At the last second, he tried to turn it into a horizontal swing. He kept a little distance as he swiveled, transforming the chop into a flat stroke, as if to separate me into halves.

Our swords met in a shower of sparks.

I don't know how I knew how to do it, but I easily parried the attack. It came naturally to me, like I had been born for it.

Cool.

He started swinging, slicing, and stabbing at me. Even though he scattered two shelves' worth of canned goods in the process, he couldn't get past my defenses. My sword was a bright blur, matching his black blade, flares of muted fire marking each blow. I was patient, content to defend for the moment, already thinking of the end.

After a minute of frantic attack, his coal-like eyes bulged. His growling gave way to panting. His swings became more desperate, especially when he noticed I was driving him toward the corner of the store. There was already little room to maneuver, and I was taking even that away.

The panic that first showed in his moves registered on his face. His brow furrowed and his eyes darted, apparently looking for an escape. I guess I should have felt sorry for the guy.

Nah. Not so much.

Instead, I was serene. I eluded his swings and began to test his defenses. A jab here, a slice there. He met them all but was sloppy.

He was fatigued and obviously wanted a way out. You could tell he thought he was being sneaky, though. He kept scooting toward the door with each swing.

As if I wouldn't notice.

At long last, he faked a rush at me and took one last mighty swing. Apparently, he hoped that would give him room for a quick exit. He dove for the door.

Great idea, bad execution.

He hastily reached with his free hand toward the door, trying to escape. By doing so he left that extremity exposed. Without hesitation, I chopped down with my silver blade, severing his extended arm just below the elbow.

Instead of the limb bleeding or falling off, the flesh below his elbow disintegrated into ash and then disappeared. Seriously, specks just melted like snow on a hot day. It would have been sort of cool to watch, if it hadn't been for the screaming and hollering.

For such a little dude he had some lungs.

He cradled the stump against his body and began to curse me in a foreign language. I actually understood some of it, too. It wasn't very nice.

My ADD must have really kicked in for a second because I was distracted by the lack of leftovers from his arm. No blood, just a few fading flecks of black left here and there. So weird.

Focus, Jamie! I shook my head and looked back up at Dark Sword.

He was still breathing hard and holding his stump. He stared directly into my eyes. Then he said something very strange in a chilling, deep voice. "Let me go, and maybe we let you live. Else, you die with the others. Make your choice, boy."

I heard what he said but didn't understand what he meant. I got the "we'll kill you" part, but what *others* was he talking about, and who was he calling "boy"?

I took a deep breath and looked to the ceiling. What are my options? Hmm.

I was never very good with multiple choice questions, but I thought I knew the answer to this one. I took a step toward him and looked him in the face. "I vote for the not letting you go part . . . boy."

I swung my sword in a broad arc, instinctively letting loose a battle cry.

Eyes panicked and, still gripping his black sword, he sluggishly raised his good arm to ward off the strike. It was too late.

My sword caught him squarely below his jaw. It passed cleanly through his neck as if it met no resistance at all. His body exploded into dust and ash, and his sword vaporized like a breath on a cold winter day, disappearing with the last vestiges of his body.

CHAPTER 2

Heart hammering, I opened my eyes and took stock of my surroundings. Gone was the mini-mart. Good. Gone was Dark Sword dude. Even better.

I was home.

I carefully scanned the room from the relative safety of my bed. Old dumpy furniture . . . Check. Wall full of pictures of life I left behind . . . Check. Clock rudely insisting I get out of bed . . . figures.

I took a deep breath and stared at the overhead beams for a minute, vaguely aware of the insistent *WAH . . . WAH . . . WAH . . .* of my alarm.

I was shaken. And shaking, for that matter. The aftereffects of adrenaline would wear off soon enough.

But seriously? What was that all about?

Okay. That had to have been a dream. That's the logical explanation. You don't get attacked by a sword wielding crazy-face in the middle of a store and wake up in your bed if it's not a dream. There's gotta be a rule about that somewhere.

Something didn't add up, though.

If it was a dream, it was unlike any I had before. I could still see everything in startling detail in my mind, including my sword. If I didn't know better, I could even believe that my foot was a little sore on the spot where I had tripped Ugly-Face. To my knowledge, no other dream had ever left me with high-def playback and bruises. But if it wasn't a dream, that could only mean I was losing my mind. Or something infinitely worse.

Get a grip. You probably just had one too many burritos with secret sauce. Let it go.

Right. That was probably it. Anyhow, I had enough issues in my life without adding psychotic episodes to the list.

I could almost hear my old drill instructor sarcastically yelling at me, *The room is clear, hero! You may exit your foxhole.*

Fine.

I drug myself out of my bed and slapped at my alarm until it stopped bothering me. I really didn't enjoy getting up early, but I was used to it. For better or worse, a few years in Uncle Sam's Air Force changed me. Getting up early every day is one of the lesser changes, really.

My right knee ached as I limped toward the bathroom, which is another change, courtesy of the same Uncle Sam. I took some shrapnel to the leg and I didn't heal fast enough, or well enough, to suit the powers that be. So the military kicked me to the curb and wished me well after just a few years of service. In the end, a small piece of metal in said knee, some mild hearing loss, and fading pictures were all that remained of those days.

At least that was what I thought until that night.

Given all that had happened to me, I always considered myself blessed to have come out of some tough situations in one piece. I prided myself on being a well-adjusted member of society. But now, I was beginning to wonder . . .

Come on, Jamie. Snap out of it, dude!

Right. Get some coffee and a couple of aspirin and all would be right as rain. Keep going.

One glance at my watch told me I didn't have time to dwell on it, anyway. I had to get to work. Step one, brush teeth!

I quickly fell into my comfortable morning routine, but a passing glance in the mirror didn't do any favors for my self-esteem. My brown hair was tangled, I had day-old stubble and there was something of a pained look in my greenish eyes. I stared at my troubled reflection for only a few seconds, then moved on.

After a couple of minutes, my mind began to clear and I actually felt better. I hopped in the shower and immediately washed my hair. Because it was pretty short, it didn't take long, but I did an extra rinse when I noticed little pieces of black dirt going down the drain.

Huh. I could have sworn I got clean after work yesterday. Well, the wind was blowing pretty hard and that one crew blew jet exhaust all over us. I must have missed a spot. Yeah, I guess that's it.

I really should have paid attention to the touch of mental dissonance I had right then. My brain was trying to tell me something, but I was too busy to listen. Or maybe I didn't just want to hear it. Either way, I missed the proof that my world had just changed.

* * *

I had to hustle to make it to work on time. The previous night's foray to the corner store of crazy had me distracted, and I left a little later than usual. I skipped my morning coffee, gunned my little sedan out of the apartment complex parking lot, and tried to make up for lost time.

I had the windows down that morning and the cool, late-summer air helped clear my head. The faint smell of pine was naturally comforting, at least for those of us who grew up in the south. The sun was already threatening to peek above the horizon. Though it was a beautiful sight, I couldn't properly slow down and appreciate it. I hate being late for things, especially work.

I did well until I hit the line of cars waiting to get into the gate at Columbus Air Force base. It took only a couple of minutes to get through, but that kind of thing feels like hours when you're running late. The gate guard gave a friendly wave as I passed. You got to know the early morning crew at this little base pretty quickly, and it was nice to see a welcoming face.

I swerved into the parking lot and my tires made little *chirps* when I stopped.

I might just make it on time, after all. Whew.

The irony of working on a military base wasn't lost on me. When the Air Force said adios, they thought they were done with me. They were, sort of. But I needed a job, and I loved airplanes.

As luck would have it, there happened to be a big flying training base in my hometown. I applied for an open contract maintenance job, and they picked me. That was how I found myself working with the flight line crew.

I jogged from my car to the building with a big T-38 on the side of it. I always felt lucky to work on the T-38s, as they were the closest thing to fighter jets that Columbus had. As I reached the entryway, the sun just crested the tree-lined horizon, its rays sparkling off of the sleek jets' paint.

Man, they were pretty.

I burst through the door and joined the crowd moments before our supervisor began speaking. Peggy, the crew's secretary/mother-figure/enforcer, saw me and raised her eyebrows in concern. She eased over to where I stood as the supervisor began roll call.

Her dangly earrings swayed as she leaned over and whispered, "Are you okay, hon?" She was way too sharp for her own good, if you ask me. Maybe I just thought that because we could never get anything by her.

I winked and whispered back, "I'm okay, just a big night." Her eyelids narrowed and she stared at me for a long moment. I could tell she didn't buy it. She knew I wasn't a partier and was one of the most boring guys on the crew, at least as far as their version of "fun" went. However, I think the mama side of her eventually kicked in because she whispered back with a genuine smile, "I'll get ya some coffee."

She had just turned away when I heard, "Jamie!" from Ed, one of my fellow crewmen.

"What?"

I looked up to see the whole crew, including the supervisor, staring at me.

"Um . . . here?"

The laughter broke the tension. Even the supervisor's mouth turned up in faint amusement. He went back to his announcements as I felt a short tug on my shirt.

Peggy was holding a steaming cup of coffee out to me. "Be careful, it's really hot."

"Thanks, Peggy, you're the best," I said softly. She gave me one more "concerned mom look" before winking and walking away.

However, there was something else in her eyes that I couldn't quite place. She looked almost . . . sad.

Our supervisor wrapped up his announcements with, " . . . and that's it. We've got a twelve front this morning, so all hands on deck. Stay safe and see you in a few hours."

The crew broke up and began moving toward the door. I drank the coffee as quickly as I could. Somehow, I managed to keep from hurting myself, although I inhaled most of it in one gulp. I tossed the Styrofoam cup in the trash and then banged the exit open with my shoulder.

As I jogged to my place on the line, I realized my knee was still a little sore. I sighed and kept moving.

Oh well, it was worth it. I needed to make a livin'.

If I were honest though, I'd have to admit it wasn't just the paycheck. The sight and sound of the jets got my blood pumping. Working on jets isn't the same thing as flying them, but even if that was the closest I would get to clouds between my feet, at least I got to be a part of something special.

I grabbed a launch bag and made my way to my assigned jet. It was quiet at the moment, but it would get loud soon. I donned my hearing protection and watched the instructor pilots, along with their students, making their way out to the aircraft.

At that particular moment, two aircrafts' engines began howling and spewing noise. The thundering cacophony of engines coming to life would peak with primal screams before settling to muscly roars. It got so loud that the ground trembled under my feet and my insides shook.

I loved it.

My job was to help get the airplane in the air on time. I was basically part airplane mechanic, part Indy pit crew. It kept me moving and involved in the action. You had to be careful around the jets, but if you treated them with respect, they'd treat you okay, too.

During a break, I noticed one of the friendlier instructors bringing a handful of eager young students out for an initial look at a T-38. The jet they were inspecting actually had the instructor's call sign on it, Boogie. I once asked him why people called him that, but he just looked amused and shook his head.

I guess that's not too strange. Most of the guys wouldn't come out and say how they got their call sign. Sometimes it was obvious and unflattering. For instance, I once heard of a man whose first name was Stu, so they named him Pid. Poor guy.

A year earlier, one of Boogie's fellow fighter pilots, Monk, had told me Boogie was, to use fighter pilot lingo, a "no-kiddin' good dude." I guess I had a perplexed look on my face because he explained:

"Jamie, if a fighter pilot really wants to ensure that you know that something is one hundred percent true, he says 'no kiddin,' and if he wants to strongly vouch for someone, he says that someone is a 'good dude.'"

"So, you're saying that it's one hundred percent true that Boogie is a great guy?"

"Exactly."

"Got it, Monk. Thanks for the insight."

Such is the world of the fighter pilot, where words mean things.

Boogie began his walk-around of the aircraft with his students. When he reached the front of the jet, he looked up and broke into a grin. "Jamie, what's up, bro?" I couldn't help but grin back because he always seemed so sincere.

He walked over and extended a Nomex-gloved hand, but stopped short as he looked into my face. I held out my hand and shook his, but his eyes gave him away. They seemed surprised, widening and jumping between spots on my face, almost as if he was trying not to stare at something. Was my nose not clean?

"Er, um, so what's new, Jamie? Having a good morning?"

I could tell that he was having a difficult time concentrating. He kept looking at my forehead, then forcing himself to look in my eyes. I started to feel a little self-conscious.

I rubbed my face. "Do I have anything on my cranium, um, like dirt or bugs, or something?" I had unintentionally used the fighter pilot word for head. I guess I was becoming more like them whether I meant to or not.

That seemed to snap him out of it. "No, man! Sorry about that, you just look like you had a rough night or something. Is everything okay with you?"

Sure, everything's cool. Just some demented, midnight death-matches. How are you?

I hesitated.

Hit him with a little truth, Jamie, just not too much.

I answered as conversationally as I could. "I had some crazy dreams last night. It must have been the spicy food I ate for dinner. I'm sure the double-scoop of chocolate-chip cookie dough ice cream I chased it with didn't help."

Well played, Jamie.

The friendly smile never left his face, but Boogie just nodded. "Oh, really? What kind of dreams?"

Oh, come on! Drop it, dude.

I paused, ever so slightly. His gaze never wavered.

All right, just a titch more and then we are so changing the subject.

"You know, the standard kind. I dreamt about going to the corner gas station and, um, meeting weird people. How about you? Are you doing okay?"

Boogie didn't take the bait. Instead, he continued to stare at me. "Gas station, huh? Did they have what you were after?"

Before I could stop, I spouted off with, "Unfortunately, yes."

I wanted to punch myself in the face.

An awkward silence ensued. I was about to just make up a random question about flying when, abruptly, Boogie said, "Groovy, man!" I wasn't sure what was so groovy about bad dreams, but I smiled anyway. It sure felt like I had just missed something important, though.

Just then one of the students approached Boogie. "Sir, how can you tell the main struts have enough air in them?"

Boogie turned and walked back toward the aircraft. "It's easy, Lieutenant. Here, let me show you." The rest of his explanation was drowned out by jet noise, but I caught Boogie staring back at me one last time, an inscrutable look on his face.

CHAPTER 3

"Heads up, Jamie!"

The plastic water bottle bounced off my chest before I could process what Ed said. It skidded across the floor and came to rest against the wall. I slowly picked it up and put it in the trash.

"What is up with you today, man?"

Ed and I had teamed up to launch a few jets. It went well, mostly because he's a hard worker and knows his stuff. That day, I felt like I was always a step behind. I guess it showed.

"Oh, I don't know, I thought I would test you and see if you could pull your weight for a change."

He laughed. "Now that's more like it! Get some rest, bro, 'cause we've got another big day tomorrow. It'll be ninety degrees in the shade and all the fun you can stand." A fist bump later he was out the door and singing loudly. Off key.

I rubbed my eyes and took a deep breath.

I just want to go home, maybe go for a run and then veg out with a movie. Any kind of movie will probably do, as long as it doesn't have swords, or mini-marts, or creepy dudes or . . . you know, on second thought, maybe a good book would be better.

I sighed and slowly pushed through the exit.

Loose gravel crunched under my dark steel-toed boots as I made my way through the oven-hot parking lot. It would cool later, but the black asphalt just soaked up the rays and fairly steamed until after the last bit of daylight fell behind the horizon.

My mind wandered to happier days. The boiling parking lot reminded me of when we kids would go to the local swimming pool. Invariably, I would forget to take my shoes.

Summertime in the south? Who needed 'em?

I smiled as I remembered hopping from white parking stripe to white parking stripe, using their relative coolness to avoid the fiercely hot black. It was like a game, but a painful one at that. You had to be careful where you stepped, or else—

I didn't notice him until I was almost to my car. He was just a bit taller than me, still close to average, but had the lean build of an endurance athlete. I was far enough away to not be too startled but close enough to see . . . Boogie?

What's he doing here?

Boogie was loitering near my parking spot, a serious look on his face. His flight suit was sweat-stained and wrinkled, and his flight cap had a fighter pilot's dent in the top of it. He looked every bit the part of the proverbial hard-working IP. The only things out of place were the wrinkled brow and tightened jaw.

"Hey, Boogie. Ah . . . what's happening?"

My voice seemed to catch him unaware. He started, but relaxed when he saw it was me. I saw him exhale a large breath and put on a big smile, but it kind of looked a little forced. A lingering sense of concern, highlighted in his brownish-green eyes, hovered on his face.

"Hey, Jamie! Can I talk to you for a second?" He was still smiling, but something in his voice gave me pause. Uncharacteristically, he shifted from foot to foot and stretched his neck nervously.

"Uh, sure thing, Boogie."

"Great. I just . . . ah . . . well, I ran into Ed earlier, and he said that maybe you were having a tough time or something. Are you doing okay?"

No. I'm probably having a nervous breakdown.

"I'm fine. I'm just having a bit of an off day. Nothin' to be worried about."

He absently twisted the wedding ring on his left hand and stared off into the distance for a few seconds. "So . . . tell me again about your dream."

My breath caught and my right hand involuntarily flexed.

Why does he keep asking . . . ?

Wait. I've got it. I bet he thinks I've got leftovers from the war. Post-traumatic stress disorder or something.

Oh, man. I should've never told Boogie what happened to me in Iraq. But yeah, okay, that sort of made sense.

I started to relax a little. "Boogie, thanks for your concern, but you don't have to worry about me. The docs have checked me out, and I've got a clean bill of health. I'm perfectly fine."

Boogie turned to me. "So, he had a black sword?"

Okay, maybe not so fine.

My smile crumbled and my heart started triple-timing. It was suddenly as if I was back in the mini-mart. I broke out in a cold sweat, and adrenaline coursed through my veins. I was afraid a blade might magically appear in my hand.

I nodded numbly and stared at him with wide eyes.

"That makes sense," he said, as if he'd known the entire time. His brow furrowed as he quietly watched me. "I've got to go. Let's meet at the Little Pig at nineteen hundred for some dinner. This isn't the right place to talk. I'm buying."

I could think of nothing else to say, so I just mumbled "Okay" and watched him do a perfect military about-face. He marched away, leaving me alone with images of swords and ashes.

* * *

I honestly considered not showing. Avoidance is a perfectly valid coping strategy, if you ask me. Plus, I wasn't in the military anymore. He couldn't tell me what to do.

I paced back and forth in my living room and ran through everything again and again, but none of it made sense. What was I walking into? Intervention? That was probably the least of my worries.

Go through it one more time, Jamie. You got this.

All right. I experienced what had to be a dream and it was a bad one. That's not too weird. I fought an ugly guy and kicked his butt. Duh! Definitely within the realm of not crazy.

There *is* the whole flicker-face/sword-cutting-to-ashy thing, but really, who hasn't dreamed of thrashing melted-face dudes in a mini-mart . . . with a sword? Okay, not common, but whatever. Everybody's got their own thing, right?

But how did Boogie know about the black sword?

Ummmm . . . I got nothin'.

Or did I? Maybe it is actually a common dream if you are under a lot of stress. It's like when you . . . um . . . dream . . . and um . . . swords represent . . .

Okay, that's just stupid.

Could I have said something about a black sword earlier and forgotten?

You're really reaching, dude.

I realized that I had stopped in the middle of the floor and was staring, well, at me. The guy in the picture was decked out in full battle rattle—body armor, weapons and tons of confidence. That guy believed he could do anything and mostly, he did. You'd never catch him pacing and worrying like an old lady.

I could also just make out the faint image of my stressed face reflecting in the picture. The picture wasn't taken that long before, so it shouldn't have looked so different. What happened to that guy?

Dude, knock it off. No whining. Whatever is happening, saddle up and own it.

Right.

One more deep breath and I was out the door.

* * *

The sign read The Little Pig—Best BBQ in Town!

It actually was, but I just didn't feel very hungry right then. I eased to a stop in the restaurant's gravel lot about five minutes before seven and left the engine running to keep the air conditioning going.

The late afternoon heat was still sending shimmering waves up from the pavement as I waited for Boogie's SUV. Maybe he wouldn't show?

Wishful thinking, dude.

My thumb nervously tapped an erratic beat on the steering wheel while I kept an eye toward the road. It took only another minute before I had an answer. A lone auto topped the rise and coasted to the bottom of the hill.

The gray vehicle eased off the thoroughfare that ran north to south through the main part of town and turned into the lot. The SUV eased to a stop in an adjacent spot. I was a little surprised by what I saw.

Hmm. There's Boogie, but who's that in the passenger side? I didn't realize this was a bring-a-date thing. Then again, maybe it's not a date . . . but a witness?

I really didn't like where things were going.

Boogie and his friend both stepped out of the vehicle and onto the dusty parking lot, quietly resuming their conversation. Boogie paused briefly to wait for me to get out of my car. He looked a little different to me, because I almost always saw him in a flight suit going to or from a flight.

His blue jeans, hiking shoes, and simple T-shirt made him seem like a normal guy. That sounds weird, but I knew him only as "Instructor Pilot Boogie," and had never really considered his life outside of work.

Why is he suddenly interested in mine?

I cut the engine and stepped out of my vehicle.

"Hey, Boogie."

"Hiya, Jamie! Thanks for meeting us. Let's get out of the heat and I'll make introductions."

We walked through the double doors. I shook Boogie's hand and reached out for his friend's. It wasn't until that moment that I realized how big his friend was. Ouch. He had a brutal handshake.

"This is Al," Boogie said. "He's a good dude."

His friend cast an appraising look at me as he released what was left of my right hand. Good dude or not, he was strong and intimidating. Boogie led the way to the back of the restaurant as Al and I fell in behind him. Because it was the middle of the week, the restaurant wasn't crowded. We had no problem finding a spot.

We chose a table in the corner, some distance away from the nearest customers. Boogie and Al sat on one side of the table and I on the other. I was about to speak when Boogie held up a hand in a *wait* motion.

Okaay. I guess I'll just sit here.

For about thirty seconds no one spoke. Al stared at my face with startling intensity. Boogie sat quietly, not moving a muscle.

Really? More stare at the face stuff?

This was getting old, fast. I took a breath to say as much and I got another hand from Boogie.

Another hand? What am I, six?

I was about to lose it when Al suddenly sat up straight and looked at Boogie. They shared a conspiratorial look and then turned back to me. I looked back and forth, utterly perplexed.

"Jamie, I'm sorry for the theatrics, and I apologize for putting you on the spot. However, it's clear to Al and me that something is happening to you, something important, that we need to talk about before it's too late."

"Before it's too late? Too late for what?"

Hold on . . . this *is* an intervention. Oh, man, seriously?

I slumped in my seat and rubbed my neck. Here it comes. Tell me about the war . . . tell me about your feelings . . . tell me about—

"—about your dream," Boogie was saying.

Of course. My dream. My PTSD dream. I didn't have time for that.

"Boogie, look, I appreciate your concern, but like I said earlier today, I'm fine. And Al, let me guess, you're a kindred spirit who can help me work through my feelings?"

"Not unless those feelings have anythin' to do with brisket and fries. I'm *hon-gry*."

"Huh?" I looked back and forth between the two. I was so confused.

Boogie put out his hands as if to say *whoa there*. "Jamie, you've got this all wrong. You're fine. We're know there's nothing wrong with you. That's not why we're here."

Al was shaking his head and rolling his eyes at me, in a *when'd you get here?* kind of look.

"So what's this all about then? If I'm 'fine,' why are we here?"

"I promise I'll explain, but just humor me and tell us what happened last night. It's for a good reason."

"Come on mayun, just tell us." Al sounded like he had someplace better to be.

"Fine, if it will make you two feel better." I could be a bit of a jerk, especially when I was stressed.

Let's just get this over with, Jamie.

I took a deep breath and related the events of the previous evening. It was weird, though. The details were still really vivid. Whereas most of my dreams fade to oblivion within minutes of waking, this one played out more like a 3D recording than a deep-sleep-induced horror skit.

I tried to run through the events quickly, like ripping off a bandage, but Boogie said, "Slow down, and provide as much detail as you can."

I sighed. Great, let's re-live the whole thing. Maybe I'll get stabbed this time.

Settle down, Jamie. This is Boogie. He's one of the good guys, right? Right.

So I started over, going through the dream methodically, trying my best to not leave anything out. I absentmindedly picked up a fork and began to twirl it. It was a pointless habit I'd picked up as a kid, but it gave my hands something to do when I was agitated.

By the end of my story, I had recounted the entire episode with unnerving accuracy. I was even left with sweaty palms and chill bumps on my arms, both of which I tried to hide under the table.

Al interrupted only once. When I mentioned the words Dark Sword said toward the end of my dream, Al's eyes flared. "Stop! Say that part again." So I did.

Al clenched his jaw when I repeated what the guy had said about *with the others*. He sat up in his seat and loosened his shoulders before settling back into a quiet stare. I would have normally found his reaction strange, but the whole thing was already too weird for words.

When I finished my story, there was silence at the table. Boogie and Al looked at each other for a few seconds. Then Al nodded to whatever unspoken question had passed between the two.

With their mute discussion apparently settled, Boogie looked at me. "So, Jamie, what do you think about your, uh, encounter?"

I answered honestly. "It freaked me out, man! But it was just a dream. I don't see what the big deal is."

I was pretty tired of being the only person that didn't know what was going on. "Okay, I've answered your questions, so now answer mine. How did you know my dream had a black sword?"

Al spoke up suddenly. His tone was matter-of-fact. "Easy. 'Cause it wasn't a dream."

CHAPTER 4

I vaguely registered the *ping-bing-ping* of my twirling fork falling on the floor. I looked back and forth between the two of them, waiting for the *gotcha!* and the chuckling to begin.

They weren't laughing. They weren't even smiling.

Boogie did look back at me with a mildly apologetic look on his face, but Al was already consumed by the plastic menu, his eyebrows raising and lowering as he scanned the options. "Ooh, they've got a coleslaw special on! Y'all want me to order somethin' for ya?"

Boogie mildly shook his head and I just stared.

"Aaight. I'll be back. Hold my seat!" Al hopped up and went to the front to order. He acted like he didn't have a care in the world.

Boogie folded his hands on the table and sat quietly, much like a patient teacher. His calm demeanor only added to the absurdity of the moment.

"You can't possibly mean . . . "

"Uh-huh."

My heart pounded and I could feel a small trickle of sweat down the middle of my back. It was almost like one of those out-of-body experiences. I didn't float around the room or anything, but I felt a bit detached from the scene, almost like I was watching a movie.

"So, by 'wasn't a dream,' does he mean . . . "

"Yep. He means you totally thrashed a Nasty last night. You sent him to hell's waiting room. Well done." He leaned back and relaxed a little. "Personally I'm glad to see that you survived, not just because I like you but because it also sounds like you've got some decent fighting skills."

Boogie said that like, *Hey, nice home run last night. We could sure use you on our squadron's softball team.*

Are you kidding me?

"But what . . . how? And what do you mean by 'glad you survived'? It was a dream, dude!"

I suddenly realized that I was shouting . . . and the other patrons were looking at me.

I held up my hands. "Sorry."

They went back to their food.

I took a calming breath and let it out slowly. Boogie didn't seem to notice. He continued speaking amiably as if we were discussing batting averages or local football teams. "Like Al said, it wasn't a dream, ergo, it was real. Those creatures are called Malum, but we often just refer to them as Nasties."

Well, at least that part made sense.

"If the Malum had gotten hold of you with his black sword, that would have been the end of your life on this planet, Jamie. You would have died in your sleep and the doctors would have blamed it on heart failure." A smirk cracked his face. "Funny how that goes; your heart stops beating, so your death must be due to heart failure, eh?"

I didn't think any of it was funny at all.

Al returned to the table and started digging into his dinner. I looked at him in shock. He caught me staring and shrugged. "What?

I *told* you I was hongry. You gotta try some of this sauce, Jamie. It'll turn that frown upside down, brother."

Boogie smiled at Al. "I was just telling Jamie how well he did last night." Al grunted in agreement. "Hey man, show him your side."

Al slowed his chewing and narrowed his eyes at Boogie. I could read *really, dude?* in his face. However, he grudgingly glanced around the restaurant to ensure no one was looking, then raised the right side of his button-up shirt.

He revealed a four-inch scar that ran horizontally across his rib cage. A violently ragged cut, it appeared to have been cauterized. He quickly put his shirt down.

Boogie also scanned the room, double-checking for observers. "Al picked that up during his first encounter. He's lucky it was a glancing blow, or else 'poof.'" He made a dissipating movement with his hands. "No more Al."

Al looked up from dousing chicken in BBQ sauce. "There ain't no such thing as luck, but I was lucky to make it outta that one alive. There were two of 'em and they hit me at the same time. I was shocked as all get-out to find myself tanglin' with those ugly thangs, but thankfully, they weren't that good at sword fightin'."

"So . . . so . . . what are you saying, Boogie?" My chest tightened as if I was the one who got hit. "That I've been thrust into an imaginary gladiator league with, what did you call them, Malum?"

"Not 'maginary," Al mumbled through his coleslaw. "All too real."

"But this doesn't make any sense! Why are we fighting? For fun? Because it sure wasn't any fun last night!"

While his face remained neutral, Boogie's voice turned solemn. "No, Jamie. This definitely isn't for fun. Good people are dying."

Al put down his fork for a moment and nodded.

Boogie leaned in. "You've been to war. You've seen the best and worst of man. You survived, but I know you're not without scars."

Ouch. He was hitting way too close to home.

"But Jamie, did you know there is a war going on right here, a war most people can't see?"

I slowly shook my head.

"If you walk out of your house in the morning, you can't see anything, at least with your eyes. However, you can see the reflections of it in the daily news: riots in the cities, murders by the dozens, human trafficking growing to epic proportions, and even crime waves sweeping through our local neighborhoods."

Al pursed his lips but said nothing.

"Most people think those are just reflections of a good society gone bad." Boogie scooted forward in his seat. "But in reality, they are indicators of an all too real battle that is being waged behind the veil."

I guess Boogie could see the confusion on my face.

"There is a thin divide between the world as we know it and the other one where the fight is taking place," he said. "That's what we mean by 'veil.' You went to the other side during your dream."

"I went to 'the other side' during my dream? It didn't look that different to me."

"That's because the two sides are pretty much identical. Not only that, there seems to be a direct correlation between the Malum strongholds on the other side and bad areas of the world on this side. In other words, every place the Malum go on the other side brings horrible things to the parts of our world on this side."

He sighed deeply. "No kiddin' Jamie, I know you've been through a lot. I know you've suffered the worst of days. I'm sorry, I really don't want to burden you." He leaned across the table. "But the truth is this; you're a warrior. You may have tried to leave those days behind, but you can't deny who you are. You were created to fight and to lead, and we need you."

Strange. The more he explained the calmer I felt. My heart rate was slowing and my hands had stopped sweating. None of it should have made sense at all. And yet it did.

I stared back and exhaled, slowly. "Okay, maybe I sorta get the 'why me' part, but why the big push? You seem awfully eager about this whole thing."

Boogie leaned in even closer to me and whispered, "From what we can tell, the Malum are getting stronger locally. They are prepping for something big, right here on our doorstep. If we care anything about our families and the folks in this area, we'll do all we can to stop them. We need your help to put 'em down."

Al nodded as if it was the most obvious thing in the world, though it did not dampen his renewed enthusiasm for his barbecue and sweet tea.

Boogie sat back and casually said, "We'll teach you all we know. You'll learn how to fight and how to cross over the divide more easily than before. We'll prepare and train you as best we can." What Boogie said next gave me great pause. "There are more of us. Lots more. You'll meet the other guys if you join us, but only if you join us. We can't afford to let people know who we are if you're not going to be one of us." As if that wasn't concerning enough, his demeanor hardened and his next remarks came with a solemn edge.

He stared holes in me when he said, "But, Jamie, *if* you join us, there's no going back. As far as we know, you'll live a normal life, but you'll also train and you'll fight with us. We don't know how it will all end, or if it ever will, but I promise that you'll never have a more worthwhile reason to put your life on the line. Ultimately, though, the choice is yours."

The only sound was the *sluuuurrrrrpp* noise from Al finishing his huge cup of tea, followed immediately by, "Now that is good stuff, mayun."

It was like someone flicked a switch. Boogie smiled a big grin and began to get up to order his food. I threw out a question before I let him walk away. "Boogie, how did you know that I had an encounter, or that there was a Malum with a black sword?"

"Because you have one of these." He pulled up the hair from his forehead, revealing a very light, curved white line, which was about two inches long and ran horizontally across his forehead. Somehow, I had never noticed that before. Al then pointed to his forehead and it was only then I observed that he also had a similar, lightly colored mark.

While keeping their eyes on me, Boogie and Al grasped hands. As they did so, both of their marks changed, in that mirror-image lines formed underneath the original ones. The lines attached at one end to make a point and crossed at the other, creating a symbol that looked a lot like a fish. I recognized that fish; it was the Greek symbol called an ichthys.

From history classes, I knew the ichthys had been adopted by those who were viciously persecuted for their beliefs. They used the ichthys to identify each other without giving away their affiliation. When Boogie and Al broke contact, the faint lines faded to singular, barely noticeable ones. While I tried to digest all that they had just told me, one thing was clear: if I joined them, I would be a hunted man.

I sat and reflected on that while Boogie got his meal. Al seemed content to finish off the last bits of his food in silence. He didn't leave a crumb.

After a few minutes, Boogie returned to our table with a plate of ribs and fries so fresh it might make a country boy swoon. The food steamed and smelled like heaven. He then proceeded to greedily gulp down the plate as if it might be his last. Considering what I had just learned, I supposed it always could be.

Despite the onslaught of aromas, I was not in the least bit hungry. I was consumed by trying to come to grips with what I had just learned. Eventually, a few more questions burbled to the surface.

"So, does, uh, you know, this type of thing happen only while you sleep?"

Al took the lead as Boogie finished his plate of food. "Naw. Not most of the time. For some folks, sleep is where it begins, and then it moves into our wake time. Other guys are recruited on this side. It's a little tougher to get recruits that way, but we've picked up a few."

"But how do you get there if it's not from sleep? And where exactly is *there*, anyway?"

Al chewed his lip and gazed thoughtfully over my head for a moment. "Most of us were like you. We were livin' our lives, then began havin' fights while we slept, or things happened that just weren't quite right. All but a few of us were recruited while we were asleep, like we're approaching you now in your wake time, and asked to join."

Boogie nodded, but kept eating.

"You're unique. Boogie happened to notice your mark at work and decided to recruit you during your wake time. Being noticed in your wake time is fairly rare, as far as we can tell."

Boogie grunted his agreement while chewing on one last bite.

Al slid his plate to the middle of the table, folded his arms, and leaned toward me. "As far as 'where is there' goes, well, there's only one way to find out, mayun. You have to join us to find out."

Gauntlet thrown.

"So, let me get this straight. You're asking me to join your group, without me knowing exactly where this fantasy—"

Al raised his eyebrows at me.

"—I mean, different world is. How do I know what I'm getting into?"

Boogie wiped his mouth with a napkin and stuffed it under the edge of his plate. "You don't. But you *do* have something most of us didn't have in the beginning, and that's advice from someone you know. You may not know Al very well, but I hope you know me well enough to know that I wouldn't lie to you or mislead you. That's not my way."

The truth was, I believed him. About everything. And that really frightened me.

Al leaned back in his seat and threw out one more tidbit for me to chew on. "Jamie, when I said earlier that most of us began this journey in our sleep, that was completely true. But if you're like us, you'll be able to enter this place by walking through doorways while you're awake. They will appear as slim rectangles of light, about the size of a regular door, and they will be visible to only you and others like you."

"So, I can just walk to this place?"

"Sorta. You normally can't control when the doors appear. They just show up."

"An electric door will just appear out of nowhere?"

That's not strange at all.

"Yep. And there's somethin' else. If you step through the door, time, as you know it, will stop." Al made a chopping motion with one hand against the other. "I'm not sure that can sound any weirder than it does, but the point is that when you come back, you'll be right back at the same place and the same time as when you departed. And no, we have no idea how or why it works like that."

Boogie, always ready with a cheerful fighter pilot analogy, smiled. "It's the 'thermos theorem,' man!" By the confused look on my face, he could probably tell that I wasn't following him, which made his grin even larger.

"You know," he said, "the thermos theorem. A thermos keeps hot stuff hot but also cold stuff cold. How does it know?" He laughed out loud, and even Al chuckled for a few moments.

So corny, dude.

However, Boogie's manner changed once more. His smile fell, and his voice dropped low. "But Jamie, you don't have to go through the door. It's completely up to you. If you do go through, you will emerge on the other side, and we'll be there to meet you."

Al raised one finger. "But if you ignore the 'invitation,' as Boogie calls it, then we think you may not get asked again, maybe ever. We're not sure about that part." Al cut his eyes toward Boogie. They shared another insider moment but quickly moved on, their eyes returning to meet my gaze.

I tried to summarize what I'd heard so far. "So, you think I've been called to be part of your little fighting troupe, risking my earthly life in this parallel world where I can be cut to pieces by demon-looking things you call 'Malum,' and you don't know where it's all going or how it will end?"

Al stared at Boogie, and Boogie just pursed his lips and raised his eyebrows in a humorous way. They both looked at me and Al said, "That's about right."

How could I say no to that?

Boogie handed me a menu. "What would you like to eat, Jamie? Like I said, I'm buying, and it's really good."

"I appreciate the offer, but I'm just not hungry at the moment. I'll get something later"—I dropped the menu on the table—"if my appetite comes back."

Boogie nodded and shoved his plate to meet Al's. They were both done eating and I was, for the moment, out of questions.

"How about we call it a night, Jamie? I've got an early flight tomorrow, and I know you'll be up with the sun, too."

"Yeah, that's probably a good call."

As we walked toward the parking lot, one more question did come to mind. "Al, you said if I turned down my 'invitation', I might not get asked anymore. I understand that. But if I say yes, then how often will I have to make the trip to this other world? I mean, is this a daily thing, or does whoever is in charge give us a few weeks off to rest?"

It seemed like a simple question, but it provoked another few moments of silence as our little troupe stopped by Boogie's SUV.

Boogie finally spoke up. "Jamie, that's part of the reason I didn't want to wait to talk to you. When I first got started, it would be weeks, sometimes months, between doorway appearances. However . . . " He paused as he looked at Al. "Recently, the doorways have come more often. Sometimes on consecutive days. We think . . . " He paused again.

"We think somethin's up, mayun. Somethin' big's comin', but"— Al folded his arms and scanned the parking lot—"we really can't say any more here." He even looked into the clear night sky, which I found a bit strange. He then returned his attention to me.

Boogie also turned and faced me. He said kindly, "Jamie, you're one of the good guys. We would love to have you with us, but I can't force you to sign up, and I wouldn't want to anyway. This has to be your decision."

With that, Boogie gave me a friendly slap on the shoulder, Al waved, and they both climbed into his SUV and drove away into the starry night. I stood immobile, but was internally rocked to my core.

I felt exactly like I did the first time I stood in the open doorway of an airplane, twelve thousand feet above the ground. Fear lashed at my senses as my thoughts fought to be heard over my emotions. My head was screaming at me to get away, but my gut pulled me onward, to trust in something that was unproven and uncertain.

As frightening as that had been, an even scarier moment of truth had come. I was teetering in the doorway, and I wasn't sure which way I would fall.

CHAPTER 5

I remained alone in the dark parking lot and watched the tail-lights of Boogie's vehicle disappear into the distance. After the car noise faded it was just me and the stars, one of us wrestling with the future. It was a lot to take in at once.

My stomach abruptly made a *grrrrrmmmm* noise.

Seriously? Now you're hungry?

I didn't feel like walking back into The Little Pig. I'd made enough of a commotion in there for one night.

What sounds good? Got it. Bagel and a coffee should hit the spot.

My adrenals had been blasted so much over the years that a little caffeine didn't keep me awake at night. Sleep was the last thing on my mind, anyway. I needed time to do some mental "marination" of this whole Malum fighting thing. So, I climbed into my car and eased down the road to one of the few coffee shops in the area.

There wasn't much of a crowd at that time of night, so I was able to find a parking space nearby. The shop was a nice balance of southern-charm and urban-trendy. It had large framed pictures of the local sights but modern furniture that somehow managed to remain comfortable. The ubiquitous chalkboard was decorated with curly letters and advertised the specials of the day. I quietly walked into the café and looked around. The smells of fresh coffee and baked goods were welcoming and the atmosphere was calm, all of which I appreciated.

If there is such a thing as comfort food, then surely there is comfort in caffeine. I ordered a medium-size cup of fresh-brewed and a bagel from the barista, who promptly asked for my name. I told her, which she placed on my cup. *Jay-me.*

Close enough.

I watched the barista work, if that's what you'd call it. She kept pausing to look at her cell phone and tried to text with one hand. She actually knocked my first drink over before it was full and had to start again, though she used the same cup as before. My coffee smudged name was now just -*me.*

I would've said something to her about it but, honestly, I was too distracted by my own thing to really care. My brain was like an old computer trying to open a new, big program. All of the data was there, but it was taking a while to sift through it and get everything into its proper place.

The barista eventually finished preparing my coffee and bagel and placed them on the counter without saying a word or looking up from her screen. No matter. I took my stuff and eased into a corner booth. Back against the wall, I settled my gaze on the window beside my seat.

The place was nearly empty. It was just me and some college students, most of whom had their noses within inches of smart phones or electronic tablets. I could have started dancing in the middle of the store to the nondescript music they were playing and none of them would ever be the wiser. Their loss.

As my coffee steamed, I sat and stared through the window, not knowing where to begin or what to do. I did occasionally remember to take a sip of the four-dollar drink and a bite of my bagel. Despite the inattentiveness of my server, the coffee was smooth and the plain bagel fresh and soft. Though it was still warm outside, it was cool in the air conditioning, so the hot mug and warm bagel felt soothing in my hands and in my stomach.

When I've got big problems, I learned from my dad to just sit and let things ramble around in my brain. He explained it like this when I was a kid: *Son, it's a little like chasin' butterflies. You can run after them for all you're worth, and probably come up empty-handed. Or, you can sit quietly and wait for them to alight on your shoulder.*

Over the years I found that I usually have better luck with the latter. So I just tried to still my mind and let things sort themselves out for a while.

I sat and stared through the smudged window at the world outside. That is, when I could see around the decorations and child-sized fingerprints. After a while, my gaze came to rest on the reflection of the inside of the establishment, which clearly showed the cashier's counter. My little barista was still apparently texting her bestie with the latest gossip, to the detriment of her duties.

Movement caught my eye. A person came out from behind a tastefully hidden door in the back. She began speaking to the vocabulary-challenged worker with a calm but stern look on her face. The employee quickly put her phone away and started acting busy.

Ah-hah. Methinks the manager cometh and catcheth thee not working.

My suspicions about her managerial status were quickly confirmed. After she encouraged the barista to clean and restock the shelves, she made her way from behind the counter to walk the floor to check on her evening customers. I watched in mild interest as she began at the far side of the room.

The collegians barely acknowledged her, even as she stopped by each one of them and asked, "How are you tonight? Is there anything I can get you?" I guess the siren songs of their electronic worlds wouldn't let them leave their screens.

One of them did actually look up. He had ear phones in and just gave a tight smile and a shake of the head. I felt a little sorry for her.

Despite the lack of affirmation, the manager still smiled and continued to make her way around the floor. She was friendly and apparently unfazed by the non-replies she got from most of the customers. I could see why she was the manager and not the barista at the counter, who was not so covertly texting again.

The manager eventually got to my table. When she stopped by the end of the bench she delivered a practiced, "And how is everything tonight?"

I took my gaze away from the window and turned and looked into her face.

Whoa. She's a lot cuter than I thought.

She had dark brown eyes that were smart and alive, brunette hair pulled back in a ponytail, and a natural beauty's smile. I wasn't sure why I had never noticed her on my previous coffee runs. I guess I have been known to miss the obvious once or twice.

In this type of situation I normally get shy and just say *everything's good.* This time though, I was determined that it would be different. I was gonna rock it.

All right, Jamie, something suave and engaging. You know, be cool. Ready . . . go.

I blurted out, "Everything's good, except the coffee."

Really? And . . . fail.

She stared at me like I was speaking Swahili.

Okay, Plan B. Give her your best hey, I'm witty, funny, and handsome smile. Maybe she'll see the charm oozing from your pores.

I smiled . . . and immediately realized that I probably overdid it. For some reason a Cheshire cat came to mind.

I do think she saw something in me though, but I'm not sure it was charm. She politely smiled and, half-turning to walk away asked, "Is there anything I can get for you?"

I tried to cover my flop with my lame sense of humor. I don't know why I thought that was a good idea . . .

I popped off with, "Not unless you've got a big black sword I can stab myself with to keep from making any more jokes."

You know, some girls sort of like guys who can make fun of themselves. I thought I might be able to connect with her by proving I was aware of my woefully inadequate one-liners.

I was wrong on each account.

I stared into her eyes . . . and watched her smile dissolve on her face. It was replaced by a look I did not readily recognize, but which I knew did not represent a desire to take long walks with me and call me pet names.

Uh-oh.

In fact, she looked a bit scared, like I was a wanted criminal. I was becoming concerned that she was going to yell, *Call 911!* and run away, leaving me with my last moments of freedom and a half-drunk cup of coffee.

"I'm just kidding!" I ran a hand through my hair in exasperation. "Sorry about that, I guess I'm not as funny as I thought. I've had a rough day. I apologize if things aren't coming out right."

She settled down from her fight-or-flight moment. For a few seconds, she just stared at me, a curious light settling in her eyes. Then she put on an embarrassed smile.

"Oh, no, um, I'm sorry." She quickly regained her composure. "I guess I've had a long day too and didn't quite catch what you were saying. I hope you have a good evening." With that, she abruptly walked away.

I'd been rejected before, but after such a long day all I could do was shake my head and remind myself what a smooth idiot I could be. I guessed I wasn't as handsome or amusing as I had hoped. What a shocker.

Hoping no one else had seen or heard the encounter, I returned my gaze to the window. The reflection indicated that the other patrons had, thankfully, been too wrapped up in their social media worlds to notice the king of dorkdom getting shot down. I sighed.

Okay, Jamie, I think it's time to leave the scene of the crime, dude.

At that moment I noticed Ms. Manager had stopped in the back doorway. She was looking intently in my direction. I couldn't see her eyes well enough to read her.

I stared back at her in the window, though. My gaze went unnoticed as she hesitated, unmoving, at the back of the room. I was about to turn to chance another glance in her direction when, without a sound, she disappeared through the door and out of sight.

* * *

My head was spinning like a novice swimmer caught in a whirlpool. I had received a crazy invitation and an unambiguous declination, all within the span of a couple of hours. My night was pretty much complete. For some reason, it felt like a win to make it back to my car without incident.

Thankfully, the streets were mostly empty and I knew the way home by heart. It was so familiar, my car traveled almost of its own accord. My headlights easily brought the street in front of me out of darkness, allowing me to see the way to go. If only they would do the same thing for my head.

I kept replaying the discussion with Boogie and Al. Their bid to pull me into their little army had me in knots. I couldn't dissect my emotions quickly enough to gauge how I felt about the Malum thing. To top it all off, the uncomfortable encounter with the girl at the café only added to the absurdity of the day.

Once home, I plopped heavily on my bed. Little black bits of what I now knew were deceased Malum flew into the air from my pillow. I put my head in my hands in a fit of frustration. That is, until I realized that I had dark specks on my hands too, and was now likely inhaling them.

Are you kidding me? Gross!

I jumped up, pulled off the sheets and began to vacuum the floor.

Would this day never end?

Come on, Jamie. Hang in there.

I busied myself with the Malum cleanup job. While I cleared the floor I left my brain on autopilot, hoping it would clear things out, too. As I watched small bits of Dark Sword being removed from the floor by my vacuum cleaner, I realized two things.

One, this was one of the strangest cleanups I'd ever done. Vacuuming dead Malum from your floor? Seriously, who does that?

Two, I was really conflicted. While the thought of fighting creatures over there was weird, I guessed it might be worthwhile.

If it helped protect our town, then it might not be so bad to belong again, right?

On the other hand, I had already given so much to *them* that I wasn't sure I wanted to give any more. If I were real honest, I had to admit that while I did make it back to good physical health, the jury was still out on the emotional side of things. It turned out the military was much better at putting your body back together than your spirit.

I know, no whining. I just didn't know what to do.

I eventually had my bed linens changed and the entire room vacuumed. I had just finished putting the old sheets in the laundry when I yawned. It wasn't until that moment that I realized that I was actually sleepy. I guess hearing about different worlds and that there were new and interesting things that wanted to kill me was a little fatiguing. I changed clothes and sat down in my recliner to try and clear my mind.

Then it occurred to me that I might start dreaming about Malum again.

Oh, man, I don't want any more of those dreams right now. I don't think I'm up for it.

I almost stood up to make coffee, but settled back in my chair after a moment's hesitation. I realized that it wouldn't help a whole lot.

First, coffee never keeps me awake when I'm really tired, and I was exhausted. Second, I couldn't run from it for long, so I might as well face it now.

I had to face things, one way or the other.

So I did all I knew to do, in that I prayed about it and left it in God's hands. I really believed He could hear me, so I just prayed that He would keep me from messing this up too badly. Lord knows I already had enough bad decisions in my past to deal with that I didn't need more.

Before I knew it, I was nodding off in my recliner, so I moved to my bed. I slipped silently into a cozy unconsciousness and began to dream. But this time, I dreamed of my recently deceased father. I loved and missed my dad, and he was always a welcome part of my dreams.

In this particular dream, he gave me words of wisdom in his old southern drawl. He always had a way of cutting through the world's confusion with sage advice. Though I would not remember much of this particular dream later, his final words clung securely to the part of the mind that holds such things until daylight.

Before his weathered face faded from my mind, he simply said, *It's time, son.*

* * *

For being such a supposedly hardened combat vet, I felt like a bit of a weenie when it came to certain things. As it sometimes happened, I opened my eyes to the sound of my annoying alarm clock, only to find tears easing down my face. The reality of my dad's passing sometimes invaded my dreams and crashed back with my consciousness.

It hadn't been all that long ago when he passed on to the other side. Not quite a year, actually. It still hurt with a dull ache that was slowly, very slowly, being overtaken by the good memories.

I guess it's okay, even in manly-men quarters, to cry over losing your father, but I didn't like showing what I considered to be weakness. I hated crying in front of others when I was a kid, and I hated it even more as an adult. Fair or not, when I see a dude bawling I don't think of strength and stability.

So I wiped at my tears with the back of my hand and slowly sat up. I made a drowsy grab for the offensive noisemaker and caught it on the second try. It seemed to gleefully mock me, so I hurriedly shut off the alarm, turned on the radio, and rolled out of bed.

I was a little old-fashioned in that I still listened to the radio. That morning I wasn't so sure it was such a great idea. I had no sooner powered it up than the commentator led his segment with "In addition to the wave of home invasions that has hit the Memphis area and is bleeding to the south, there is now a string of murders following closely behind . . . "

No. I can't handle that this morning. Radio . . . off. Whew.

Maybe a quiet morning is the way to go. Yeah, let's do that.

Then the only sound was the *swish, swish, swish* of my shuffling feet on the tile floor.

Hey! No dreams last night. Thank you, Lord, for the little things . . . like Malum-dust free bedding.

I did my best to think positive and get pumped up for another day.

Okay, Jamie. It's a new day. You can chill and think things through some more. Maybe even talk to Boogie again. Yeah, that could work. I might even be able to catch him on the flight line during a lull in the action.

Within thirty minutes I had finished most of my morning routine, including my shower. I was walking into my bedroom to finish dressing for work when a small light grabbed my attention.

Huh? Is that the furnace? Weird. I've never noticed that light before . . .

I turned so I could trace the light to its source. When I did, I noticed that it was not a *point* of light, it was a *line* of light . . . that stretched from the floor to above my head, then horizontally for about one meter, then down again the other side to the floor.

A doorway.

In retrospect, I should have taken a deep breath and calmly thought about what I should do. I really hadn't made up my mind as to what I would do if a doorway appeared, but the sight of one right there in my apartment startled me.

I did what most trained soldiers would do when faced with danger or opportunity. I didn't think, I reacted. I reacted in a decisive and commanding way that would have made my old teammates proud.

Without hesitation, without preamble, and . . . without thinking, I stepped through the doorway.

PART II
SPARKS

CHAPTER 6

I wasn't at all sure what I expected to hear when I stepped through the door. I would have guessed silence, or the howling wind, or even a pitched battle between good and evil. But what I actually heard, loud and clear, was laughter.

That is so weird. What is going on?

The sound I heard wasn't just chuckles, but the all-out you're-the-butt-of-the-joke laughter. It started with a few voices and grew with a loud crescendo. Within seconds, dozens of people were enjoying a hearty belly laugh at some unsuspecting fool's expense.

Initially, all I could see was white light. However, as objects came into focus a few things became clear. First, I was standing in a clearing in the woods. The sun shone brightly as if it were the morning, and there were few clouds in the sky. The flora and fauna were very similar to our area of Mississippi.

Second, I was standing among a rather large group of tough-looking men. They all looked and acted as you would expect them to. That is, if you expected a group of rugged American males to greet you in this brave new world. However, it wasn't their muscles or tattoos that made them look tough. It was their eyes.

The last thing that occurred to me was that absolutely everyone was laughing. Except me. And they were all looking at me. At first, I didn't know if this was how they treated newbies or if I had something hanging out of my nose or, as the realization hit me . . . I had just gotten out of the shower and was wearing only a towel. The great warrior had come to the brave new world in barely more than his birthday suit.

Awesome. Welcome to Tough-Ville, towel-boy.

My face flushed hotter than it ever had before, tingling sharply with embarrassment. There was nothing to do but stand there and take it. I smiled a thin smile at my adoring fans, and I would have waved, but didn't want to risk losing the only "clothes" I brought with me.

What an entrance, hero. Unbelievable.

Momentarily, Boogie stepped from the crowd and made his way toward me. I could tell he was trying not to laugh, but the pursed lips and upturned ends of his mouth were indicators of the losing battle.

He suddenly succumbed to a broad grin and a hearty laugh. "I guess I forgot to tell you that you normally have a few minutes before the door closes, so you can, uh, quickly prepare for departure." He could barely get the last words out before he began laughing again.

"Yeah, I guess you did." Both of my hands grasped the towel, which now threatened to fly away in the afternoon breeze. I was not normally very shy, but this wasn't the way I would have chosen to meet my new team.

Boogie quickly motioned for me to follow him to the side of the clearing, not far from where we were standing. "We've got some extra clothes over here in these canvas bags. I think you can find something that fits you. There's a private area on the back side of this small hill where you can change clothes. When you get changed, come back to the clearing and I'll introduce you to the guys."

He smiled and shook his head as he walked away and disappeared around the side of the clearing. I was a little surprised that they would have something as normal as spare clothes here, but I obviously had a lot to learn about the place.

I rummaged through the bags until I found some old blue jeans, a T-shirt, and a pair of used hiking boots, size 10.5. The blue jeans were definitely used but had only one small hole in the right knee, whereas the T-shirt was almost new, prominently displaying the logo of a popular clothing company in yellow lettering on a navy blue background. All things considered, the clothes fit pretty well, and the shoes worked, too.

Once I finished lacing the boots, I stood and jogged back to where I'd last seen Boogie. He was clearly waiting for my return. Though he was conversing with Al and a guy I didn't know, he noticed my presence as soon as I walked into the clearing. Boogie left Al and the stranger to continue their conversation and walked over to me.

"Jamie, I'm really glad to see you. I'm sorry about the towel thing, but I think you made the right decision to come over." He said it like we were at a friend's house cooking out, and not in a strange world, entered through electric doorways.

"Since you were Air Force, you'll understand what I'm about to tell you." He gestured to the others. "What you see standing before you is the group we've been able to gather to date. Some of us have been here longer than others, so we're a bit more advanced in our training, which is primarily what we're doing." He paused for a moment. "At least so far."

"We're divided up into three different platoons." Boogie put one hand to his chest. "I'm in Alpha Platoon, since I have been here longer than most and we're a bit specialized." He didn't elaborate any further than that. "Al, who you met last night, is the leader of Bravo Platoon."

I saw Al at a distance across the meadow, casually chatting with a number of stout-looking guys. There looked to be twenty or twenty-five men standing around him. Most were in small groups of three or four, but they all laughed and joked quietly in the morning sun.

Boogie jerked his head in a *come on* motion to indicate I should walk with him across the meadow. "The most recently arrived people, such as yourself, are assigned to the newly formed Charlie Platoon. It's so new, in fact, that it's more like a squad than a platoon at the moment, as there are only a few members right now. You're actually number five, if you count the platoon's leader, Gunny."

I looked in the direction of Boogie's gaze. A lean man with short hair and a square jaw inspected me from a distance.

"Gunny, huh? As in a United States Marine Corps Gunnery Sergeant?"

"Yes, as in USMC." Boogie lowered his voice. "He really is a good guy but . . . uh . . . well . . . you will find that he's very enthusiastic about training."

Enthusiastic? Great.

Gunny didn't appear to be much taller than five-nine or much heavier than a hundred and seventy-five pounds, but somehow, he exuded intimidation and intensity. The man stared appraisingly at me, and nodded slightly in our direction when Boogie raised an open hand in friendly salute.

Standing next to Gunny were three fairly young dudes. Well, two guys who could have been the same person, cloned, and a third who couldn't have been any more different from the other two.

The two young men, for they looked to be about eighteen, were identical twins. They were both about six feet tall, lean, and had blond hair and blue eyes. They were dressed in knee-length shorts and casual shirts with clean tennis shoes and could have been on their way to a match at the local country club.

The third member of Charlie Platoon was big. I mean really big. He was at least six-three, his arms were as big as my legs, and his legs were easily three of mine wrapped together. He had a dark goatee and a mishmash of tattoos down both arms.

Boogie clapped my shoulder. "Jamie, we're about to get started, so I'm going to leave you in Gunny's capable hands." As an afterthought, he said, "I hope you're well rested."

After taking another look at Gunny, I hoped I was, too.

A man who appeared a little older than Boogie climbed onto a large rock in the center of the clearing. As he ascended to a convenient pseudo-platform on the top of the stone, the crowd immediately quieted and gathered around him.

I guessed that he was about fifty, though he looked fit and trim. However, the crow's-feet around his eyes and the gray hair above both ears showed that he had some mileage on him.

"Quickly, men," he said. "It's good to see everyone again. I need your complete dedication to training today. I don't know for sure, but I think we're going to have to soon shift from training and exercises to real-world operations"—he hesitated, as if the irony had just hit him—"of a sort, real soon."

He clasped his hands behind his back. "The bottom line is that I don't think we're going to have much more time to train, so get everything out of it that you can." His gaze swept the crowd and he got quiet nods in return. Then he shifted his tone slightly and opened his hands in a welcoming gesture. "But before we go on, I'd like to introduce the newest member of our group and the brand-new addition to Charlie Platoon, Jamie!"

I wasn't sure how he knew my name, but he smiled in my direction, as did many of the men present. A few even golf-clapped as a polite welcome. His disposition immediately shifted back toward the serious. "Boogie, take Alpha and work on your new tactics. I'd like some feedback from you when you get back."

Boogie nodded.

The leader then said, "Al, take Bravo on training route three. Expect some simulated contact from our role players. Today's role players will have on baseball caps to distinguish them as adversaries, so please do not mistake them for Malum and hurt each other."

A few of the rougher-looking Bravo teammates smiled and laughed a little under their breath. Al gave them a withering look. They immediately settled down.

Yep, Al was as tough as I thought.

"And watch out for non-role-players," the leader said. "Alpha has seen some possible Malum scouts wandering around our perimeter, so keep your heads up for the real thing. Gunny, take Charlie through training route one and tutor Jamie as much as you can. We need him to get up to speed quickly, and we need to know what we've got on our hands."

Gunny smiled broadly and gave a strong, traditional Marine Corps shout of "Ooh-rah, sir!"

The leader smiled. Many of the others of our group looked mildly entertained by Gunny's response, though they wouldn't look in Gunny's direction. My guess was they were afraid that Gunny might notice and would decide that they needed some "training," too.

"Boogie, Al, Gunny . . . brief your platoons and let's get started." The leader then stepped down from the rock and melted into the dispersing crowd.

While Boogie and Al began addressing their platoons, Gunny motioned for us to gather around him. He began to speak in the familiar, staccato tone of a military instructor. "Charlie Platoon, today we will execute training route one. We will depart in single file and you will not fall out. Jacob, Jared," he said, speaking to the twins, "you follow me. Jamie"—he looked in my direction—"you follow the Js and keep up. Tiny will bring up the rear."

He put his hands on his hips and occasionally used a knife hand to emphasize certain points. "We will double-time for most of the route. Concentrate on keeping your heads up and observing your environment. You cannot fight what you do not see." The sharp tones and deliberately emphasized syllables made me feel like I was back in boot camp, but the other members of Charlie Platoon just nodded.

"Also, if I draw my sword, mimic my movements with your swords. You have got to get used to doing everything with them in your hands. All right. Do you have any questions?"

I hesitated, but dutifully raised my hand.

"What is your question?" Gunny barked.

I felt pretty self-conscious, but said, "Um, Gunny, I've got a bit of a bum knee and I don't want to slow you guys down. I can probably keep up for a while, but it often gives out after a mile or two."

The other trainees just stared at me like I was very confused or not very bright. Then a lightbulb seemed to go off in Tiny's head and he said to Gunny, "Oh yeah, he's new. He doesn't know, right?"

"Know what?" I asked.

Gunny nodded and said, in a slightly less strident tone, "Jamie, some things are different here. They are not permanent and they do not carry back to other side, but they are consistently different."

Tiny nodded his huge cranium.

"For example, wounds heal quickly here, unless you are dead," Gunny said, quite deadpan. "Also, injuries and limitations that you have on the other side probably do not apply here. Now, you still have to get into and stay in shape, but I suspect your knee will hold up just fine."

Now that he had mentioned it, my knee hadn't ached even a little since I got there. I assumed I had just been too busy to notice. I bent my knee in a testing motion and it felt great. No pain.

"Anything else, Jamie? We are burning daylight and need to get moving."

"Yeah, I mean, yes, Gunny. Uh, where do I get a sword? Do we pick them up on the way out?"

My three teammates just laughed. The twins even broke into a mock sword fight while Tiny rumbled under his breath.

Okaay. It's definitely tease the new guy day.

"You'll see." Gunny turned and yelled, "Let's go!"

As we formed up to begin our foray into the cool forest, I turned my back on the clearing to get in line with the others. I heard Boogie give a shout of encouragement to his team and then I heard a loud whooshing noise. I glanced back toward his location and was immediately disoriented.

What in the world . . . ?

Bravo Platoon was standing alone in the quickly emptying clearing. The strange part wasn't that Al and the rest of his Bravo guys were still standing in the meadow, but that Boogie and the entirety of Alpha Platoon had disappeared into thin air. It's like they had evaporated or something.

If Alpha had indeed magically vanished, then Bravo did not appear the least bit disturbed by its disappearance. Momentarily, Al yelled out, "Let's roll!" and his team followed him down a beaten track at a moderate pace. Just as they reached the woods, I could have sworn I saw small flashes of light, and tiny glints of gold, but then they were gone.

CHAPTER 7

I barely had time to take it all in before Gunny took off into the woods like a crazed cheetah. Tiny and the twins easily kept pace but it was all I could do to keep up. I did my best to not lose sight of the Js as they romped down the trail. Their blond hair and white shirts were easier to keep sight of in the shadows of the forest than the shifting silhouette of Gunny. His old school fatigues and jungle boots blended easily into the shadows.

It was a nice surprise to not feel a bit of pain from my old wound. My knee felt excellent, just like Gunny said. However, the stitches in my side from being out of shape, well, that was a different matter entirely. While I didn't fall behind during the run, I did think I was going to collapse when we finally stopped.

"Okay," Gunny said without preamble, "Jacob, Jared, you two spar with Tiny. Concentrate on movement versus mass and use coordinated action. You flow pretty well together, but I want you to watch what moves the other is making so you can effectively complement each other."

At that, Jacob said to his brother, "My, you look good today!"

"Why, yes, I do," Jared answered. The twins laughed and continued "complementing" each other as they excitedly positioned themselves to fight Tiny. Gunny sighed deeply, shook his head and motioned for me to follow him a little farther into the clearing.

I wasn't sure what type of sparring Gunny meant for them to do, but I had no sooner turned my back on them than I heard "Hi-*ya!*" from one of the Js. I jerked my head around, and, miraculously, all three of my teammates had swords in their hands. The Js jumped and ran like hyperactive mongooses, but Tiny just calmly watched them.

For the most part, he stood motionless, his eyes following their feints and crazed antics. He moved only to parry swings that got too close. The Js took turns taking swipes at him, almost all of which were easily batted away by the big guy. Tiny moved a lot faster than you would have imagined.

Gunny must have had eyes in the back of his head, because he barely got out, "And, Js, don't get—"

His sentence was interrupted by a loud "Aaagghh!" from Jared as he got swiped with the flat slide of Tiny's blade.

"—cocky." He shook his head but kept walking, leading me in the other direction.

He yelled over his shoulder. "Set up and start again. This time, practice what I have taught you."

A calmer commotion suggested they were listening to Gunny. It was only a minute before I heard Tiny grunting and puffing. Whatever the twins were now doing, it was making him work harder to keep them at bay.

I think Gunny saw the look of fear in my eyes when Jared was hit by Tiny's sword. He told me, "Don't worry, these swords will not normally kill you. They kill Malum. However," he added, "glancing blows sting like paper cuts."

"And non-glancing blows?"

Gunny gazed upward for just a moment and then asked me, "Have you ever been stun-gunned? You know, like with a police officer's weapon?"

I shook my head.

"Well, it can feel a lot worse than that if it goes deep, especially if it stays there."

"Uh, has anyone ever died from friendly 'shocking'?" I asked, only half joking.

Without skipping a beat he said, "Not in a long time," his expression as serious as ever.

He's kidding, right?

Gunny abruptly spun in my direction. "Jamie, have you ever had any kind of martial arts training? You know, like karate or judo or anything?"

"Tae kwon do, but that was a long time ago."

"Well, when we fight I want you to concentrate on my torso. Use your peripheral vision to see the blows and block them or move out of the way."

Huh? What was this fight Gunny thing? And with what?

"You want me to spar with you? You mean do some tae kwon do?"

"No. We fight with weapons." He had no sooner uttered those words than a sword appeared in his hand.

It was just like the one from my dream. It had a gold handle and the shiny silver blade even sparkled. He looked at me expectantly.

Sweat broke out on my forehead. I backed away.

What kind of crazed place is this?

Come on, dude. Stay calm.

"How did you do that, and where am I supposed to get one?"

"You've already got one." He smiled, but it wasn't a happy one. It was more like a smirk. That bothered me less than his eyes, though.

They were filled with malice.

Oh . . . no.

He attacked.

Gunny's first swing was perfectly horizontal. It was clearly aimed to separate my head from my shoulders. I stumbled back wildly. "Wait!"

As if that would help.

He showed no signs of stopping. Or hesitating. Or anything else that would be considered fair.

His blade passed precariously close to my jugular vein. There was a brief flash of heat as it passed. It felt like the tip of a hot fireplace poker being waved in my face.

Move, Jamie!

He immediately followed through with a reverse swing. It came awfully close to searing my heaving chest. I even heard a sizzle as it passed.

I was barely able to stay on my feet. I stumbled over rocks and tree roots, but Gunny mercilessly stalked me. Another swipe had me diving out of the way.

Enough of this.

I intentionally rolled an extra few feet from him to gain some extra space. When I regained my balance I popped up in a fighting stance. I squared on Gunny and his gleaming saber.

Okay, what now?

Come on, Jamie! Where did you get the sword last time?

I looked around furiously.

Gunny paused briefly, and then pursued me. With deliberate steps, he quickly got within striking distance. He brought his sword down in a vicious vertical arc. It was aligned to hit the middle of my head.

I had nowhere to go and reacted instinctively. I braced my left foot behind me and brought my right fist up.

Oh, man. This is gonna hurt!

In the blink of an eye a gleaming sword appeared in my hand. It felt natural and perfectly balanced in my upraised hand.

So. Cool. I have my own sword!

Oh, wait.

Gunny's sword crashed into mine in a reverberating shower of sparks. It sounded like a power station being hit by lightning.

Dude! Remember Gunny? The whole shock-you-to-death-with-a-sword thing?

I could almost hear my dad yelling, *Pay attention to what you're doin', son!*

Right.

I was able to absorb the blow, and his sword bounced off my blade. I stopped the momentum just inches from my sweaty hair.

Gunny stepped back and calmly assessed my reaction.

"Hmm. Glad to see you decided to fight, Jamie. Now, let's see what you've got."

He stepped in my direction again, hacking high and low. It appeared he was searching for an opening in my defenses.

What did I do to make this guy so mad?

We fought for what felt like forever. In the middle of everything, a detached part of me realized that he wasn't even breathing hard. My breathing was coming in gasps.

Keep fightin', Jamie.

I constantly moved my feet and looped around in a circle. Like boxers do. I didn't want to get cornered. My shuffling feet kicked up dust here and there.

Gunny repeatedly attacked. He was relentless.

Yet, I was getting better at blocking the blows and avoiding attacks altogether. I guess a little on-the-job training can make you sharp.

Even my breathing settled into a sustainable rhythm.

I would like to brag and say I was a natural at sword fighting. Maybe I was. But all I cared about right then was that I was good enough to keep from getting fried.

The only sounds were crackling pops of swords meeting in air and sizzles of near misses. We kept circling.

Now what? How do I get outta this one?

The words of one of my old instructors came to mind. *Just mimic what I do, your body will pick it up.*

I decided to give it a shot.

When Gunny attacked, I memorized his moves. When I had a chance, I tried the same moves on him. He feigned, then sliced. I blocked. I feigned, then sliced. He blocked.

I turned his attacks into a "monkey-see, monkey-do" for me.

It actually worked, at least for the first few minutes. I threw in a few more attacks where I could. One of them actually came close enough to Gunny that I saw surprise in his eyes.

Yeah, boy! That was how I roll!

I began to feel good. In fact, I began to get fairly confident. Some might say overconfident.

I smiled. And . . . that was the moment my enthusiasm outran my capabilities.

Gunny saw me smile, and his eyes darkened.

Uh-oh.

He suddenly stopped and looked at me. With a patronizing stare, he said, "Didn't you say you were in the Air Force?"

When did I ever tell him that?

Still breathing hard, I said, "Yeah, I was."

What did that have to do with anything?

He verbally blindsided me. "I can see why they ran you off. You don't seem to be much of a fighter."

What . . . ?

"Yep, I think you and the Air Force are better off with you as a civilian."

Oh, uh-uh.

My fist went white-knuckle on my sword. I could feel myself losing my cool, but I couldn't stop it.

Through clenched teeth I growled, "You don't know what I've been through. You've got no right." I could feel my face flush.

"Whatever, son. I suppose your poor little knee was a good excuse to get lazy again. You'll do the same thing here. I can tell you'll quit when the going gets tough."

His words were raw fuel on my fury. It was like someone suddenly flicked the rage switch inside me.

Oh, Gunny, you're gonna pay.

If I had taken a moment to look, I would have seen that the Js and Tiny were rooted in place, faces filled with shock.

I attacked.

My blade became a silver blur. I jabbed from every direction. I swung for all I was worth, aiming primarily for his face. It was almost as if my body was on autopilot, set to destroy mode.

Come on, Gunny. Step right up. I'll fix that smirking mug for ya.

Our swords were like bright flashes of light. They created a constant shower of sparks as they met in midair. Cracks and pops snapped in the breeze.

I began to physically back Gunny toward the tree line that surrounded the clearing. I was winning. I was going to get him.

He suddenly lurched at me. He froze me by grabbing my sword-bearing arm with his free hand. Our swords were effectively locked between us. They crackled and hissed.

He stared in my face for a moment and then laughed. "I guess you couldn't cut it, huh? I always knew you Airmen were a bunch of pansies."

He shoved me backward, as if I wasn't worth his time. He began to walk away.

My vision turned red. All sound, save the pounding of blood, ceased. I could see nothing but the slowly retreating form.

Nothing else mattered.

With the scream of a wounded animal, I charged.

I was on him in a second. I leapt forward in a fury and swung my blade. I aimed for the center of his torso.

Gunny spun, bringing his sword up. He blocked my swing. His sword took the brunt of my initial stroke with a loud crash. The sound echoed off of the trees.

He was unprepared for my follow-on. I hit him with a part martial arts, part backyard brawl spinning leg sweep. A surprised look enveloped his face as his world began to rotate clockwise.

His feet seemed to defy gravity. They spun higher than his counter-rotating head. Gunny hit the ground hard with a bone-rattling thud and an audible "oof!" A small cloud of dust marked his impact.

His sword lay still in his motionless hand.

He was flat on his back. It looked like he couldn't find his breath . . . which left him wide open. I didn't hesitate.

Two steps covered the distance between us.

I brought my sword down in a harsh vertical ellipse, swinging toward his torso with enough torque to split a tree. I wish I could say I knew my blow wouldn't badly hurt him. I have to admit part of me wanted to find out if that were true.

I stared into Gunny's eyes as I brought my sword down. I hoped to see confusion, or anguish, or better yet, fear.

I didn't. His eyes were different. They were full of . . .

. . . something that took a moment too long for me to comprehend.

A searing blade entered my chest, just below my sternum. The light of his sword was so close and so bright I could actually see the morbid scene reflected in Gunny's eyes. The whole thing had been an act.

Gunny had feigned his fall and was only waiting for an opening. An opening that I had all too quickly given him. He buried his sword to the hilt in my chest and stared intently into my dismayed face.

I could not speak. I could not move. I could not think.

The only sound was the crackling of his sword in my chest. Instead of stabbing and removing the sword, he left it there. I felt as if my insides were being microwaved on high and my finger was stuck in a high-voltage outlet.

My mouth opened in a silent scream, and the world faded to black.

* * *

My next memory was of cool green grass on my face and of the contented chirping of small birds. I did not feel the terrible, jolting pain anymore, but I did feel like I had gone a few rounds with a professional fighter, and lost badly. A deep and pounding ache in my chest was very slowly abating.

I gradually opened my watery eyes, only to see a serene-looking Gunny standing over me. His sword was nowhere in sight. He had one hand open to show no ill intent and the other extended to help me up.

You gotta be kidding me.

Well Jamie, you can either lie there on the ground like a loser or get up.

I didn't want to, but I accepted Gunny's hand and slowly stood.

My chest ached and my back throbbed. I instinctively rubbed the sore spot on my upper torso. Little flecks of burnt T-shirt came off in my hand, but my skin felt okay.

Wonderful. Fried to a crisp and back again.

The world was spinning, so I put my hands on my knees and tried to steel my balance. The Js and Tiny walked over and watched Gunny and me very carefully. When I glanced at them, their faces were filled with fear and apprehension.

Gunny's countenance had changed considerably. He didn't look aggressive. He didn't even look angry. In fact, he had an unexpected, fatherly look on his face.

"Jamie, can you hear me?" He stood barely a foot away. I nodded and slowly straightened up. For many reasons, I did not trust myself to speak.

Gunny looked intently into my eyes. "I need you to listen very carefully to what I'm about say, because it is important."

Whatever, man.

I stared at him and nodded again.

"Jamie, that was the best fighting I have ever seen from a new recruit."

Huh?

"I will add that, right up to the point where you became careless, it was some of the best fighting I have ever seen. You have got a gift. It is something really special and we need to develop it. If we *can* develop it, I think you can be one of the best. Ever."

I didn't know whether to say thank you or take a swing at him. So I just stood there and did neither.

His eyes narrowed as we peered at each other.

He addressed the whole group. "However, there is something that you have got to understand. These things that we're up against, these Malum, will use anything they can to distract you. They want to hurt you, to kill you, and they do not play by the rules."

The trio of trainees raptly followed every word he said.

"They sometimes know things that there is no way they should know. They will use that knowledge, and any kind of weakness they can find, to distract you and defeat you."

"You mean like what you just did to Jamie?" Tiny said.

"Yes, Tiny. Just like I did to Jamie. Malum are ruthless and merciless and they will attempt to win at all costs. Now, do all of you understand today's lesson?"

Everyone nodded, except me. I wasn't buying it.

He set the whole thing up. The teasing, the taunting. It's like he wanted to humiliate me. I think he actually enjoyed it.

"If you let them get inside your head . . . "

"Then you leave them an opening. An opening that can kill you," Jacob finished.

Gunny nodded and smiled slightly. "You must remain calm, and focused. Remember, anything they say or do is to hurt you. Ooh-rah?"

"Ooh-rah, Gunny," the other three said.

He turned and looked at me.

"And you, Jamie? Do you have anything you would like to add?"

I didn't dare say what I really thought.

"No."

"I see." For a few moments, the only sound was the breeze through the trees.

"Okay, enough lollygagging." Gunny clapped his hands together and rubbed them. "I think we're ready for some more double-time." After a last glance at me, Gunny turned away.

Everyone quickly lined up and I fell in at the back of the formation. I needed to cool off. Surprisingly, other than a tad of vertigo, I seemed to be no worse for the wear. We accelerated through the woods, running back along the trail by which we had come.

I replayed the whole thing over and over, which was probably the wrong thing to do.

Come on, Jamie. Settle down.

Well, he didn't have to embarrass me like that. And he sure didn't have to stun me until I passed out. That wasn't cool. And for what? So we can zap Nasties here in la-la-land? I just don't get it.

I mean, really. Is it worth all this?

CHAPTER 8

While I wrestled with my thoughts, we ran. We ran for miles. We didn't stop until we made it all the way back to where the day's odyssey had begun.

We were all winded, but unhurt. Except for my pride, that is. I calmed down on the outside but couldn't shake a tinge of residual anger.

"Everybody take a breather," Gunny said. "We'll debrief in a few minutes."

I wandered away, looking for a minute to myself.

Well, that was fun. Not.

At least my knee felt good. That was something, right?

I bent over and put my hands on my thighs again, trying to catch my breath. A slight movement on the far side of the clearing caught my eye. I squinted from the sunlight into the shadows.

I looked up in time to see our leader in earnest discussion with a young lady. This seemed really odd to me. It wasn't the fact that he was talking to someone, it was the realization that I had not seen a woman here since my arrival.

I could see only the girl's back from where I was standing. She had shoulder-length brown hair and was of average height. She wore blue jeans, a tan jacket and held a pair of sunglasses in one hand and a cap in the other.

At that moment the man glanced up. He saw Charlie Platoon in the clearing and said something to the newcomer that provoked an abrupt end to their conversation. She began to walk away, her back still to us. However, she momentarily turned and glanced in our direction.

I don't know what I expected, but I didn't think I would see a beautiful girl standing here in Nasty-land. Even from here I could tell she had a striking, but delicate, appearance. There was a deliberateness in her movement that I found intriguing. Her pretty eyes scanned the faces of Charlie Platoon.

No, it can't be. It is! It's the manager from the coffee shop. What's she doing here?

I was staring intently at her face when she turned her head a bit more. The moment she looked in my direction, recognition flashed across her features.

Of course, my inner nerd decided that would be a great time to show up.

She remembers me too!

I reflexively rose, smiled at her and gave a big wave.

Not awkward. *At all.*

Her deep brown eyes grew as wide as coffee cups. I could swear she blushed. She almost seemed transfixed my presence.

My first thought? She really does dig me! I knew it.

Second thought? Oh, wait. I'm in thrift store leftovers, and I probably have dried drool right beside the big burned spot on my shirt.

Welcome back, reality.

She transformed pretty rapidly by donning her sunglasses and tucking her hair inside her cap. It was like she was a superhero putting her disguise back on. She abruptly walked away from our leader and departed into the forest.

I would say that I watched her go, but she, in fact, disappeared into the foliage. It was like the forest swallowed her. So mysterious.

Our leader observed me with an intense stare.

Oh, boy.

His serious expression reminded me of the look my father would give me when I had just disappointed him. Actually, maybe it was more a look of concern. But I wasn't sure about whom he was more concerned, me or the pretty girl I had just seen disappearing into the woods.

I guess I'm about to find out. Here he comes.

He strode across the clearing and walked straight up to me. Without prelude, he offered his hand.

"So, Jamie, how did it go with Gunny today?" The tone of his voice gave him away. I could tell he already knew.

I wasn't sure how to respond. I mechanically shook his hand. "It was okay, I guess."

"It was? Are you sure?" he asked with a not-unkind voice.

Come on, man. There's a big hole burned in my shirt. How do you think it went?

"Gunny did say that I have a knack for fighting, so I'm hanging my hat on that. One step at a time, right?" I wasn't very convincing.

He had a pained look on his face. "Look, Jamie. I know we're asking a lot from you. My guess is that you feel like you were treated unfairly today."

You think?

He waited for a reply, but I just shrugged.

He put his hands together in a plaintive gesture and steepled them together under his chin. "I am sorry about that. I hope we can figure out a way to help you understand the *why* a little better. I can't explain everything right now, but would it help if I told you a bit more?"

"If you think it would help this 'pansy' get it," I said, dripping with sarcasm.

Nice work, Jamie. Are you going to offend everyone, or just your new bosses?

He looked back with sorrowful eyes.

I took a deep breath and tried to start over. "Listen. I am sorry about that. It is hard for me to understand what's worth all of this." I gestured at the gathering crowd. "I took a leap of faith by showing up today, but I guess it has sort of left me with more questions than answers."

I realized I was absentmindedly rubbing my chest where I had been stabbed. I tried to act like I was dusting off my shirt, instead.

Real smooth, Jamie.

Before he had a chance to respond I asked, "Sir, what's your name?" I didn't want to be impertinent, but I didn't think "Hey . . . man!" would work very long.

He smiled and casually put his hands in his pockets. "You can call me R.B. I'm not sure if you've noticed or not, but for reasons of security we try not to use full names if we can help it."

Actually, I hadn't noticed it. What, was it like a secret code or something?

He must have seen the confusion in my face. "It's like this. These guys take care of each other and watch each other's backs when they're here. When they go back through the veil, they are mostly on their own. Except for when you see Boogie and Al, or other members of our team, you will be, too."

"Okaaay." I still didn't get it.

"We believe that the things we fight here are also present on our side of the world. Though for various reasons, they usually stay hidden"

"Hidden? On our side of the world?"

"Right. They roam, more strongly in some areas than others, but they roam nonetheless. And they listen carefully to whatever might help their cause."

"Wait a minute. I thought we came *here* to fight the Malum."

"We do come here to fight them. That is true. But honestly, the main reason we don't fight them on the other side is because they don't want to have an open war over there. At least not yet."

"Why not?"

"Truthfully? They're having a lot of success by running reconnaissance there and fighting here. They have no reason to change their tactics so far."

I massaged my forehead and exhaled. It was an awful lot to try to take in.

He pointed at the ground as he spoke. "I'll give you the bottom line up front. The things we do here have an effect in our world. If we kill Malum here, their effects are gone from our families' side of the veil. In total, we make life better over there by fighting here. It's as simple as that."

Hmm. Maybe.

"R.B., I hear what you're saying but are you sure about all of this 'Malum influence' stuff? Maybe people are just doing bad things because they are bad people. Are you sure Malum are behind every-thing bad?"

"No, son. Not everything."

He glanced at the almost-filled clearing. "I guess you can consider this a shadow war. We know they are on this side of the veil. They know we are here, too. And we're each preparing to fight the other. I don't know exactly why the war is heating up here, but it's just the way things are at the moment."

"So, you're saying they're getting ready to attack?"

He tilted his head back and forth in a *perhaps* kind of motion. "My—" He began, then caught himself. "—sources say the Malum have a local group that has recently grown. They hope to find us and crush us before we can become a potent fighting force. Does that make sense, Jamie?"

I got it, I just wasn't sure I believed it. I nodded anyway.

He put his hand on my shoulder for a moment. "If you'll apply yourself to your training and give us all you've got, we'll do our best to make all this make sense to you. I would be lying if I said I under-stood everything about this world, but the longer you're here, the more things will fall into place."

If you say so, dude.

"What's the difference between Alpha and Bravo Platoons? They both seem pretty experienced to me."

What I really meant was that I would love to get away from Gunny. Surely there was a way for me to move over to Boogie's platoon.

If I kept coming back to this place at all . . .

At that moment Bravo Platoon came barging into the clearing, clearly agitated. A few of the members were talking excitedly to each other, which was to say they looked a little upset. Al looked around the clearing. His eyes searched until he found R.B.

He strode toward us at a quick clip.

We could both see the stressed look on Al's face, so he answered quickly, "Bravo Platoon are some of our best ground fighters. They excel at sword fighting and squad-level tactics. They are also some of our fiercest warriors."

"And Alpha Platoon . . . ?" I asked.

Still looking at Al, R.B. said, "Why don't you ask Boogie?"

"Uh, sure. I will as soon as he gets back."

"He's back." He glanced momentarily upward, then turned and walked toward Al. They met in the middle of the clearing and began to confer.

Al was quite animated. He pointed toward the area from which they had come. I turned away from Al and R.B. and, not knowing what else to do, glanced in the same direction as R.B. had.

All I could see as I looked over the tops of the pine trees and into the sky was a flock of birds. They were really big birds . . . that didn't have wings . . . and were flying toward our clearing at a high rate of speed.

With R.B.'s warning about Malum fresh in my ears, I assumed the worst.

Oh, no! The Malum have found us and are attacking with bird-Malum-men! We're not ready!

I spun and ran, shouting, "Look out! Incoming!" And . . . I promptly tripped over my shoes that didn't fit quite right. I landed on my stomach with an "unngh!"

I managed to draw my sword and tried to regain my feet. A heavy foot stomped down on my sword-bearing hand while the bright light of the sun blinded me.

My only thought was that I didn't even make it through my initial day of training before getting it. I was about to lash out with my free hand with a last-gasp attack when I heard, "Easy, Jamie! It's me, Boogie."

I blinked a couple of times and the "large birds" came into focus. It was Alpha Platoon. They had just returned. From flying. And they were laughing at me. Again.

It didn't last long. One look at the blood-soaked Bravo troop was enough to end it.

"Get him over here!"

Some guys from Bravo carried a wounded man over to a cot. A guy I later found out was called Fudd quickly began working on him, trying to stop the bleeding.

"Everyone, to the clearing!" R.B. called.

Alpha and Charlie troops walked to the center of the gathering spot, as did Bravo, albeit grudgingly. They kept looking over their shoulders at their wounded comrade.

"Men, I've heard from Al and Boogie. Given the circumstances, I think it is important that everyone knows what happened. Al, you lead."

"It's like this. We screwed up, y'all. We let our guard down. I sent guys to screen our training area, and Marco stumbled into a Malum scout. Marco got him, but not before the Malum got a good swing in on him."

I glanced at Marco, who was writhing in pain.

Al continued. "Even with R.B.'s warning this morning, we just weren't expecting to see 'em. I take full responsibility. I shoulda known they would be there."

All at once, the Bravo guys began defending Al.

"No, that ain't right!"

"Uh-uh! It's not his fault."

R.B. held his hands up in a calming gesture and yelled, "It's no one's fault, least of all you, Al. This is dangerous stuff. Unfortunately, sometimes things happen."

This settled everyone down a little. The next bit of news helped, too.

Fudd jogged over. "He's going to be fine. We stopped the bleeding."

You could almost feel the collective exhale.

He continued. "He'll have to come up with a good excuse for being weak tomorrow, but he should recover quickly. As long as no one sees the leg wound while it heals, none should be the wiser."

One of the Bravo guys shouted in Marco's direction, "That won't be so hard. He was already weak!"

All we could see from the cot was an arm shooting straight up in the air with a thumbs-up.

Warrior humor. Laughter rippled through the crowd.

R.B. turned to Boogie. "From your vantage point, what happened?"

Boogie's normally-calm exterior appeared very strained. Uncharacteristically, he fidgeted and there was raw emotion in his voice. "R.B., first off, we had no idea Bravo had gotten hit. You know we run patrols over Bravo and Charlie while they are training. We checked on both of them today, but it just wasn't enough. It might be time—"

R.B. cut him off. "Understood, Boogie. It's okay. You guys were doing your job right. Please continue with your report."

"Okay." Boogie took a breath. "Weasel and I had just finished dog-fighting practice, so we decided to do a perimeter sweep." When he said Weasel, he pointed to another guy about Boogie's height and weight, but with a shaved head and a goatee. His facial features had a mischievous sparkle to them, and he stood quietly with arms crossed. His blue eyes darted back and forth.

As Boogie recited the story he began to calm. "We knew the areas where Bravo and Charlie were training so, as I mentioned, we did a few passes to check on them."

He glanced in my direction and nodded as his eyes flicked toward the burned mark on my shirt. I guessed he had seen me getting my butt kicked.

Could this day get any worse?

He returned his attention to R.B. "However, when we did our last pass, I noticed something. There was an unidentified individual lurking near Bravo's training area. At least we thought it was only one. So Weasel and I decided to intercept him."

I was doing my best to follow what Boogie described. There was somebody, or something, that was hanging out near Al's group and they wanted to ensure it wasn't something bad.

I guess they only saw one of them.

Oh. That's why Boogie was upset. They missed one.

"Weasel and I approached the area as stealthily as we could. I signaled that we needed to do an ID." He looked toward the new guys. "An identification maneuver. Weasel and I climbed pretty high, then we split up to bracket him. The Nasty didn't make things easy. He kept close to the woods with thick forest at his back." Boogie looked toward us newbies again. "Some of the Malum are really good at tearing through the forest, which makes it difficult to run them down."

Malum can run fast? I hadn't considered what they might be like outside of a mini-mart. What else could they do?

He continued. "As soon as Weasel saw that I had made it to a blocking position, he flew straight down at the bogey and startled him so badly that he flickered."

Interesting. That's exactly the same thing the Malum did when I startled him in my so-called dream.

"At that," Boogie said, "the chase was on. Weasel?"

Weasel took a few steps closer to R.B. "Once he flickered, I knew he was a Nasty, but he was already tearing away from me like a scalded dog." Weasel said this in an easy cadence and sounded remarkably similar to Al. I guess that stood to reason, since most of the guys in our group appeared to be from the area. "Unlike Bravo's guy, this one didn't try to fight at all. He just ran through the woods at breakneck speed, tryin' to lose me." Weasel grinned. "And no, he didn't lose me. But he did find Boogie." Weasel pointed toward Boogie, who then resumed the story.

"I positioned myself at the most likely avenue of escape, and Weasel did a masterful job of herding him in my direction. I didn't think it likely that we could catch him without suffering injury, so I dusted him."

"What he did was an amazing dive"—Weasel mimicked the moves with his hands—"from very high altitude to very low, ending with a killer attack pass. He leveled off about six inches above the ground. I've never seen anything like it."

All I could think was "Awesome!" This might seem a little strange, but imagining flying and cutting down Nasties with a sword brought a smile to my face. However much harm they might or might not have been doing, it was Malum huntin' season! Maybe there was a good reason to stick around after all.

Boogie looked as blasé as if Weasel had described a Sunday stroll. "At that point, we thought we had de-loused Bravo, so we came home."

"You did, brother. If we woulda bumped into the second one in the wrong place, the result coulda been much worse." Al fist-bumped Boogie.

R.B. took this all in, his forehead creased by a frown. "Alpha, Bravo . . . I am extremely proud of how you handled yourselves today." While his praise was well deserved, the look on his face gave away some unspoken concerns. "I'm sorry we put you in a spot where that could happen, and that's my fault." He held up a hand to ward off the protests. "The buck stops here. The end."

He spoke to the fatigued crowd. "Okay, guys. It has been an exciting day. I think it's time we wrapped things up. Al, make sure somebody helps Marco through the door and also checks on him on the other side, okay?"

"You got it, Boss."

While I knew that time worked differently here, the sun was still beginning to ease toward the horizon. The fading light gave away the location of multiple "electric" doors, which I hadn't noticed earlier.

"I don't know how many days it will be before we are back, but I suspect it will be sooner, rather than later. Until next time, God be with you." R.B. smiled and motioned for us to continue through the doors.

I jogged up to Boogie, who was walking toward an exit. He looked weary, but smiled when I approached.

"Hey, Jamie. So, what do you think?" It was a simple question, but I found myself at a loss for words.

Boogie nodded thoughtfully. "I know, dude. It's a lot to take in." He shifted gears. "Gunny told me about your training today."

Great. Why was everyone on my case?

I shrugged.

"What he told me was that you're a natural."

Wait for it . . .

"He also said that you may not be 'all in' with your training. That something's holding you back."

There it is.

I was about to protest when he stopped me. "Jamie, it's okay. It's my fault we're running you this hard. I told R.B. to really put the pressure to you."

Boogie was in on this?

"I figured that if you can break out of . . . well . . . whatever's holding you back . . . " He shook his head in apparent self-recrimination.

I didn't know what to say.

"Jamie, despite how you're probably feeling right now, I still think you're cut out for this. You just have to find your way. I hope we see you over here again." He walked away.

"Wait!" I really wanted to explain. I took a breath to begin . . .

Wait what, dude? What are you going to say? You're tired of being abused and hurt? Are you going to talk about your feelings? Let. It. Go.

Yeah.

"Um, does it matter which door I pick?"

With understanding eyes, Boogie shook his head. "Nope. Pick any you want, they'll take you home."

Boogie nodded and stepped through the nearest door, disappearing from sight. Without a second thought, I followed and vanished into an electric door in the woods.

CHAPTER 9

I found myself standing in my quiet apartment.

All right then. Welcome back, Jamie.

I glanced down at my borrowed clothes, complete with burned spot in the middle of my shirt. At least I knew it wasn't a dream. That was something to hold onto.

I turned to look at the door, and it was gone. Not a flicker of light was left behind.

So that's how the whole thing works, huh?

At that moment I realized I felt different, but in a good way.

It was sort of like someone had pushed my reset button when I came back through the door. I took a deep breath and realized that I felt refreshed, almost like I had just risen from a good night's sleep. I looked at the wall clock and realized that, for all intents and purposes, that was exactly what had just happened.

Al wasn't joking. I had returned to the same place and the same time from which I had departed. The only difference was that I was sans one towel and had added some less-than-gently-used articles to my sparse clothing collection.

That also meant it was time to go to work.

In short order, I changed out of my borrowed duds and put on my work clothes. I didn't feel dirty or smell bad, despite the fact that I had spent the last "day" training in the woods. It was a little unseemly, but I actually sniffed my armpits to make sure. Nope, smelled like clean skin and soap, at least for the time being.

On the way to work, I let the training day's events replay in my head. For better or worse, it made my normal work day seem quite boring.

I was far from knowing whether that was a good thing or not.

I made it in a bit early and decided to relax for a few minutes. I slipped through the door and helped myself to the snack bar. I was sipping coffee when Peggy rounded the corner.

"Jamie! I'm glad to see you."

Her eyes were bright and she almost clapped her hands. She looked exceptionally pleased that I was there. She even came over and did what I call a Southern Mama hug on me. It's like a bear hug, but much nicer.

"Um, I'm glad to see you, too, Peggy. Is everything okay?"

"Sure! Yes!" She seemed to realize she was being very enthusiastic. "I'm . . . just really glad you decided to make it to work on time."

Not *even* awkward. You are getting so weird, Peggy.

I liked her though, so I didn't mind the attention. Even if she was beginning to push the strange meter to the limit.

"Yes, well, I had to make up for my last-second show before. It all evens out, right?"

"Yes it does, Jamie. Have a good day, darlin'."

She spun around so fast her floral skirt swirled. Just like that, she was gone.

I shook my head and sighed.

Bless her heart.

Okay, Jamie. Step one, get to work. Check. Step two, actually do work.

I will, as soon as I finish my—

Ed banged through the door and yelled, "Jamie, let's go!"

—coffee. Oh well.

"Coming, dear!"

I hopped up, trashed what was left of my brew, and headed for the door. I was the last one out of the room, so I charged ahead. As I moved to step outside, the hair on the back of my neck stood up and a jolt of electricity surged through my body.

Old senses, long dormant, were suddenly tingling. Someone was after me.

Too late, I realized that I couldn't stop myself from crossing the threshold.

Move, Jamie!

I spun hard left as soon as I exited. My maneuver put the door between me and whatever was after me. I braced for impact.

Nothing happened. The only sound was my heavy breathing.

Check your six o'clock, dude!

I spun around. Nothing there either.

Wha . . . ?

Slowly, I peeked from behind the door.

Nada.

Seriously, dude? Come. On. This Malum stuff is already making you crazy!

I glanced around one more time. The only person who seemed to actually be watching me was a student pilot. He was big-eyed, helmet in hand, just staring at me. He looked very confused by my gymnastic dismount from the building.

I waved.

He haltingly waved back and resumed walking. You could almost see him thinking, *Crazy maintenance guys!* I couldn't blame him.

I crept from behind the door and incrementally increased my speed to a trot to catch up with Ed. By the time I did, he was already servicing a tire and singing loudly. That little bit of normalcy felt comforting right then. One more scan confirmed that we were alone.

You must have a wire loose, bro. There's no one there.

I kept telling myself that all morning, despite the fact I still felt like someone was lurking nearby. The feeling lasted until almost noon, before it finally faded.

Get a grip, Jamie. There is no one watching you.

* * *

I felt a hand on my shoulder and jumped. I instinctively spun, tire tool in hand.

Boogie looked back at me with concern.

"Boogie, hey! Sorry, I didn't hear you walk up."

No wonder, really. There were no fewer than three jet engines running nearby, and I had my hearing protection on.

"Sorry about that, man! I didn't mean to startle you."

He looked as together as ever. I felt like I was the proverbial cat in the room of rocking chairs. I tried to act normal, though I was less sure what normal was.

"So, are you coming next week?" he said.

Next week? What's . . . oh, right, the cookout at his house. I forgot.

My training shenanigans flashed to mind. I think I offended pretty much everyone I could. It hadn't exactly been my best day.

Oh, boy. I figured I might as well get this out in the open.

"Do you still want me to come? You know, since my . . . performance the other day. You know—" I whispered just loudly enough to be heard by him "—over *there?*"

Boogie grinned and nodded. "Of course, Jamie. Whatever you decide about . . . that, well, I hope you still consider me a friend."

That made me smile. He really was a good dude.

"In that case, sure. You know . . . I have been thinking about what you said over there and I—" Boogie coughed and then shook his head. He gave me a *not here* look just as another IP and student walked by.

Right. Act like our training day never happened. I can do that.

Considering how I'd felt watched all morning, the no-talky-talky-about-our-training thing didn't seem quite so silly anymore. My senses had never failed me before, and they had told me something was sneaking around that morning.

It all made sense. Or . . . I was completely losing my mind.

You're in it up to your neck, Jamie. Nothing to do but keep rolling and see what happens.

So we chatted about a whole lot of nothing for a few minutes. Small talk. The only acknowledgment Boogie gave that our training day ever happened was to say, "Take care of yourself, Jamie. You're a valuable member of our team."

It was something that he could have said to anyone working the flight line, but I understood it for what he really meant. *Watch out and keep your mouth closed. Malum are listening.*

* * *

Workdays continued and time passed quickly. Before I knew it, a weekend had already come and gone without any electric doorways appearing.

Was something wrong? Could I have been uninvited? I couldn't blame them if it were true.

But there was no use worrying about it. Carry on, dude.

So, carry on I did.

I went to work and fixed airplanes. I came home and exercised. Things actually began to feel pretty normal. No paranoia, no sword fights, no electric shocks.

In other words, I was bored. My adrenaline hadn't spiked once that week.

Yeah, I was aware I didn't exactly thrive last time out. But . . . you know. Maybe the whole thing was growing on me.

The following Saturday afternoon I was tinkering around my house, trying to stay busy. I was in the middle of fixing a faulty toilet seat when I saw a familiar light emanating from the hallway. I quickly stowed my tools and prepared to depart.

Slow down, Jamie. Remember last time.

How could I forget?

I took a minute to ensure that I was appropriately dressed before stepping through the door and into the now-familiar light.

Fool me once . . .

The whole crew arrived at the same time.

I saw Boogie and Al, who both gave slight nods, apparently in approval of my presence and attire. Their men quickly gathered around them. I jogged over to join up with my Charlie Platoon teammates, who huddled on the far side of Bravo Platoon.

I was surprised by our numbers. It appeared that we had picked up two new recruits since our last outing. It didn't take long to figure out a little about both of them.

Mike was a tall, slim guy. He had brown hair and a lanky frame and didn't have any type of military background. But he was athletic and a fast learner. He also had a long reach with a sword.

Kevin was short, had sandy blond hair, and was cut from the same stock as Gunny. I began to suspect that he, too, had spent some time in the Corps. At least outwardly, Kevin appeared to relish physical training. At first, I wasn't sure how well his short arms and legs would work during our sparring sessions.

It didn't take long to find out. For the next week, it seemed like we were there every day. All of Charlie worked on tactics and weapons employment. The newbies improved rapidly, along with the rest of Charlie.

I did too. Well . . . most of me did.

Honestly, I really tried to improve my attitude, but it just wasn't easy. It felt like I was trying to run with an emotional rock in my shoe. It was bad enough that I couldn't quite put a name on it, but I didn't know how to remove it, either.

I kept plugging away, hoping things would work themselves out.

I did pretty well when Gunny and I worked on my one-versus-one fighting. I even managed to keep my cool most of the time. He was still better than me, but I was progressing.

I knew I was getting better because he, without warning, began to get the Js or Tiny to join in the attack on me. I got stung a few times, and even stunned by Tiny, but I kept improving. It became extremely difficult for them to surprise me.

Only a few days after Mike and Kevin appeared, Gunny took us on Training Route Number Two. It seemed pretty much the same as Training Route One, right up until the point that simulated bad guys poured out of the woods on both sides of us and attacked. Gunny just stood to the side and observed our reactions.

My first opponent wasn't that great. I mean, he wasn't bad, but he wasn't as tough as what I'd faced over the last week. I was able to fight him while keeping one eye on the rest of the platoon.

Mike did okay by swinging his sword in wide arcs. That being said, he tired quickly. His attacker was able to zap him a few times and then knock his sword from his hand. Mike was not pleased, but he knew he was beaten. He raised his hands in mock surrender.

Kevin was a maniac. I'm not saying his sword-fighting skills were very honed, but what he lacked in skill he made up for in enthusiasm. He yelled and ran and jumped, and swung in every direction like he had just downed four cups of coffee. And he laughed maniacally as he did so.

It took his trainer a little longer to subdue him, given Kevin's favorite sword-wielding technique. He swung his sword in a figure-eight pattern as quickly as he could. He seemed to have figured out a way to make it go really fast, so much so that it was a bit of a blur. It looked very impressive.

However, his opponent was experienced and waited until just the right moment to implant his sword with a clang! It stopped the crazed sword swinging in a reverberating crash. His trainer followed up with a shove and a leg sweep that left Kevin sprawling. Kevin caught his balance, but at the cost of opening his guard, which let the "bad guy" step inside his defense.

He placed his blade dangerously close to Kevin's neck.

The crackling underneath Kevin's chin convinced him that his fight was over. He dropped his sword, smiled, and slapped his new best friend on the shoulder. "You've got to show me how to do that!"

I took an immediate liking to Kevin.

Whether by coincidence or prior agreement, the Js and Tiny fought very differently, and fared much better. Instead of fighting their opponents one on one, the three Charlie Platoon members backed toward each other and covered each other's blind spots. I have to admit, I almost stopped and stared.

The Js and Tiny worked masterfully together. Tiny used his size to anchor the middle of their fight, and the Js darted and rolled to keep the attackers off balance. They did extremely well.

In fact, the Js had clobbered one attacker and Tiny threw another down the hill before most of the other role players joined in the attack. Tiny eventually tripped and had to surrender at blade point, but the Js continued to fight effectively. At least until Jacob took a harsh sword tip across his arm, causing him to lose his sword.

Even so, he might have lost his blade, but not his fighting spirit.

He jumped on the back of one of the two remaining attackers. It was actually pretty effective, right up until the point Jared tried to stab the guy on whose back Jacob was riding. He accidentally electrocuted Jacob instead, who went flying to the ground with an "Owww!"

The fight resumed, but not between the Js and their attackers. Nope. The battle was now fought solely between the twins. They both left their swords on the ground and wrestled and tumbled with each other in frustration.

The remaining attackers were dumbfounded. They stared back and forth between the twins and Gunny, apparently unsure of what to do. Gunny had his face in his hands, rubbing his temples.

The raucous rumble continued until Tiny walked over and picked the twins up by their ankles, one in each hand, and unceremoniously dumped them beside Gunny. They were sullen for a moment . . . and then started laughing and complimenting each other on their fighting prowess. Gunny acted like they weren't even there.

As for me, I had my own problems. My one opponent had conveniently become two and the new guy wasn't half bad. I was just about to shock one of them when I caught a slight movement out of the corner of my eye.

I spun and swung horizontally, expecting to make contact with the interloper. I got nothing for my trouble except air and a sharp sting in my right shoulder.

"Ow!"

How could I have missed?

I turned in a complete circle but saw only the original attackers. Something wasn't adding up. Where did the other guy go?

Come on, Jamie. Keep looking!

A moment later I caught a glimpse of a shadow moving rapidly across the ground. On instinct, I dropped to the turf.

As I did, I felt a sharp breeze and heard an electric crackling by my right ear. I glanced upward this time.

You sly dog. No wonder.

There was a third guy, and he was flying. To be accurate, he was flying, then pausing by holding onto a tree, and then attacking again.

Having trouble with the hover, bro? Come down and let's talk.

It was three versus one, with one of the "bad guys" airborne. I guessed I'd moved on to the next level of training.

I glanced toward Gunny. He just stared at me with a look like, *Well, what are you going to do about it?*

I could always count on Gunny for an emotional hug.

Pop! The flyer almost got me on the head that time. I could have sworn I smelled burnt hair.

Okay, enough of this victim stuff.

In a flash, I remembered the old proverb that the best defense is a good offense.

What did I have to lose?

As best I could tell, the two ground attackers were content to just keep me tied up. They would engage me just long enough for the flyer to turn around and fly back again. I think they enjoyed making me good sport for the aviator.

Having fun, men? I hope so, 'cause this might hurt a little . . .

I waited until the next aviator's pass and met his sword attack in a shower of sparks. I tried to make as big a commotion as I could. As soon as our swords parted, I turned and charged the two on the ground.

They weren't ready.

I screamed and raised my sword high. The guy on my right was careless and had his sword hanging loosely by his right side. I swung in a tight arc and caught him squarely in the torso. My strike knocked him off his feet.

The guy on the left had just enough time to adjust his blade to meet mine. He didn't get hit by my sword, but my left shoulder caught him squarely in the chest. I took him down like a linebacker tackling an off-balance halfback.

The back of his head hit the dirt and his eyes rolled backward in his head. His sword went flying. I also zapped him for good measure. I didn't need him coming back at me while I fought the aviator.

How do ya like me now, boys?

By the time I looked up, the aviator knew his buddies were down. He pushed hard off the tree and swung at my rotating figure.

Zzzooocck! I just managed to bring my sword around in time to prevent being electrically cut in two. Unfortunately, the impact knocked the sword from my hand, and it went flying into the bushes.

Aw, come on!

The aviator smiled. He had zero mercy and swooped at me like an angry bird. I tried to get out of the way, but still he popped me at will as he flew by.

It wasn't even close to being fair! No one was moving a muscle to help me and I was getting quite angry. Which was probably the point.

I *hated* losing and Gunny knew it.

Oohh, he wants to see if I can keep my cool when I'm losing. That dude is vicious—

Zzzztt! "Ow!"

Think quickly! Wait . . .

At the aviator's next pass, I acted like I was going to duck, then quickly jumped upward at him. My idea was to knock the sword from his hand. I missed the sword and realized, too late, that my trajectory was not what I had planned at all.

I actually continued upward for five to six feet, before "apexing" and accelerating back toward terra firma. I was flying!

No. Stinkin'. Way.

I was so excited, midair, that my ADD flared up again.

Oh, man I really wish I could see my face. This is so epic . . . uh-oh, earth!

I saw the ground rushing up to smack me. In an instinctual act of self-preservation, I desperately willed myself away. I still hit the ground, but gently, and with spring.

I bounced off the ground and re-lifted into the air. Through a stroke of good fortune, I was flying toward the aviator. When he turned, he saw me. Whatever I lost in style points was made up for by the look on his face.

Surprise, tough guy!

The bad news . . . I was out of control and he wasn't.

He recovered quickly. He launched in the opposite direction and zoomed by me, but not before smacking me again, hard, on my back. It stung like fire and stunned me.

My flailing flight turned into a fall. I crashed into a large bush and tumbled toward the ground. I landed on my side with a jolt. I was hurting, but I was still in the fight.

Everyone, except for Gunny, had an astonished look on their face. I suppose not many people flew and fought this early in their training. Probably for good reason.

No matter. I got this!

As I rose to my feet, Gunny stepped forward. "Okay Jamie, you have done well. I think you should stand down now."

That made perfect sense, but I didn't want to. I looked back at Gunny with a *Please?* expression on my face.

For the first time since I met him, I saw him smile. He actually grinned really big and stuck out his bottom lip like, *Okay, if that's what you want.* He waved his hands forward as if introducing combatants at a mixed martial arts match.

Ooh-rah, Gunny.

The aviator sat on a limb about ten feet off the ground. He was about twenty feet away from me. Without a word, I ran and launched myself at him.

I threw myself into the air, hoping that my last flight wasn't a fluke. It wasn't.

My vector was pretty accurate and I flew, uncoordinated though I was, directly at the guy. He sat calmly as I sailed at him. In my estimation, I was going to get close enough to hit him. I lowered my shoulder and braced for impact.

You know, I should have listened to Gunny.

Just as I was about to crash into the aviator, he dropped silently from the limb. Almost all of him was gone. Except for his sword.

The tip of the sword made contact with my chin, then skipped to my jaw. After that, it entered my chest and sliced neatly in a diagonal from the center of my chest to my right hip. I don't remember screaming like a little girl, but I do remember the searing pain.

I also remember seeing the world go end over end as I somersaulted over the branch. I fell in a rotating heap through the branches and onto the ground. I would venture that it hurt to hit the dirt, but I think my fried insides were overloading my pain receptors at the time, so I'm not sure I really noticed that part.

Everything became very quiet. To tell the truth, I think I passed out. On the sort of positive side, as the intense pain subsided my wits returned.

I slowly opened my eyes. At first, all I saw were the tree's branches gently swaying in the wind. They appeared to wave "bye" to the pain-racked idiot lying on his back in the dirt.

Welcome back, Jamie. You really are a piece of work, dude.

I heard Gunny say, "Well, that about wraps up today's training engagement." He continued. "Attackers, debrief your attackees on their strengths and weaknesses, and what they can do better next time. Then you're cleared to depart."

"Ooh-rah!" they shouted in response.

I sat up very, very slowly. I guess my thoughts were a little out of whack, because the very first thing I did was check to see if my shirt was burned like last time.

It was.

At the rate I was "training" I was definitely gonna need more shirts.

My three attackers and Gunny walked up. Gunny extended a hand and helped me to my feet. I was still a little woozy, but I don't think anyone cared. Without preamble, Gunny directed the two ground attackers to critique my performance.

Attacker number one was a lanky guy with a sly smile. "I have to admit, we underestimated you. We assumed you would be over-whelmed by our numbers and the airborne attack and we got lazy. I'd say your sword fighting isn't perfect yet, but it's well above average. But your unpredictability was what carried the day." He looked at attacker number two. "Wouldn't you agree?"

This was the guy I had leveled with my shoulder. He was at least six feet tall and had the eyes of a hunter. He did not look happy at all. From the look on his face I thought he might tackle me and start all over again. "Yep. Didn't see that one comin' until it was too late."

The aviator jumped in. "I agree. Your flying isn't very good yet, but the fact that you threw yourself into an airborne attack without any training indicates that you are very creative, or very reckless. Or both. Either way, it was completely unexpected."

"So, Jamie," Gunny said, "where did things go wrong?"

"Can I talk about what I did right, first?" I joked.

Stares.

All righty, then.

"I was clearly outmatched. I should have withdrawn while I still could. I let my desire to win override good sense."

The attackers nodded but I could see Gunny's wheels turning. His stare was so intense I began to get uncomfortable.

"That is close enough for the moment." Gunny continued to eyeball me and, with a curious expression creasing his face, softened his voice. "All right, then. Take a minute to gather yourself, Jamie. We've got one more thing to do before we call it a day."

"Ooh-rah, Gunny."

He nodded once more, then walked away.

The aviator and number one followed him, but the hunter stayed and stared at me. There was something recognizable in the way he carried himself. Almost like he was—

"You look familiar. Did you spend some time downrange?"

—one of the men I used to do ops with. "Yeah, I did time with some of the teams in Iraq. I was a PJ."

I normally didn't talk about this sort of thing, but something about his look told me he got it.

"I thought so," he said. "You look just like a guy that ran with us on some hairy missions in Anbar. We lost him to a grenade and I never saw him again." He said this in a half-statement, half-questioning manner.

"Yep. That was me. I still set off airport metal detectors from time to time."

He smiled and his countenance shifted noticeably.

"Jamie, right? Listen, man. I think I know what you're going through. We lost some guys not long after you left, and it messed me up pretty good. When I got back stateside, things just got worse."

I cringed. The memories of my own return ate at me.

He said quietly, "I lost my best friend over there. I swore I'd never go through that kind of pain again. But when I got here"—he gestured toward our surroundings—"it brought me back to the land of the living. You can make it back too, bro."

I didn't know what to say. I nodded to express what I could.

He offered his rough hand. "I'm Rick."

"Nice to meet you, Rick. And . . . thanks."

He walked with me toward Charlie Platoon. The attackers were forming ranks and preparing to depart while Charlie did the same.

We fist-bumped goodbye. "Train hard, Jamie, 'cause we'll be ready for you next time!"

"It's a date, Rick. Bring it!"

He laughed. Before he disappeared into the crowd, he yelled over his shoulder, "Wait till Al finds out you were downrange at the same time!"

Al was there, too? Small world.

Despite my thrashing, Charlie welcomed me back with smiles and slaps on the back. The Js were discreetly hopping up and down to see if they could fly. Mike and Kevin gave me thumbs-up, whereas Tiny walked over and, with brotherly affection, bro-punched me in the chest.

Unngh! My heart almost stopped from the impact. I had no idea he liked me so much.

"You're pretty good at flyin', Jamie."

"I really"—*cough, cough*—"appreciate that . . . Tiny." I could barely get the words out.

Oh, man . . . I can't breathe!

I wasn't sure why, but he looked very pleased. Bless his heart . . . and my poor heart for that matter. Owwww!

I was still coughing when Gunny strode up to me and knife-handed me in the chest. "Follow me." His tone gave no doubt that it wasn't a request. He spun around and marched away.

What did I do now?

His walk was more of a quick pace that bordered on a jog. I followed and tried to keep up, but I felt a little worn out. I guess electro-shock, a two-story fall and getting death-punched in the chest was a little fatiguing.

We strode through the clearing, past the doorways and into a part of the forest that I had never seen. I dutifully followed in silence. We walked for what seemed an hour before Gunny paused. He spun on me and said, "You know, I had you all wrong."

"What do you mean, Gunny?"

"Well, I thought that if I stressed you hard enough you'd break, then blossom. I see it all of the time in guys like you. You lose your confidence and you just need to see what you are made of . . . again."

Guys like me?

"Not you. Uh-uh. Your confidence is fine."

Well, that's good to know. I don't want my sarcasm to get lonely.

He was just getting wound up. "Sure, you're angry, but I just saw you control your frustration and make rational decisions in a very stressful situation. Plus, your desire to win, for yourself at least, is through the roof! No, that's not your problem."

The lecture was getting a little old. It was starting to sting a bit, too.

"But here's where we start getting closer to the truth. You are confident, you are capable, but you are not sure anything, or should I say anyone *else*, is worth going through the pain that you've experienced. You feel wronged and alone and don't want to be suckered again. Isn't that right?"

I felt short of breath. In my head, I blamed it on Tiny.

"You don't know me," was the best I could muster. I admit, it sounded much tougher in my mind than in my delivery.

In a calm voice he said, "Oh, Jamie. I think I do. I can't tear down your walls, that's up to you. But maybe it will help if you understand a few things. We can call it an 'informed opinion.' Let's go."

When he turned his head I followed his gaze. What I saw made my world spin.

"Oh," was all I could think to say.

Gunny turned and started walking downhill . . . toward a bustling town that looked eerily like my own.

CHAPTER 10

Déjà vu didn't accurately describe the sensation. It was way too real for that.

We strolled into what had to be a copy of my hometown like it was the most natural thing to do. Just two dudes out for a walk through bizarre-o-land.

I knew we were still on the Malum side of the veil because we walked *past* the doors, not *through* the doors. But could we have somehow gone back over to the real world without knowing?

I doubted it. But it sure looked like Columbus . . .

I was at a loss.

Gunny wasn't much use. He kept walking and said very little. In fact, the only thing he did say was in his staccato instructor's voice, "Do not talk to or touch anyone!"

So helpful.

I looked away for a second and almost slammed into a pregnant lady—face first. I jumped sideways, barely missing her baby bump. Yikes!

"Sorry about that!"

I cringed and waited for recrimination . . . from both of them. I got nothing from either. Gunny was apparently too distracted to notice my run-in, and the lady just kept on going.

Not only did she remain silent, but she didn't even look in my direction. She carried on like she never laid eyes on me. How was that possible?

I could see Gunny and he could see me, and we could see everyone else. So what was the problem?

Best guess? We were invisible to the rest of the town . . . or we were being ignored for an episode of a new reality show called *Scorned and Confused.* At the moment, both seemed equally plausible.

We continued our walk into the downtown area, concentrating on avoiding physical contact with others on the narrow concrete sidewalks. Gunny's eyes scanned the tops of buildings and the tensed muscles in his neck gave him a dangerous air. I wasn't sure why he was so nervous, but it made me jumpy, too.

We stopped in front of the county courthouse beside a bench, sagely placed under the shade of a round, leafy-green tree. Gunny peered at the clock tower with an intense stare. I followed his gaze and saw a flicker of motion in one of the open portals.

I knew Gunny saw it too, because his jaw tightened. Then his hand flexed, almost as if he were about to pull his sword from midair. I wasn't sure what was there, but whatever Gunny saw stirred him to action.

"Stay here."

He moved at a quick pace toward the front doors of the white-columned building. I called out, "Wait! What am I supposed to . . . ?" but I was talking to myself. He was already around the corner and gone from sight.

Nice. I'll just stay here and wonder what's going on. So fun.

I tried to wait by the bench, but I had too much nervous energy to be still. I paced back and forth, repeatedly glancing at the antebellum watch tower. Nothin'.

The minutes stretched and things stayed quiet, so much so that my attentiveness waned. I wandered around the tree and glanced sporadically at the clock tower for any sign of Gunny. All I saw were white clouds easing through a blue sky.

Pfft. This cloak and dagger stuff is getting old fast. Let's walk the perimeter for a minute. There's no harm in that.

I began a slow stroll around the periphery of the old building. I passed a statue dedicated to local soldiers who fought in wars of the twentieth century. It was old and grey and the words were fading. I stared at the soldiers' tags and wondered if my name would be on a memorial one day.

Probably not. Who's gonna remember you?

I shook my head. Sheesh, I was getting morbid.

Now, where's Gunny?

That was when I heard voices. They emanated from a partially hidden walkway that ran parallel to the red brick wall of the building. I heard a combination of harsh, low commands and a pleading, elderly woman's voice.

That doesn't sound right.

I carefully peered into the semi-darkness and saw a skinny, grey-haired lady desperately clutching a purse to her side. Three youths in hoodies surrounded her. There was also a fourth guy, but he stood off by himself. He had on a dark T-shirt and watched the scene with murky, bored eyes.

Maybe he's a friend of the teens but doesn't want to get involved? What a great Samaritan.

It took only a second to see that the punks wanted the lady's purse and she didn't want to give it to them. I had to give her credit. She was obviously scared, but bravely stood her ground. She refused to hand over her handbag.

Good for you, lady.

Without a conscious thought, I walked toward the showdown.

Dude, what you are doing? Is this really even happening?

I hadn't considered that.

Ooooh. Maybe this is a simulated world. Or it could be a video game–like practice area. "Malum-world 4"? Nah, there's gotta be a better name for it.

Gunny's warning to not talk or touch anyone suddenly rang in my ears.

Whatever, Gunny. It's on. I might get the high score!

As I drew closer I heard the leader of the three say, "You gonna give us that purse, woman. Don't make me hurt you."

His words had a strong southern accent, so much so that his last word sounded like ewe. I guess that was what the woman was to them, sheep to the wolves.

I shouted "That's enough!" at the top of my voice. None of the hoods acted like they heard a thing. Strangely, neither did the woman.

"I said, that's enough!"

Still no reaction.

This simulator needs some serious work.

The thought had barely crossed my mind when the skinny leader casually backhanded the lady. A sick smacking sound echoed down the long walkway. His strike drew blood from the corner of her mouth and knocked her to the ground.

Simulator or not, that made my blood boil.

Instinctively, I grabbed my sword and swung with all my might. My blade passed cleanly through the leader's back. It was a clean shot, but he didn't turn to ash.

How disappointing.

However, he did cry out and stagger away from the lady. His features were wild and motions frantic. He spun one way, then another, looking for the source of his pain.

Hmm. It's not an accurate sim, but at least the sword sorta works.

His cohorts stood rooted in place. Confusion etched their shadowy faces and fear grew in their eyes. It was clear that none of them could see me, so I calmly stepped toward the other two punks and promptly sliced through their midsections. They both screamed in terror.

Cool!

This may have been a cruddy simulator, but their reaction was hilarious.

A squatty, overfed member of the trio accidentally knocked the others to the ground as they tried to escape, thus creating a pileup of punks. All three of them then stumbled and bumbled over each other like frightened puppies. They did more damage to each other than I could have ever done with my blade. The Three Stooges would have been proud.

I let them move away from where the old woman lay on the ground, but zapped them each one more time as they ran by. You know, just to ensure they kept going. Their screams faded down the alcove as they dashed from sight.

Boo-yah! Score one hundred points for Jamie!

I stood and looked at the lady, who seemed just as confused as the future felons. Her eyes were dazed. I walked over and offered her my hand, but she ignored me.

Dude, she can't see you. Remember?

Right.

She slowly stood on trembling legs. I could hear her quietly praying and thanking God for saving her. She looked so familiar . . .

Wait a minute . . . I know her!

It was Mrs. Brown, my first grade teacher. She taught me how to spell. I adored her. What was going on . . . ?

Then it hit me.

Gunny.

Really? Abusing my first grade teacher in pretend-world to manipulate me? I knew he was mean, but how low could you go?

Mrs. Brown pulled a handkerchief from her purse and dabbed the corner of her mouth. The fabric was instantly stained with blood.

Wow. Now *that's* realistic. This is such a weird, mean game.

I watched as she made her way down the side of the building. She peered warily around the corner, and then quickly walked away on quaking legs. I was alone again.

I still couldn't believe Gunny would do this. What was he thinking?

I took a deep breath and slowly stowed my sword. There was that dissonance again. I tried not to ignore it this time.

Something doesn't add up, dude.

Think it through, then.

Okay, despite its flaws, this simulator seems awfully real. It's really sophisticated, too. How could they build something like this over here?

It took only a second before the truth dawned on my veil-lagged mind.

They couldn't. That means . . .

Oh, man.

That really just happened. We're actually traipsing around our world behind the veil, where people can't see us.

Sort of cool, except for the fact that three guys just attacked Mrs. Brown. But, what's that have to do with Malum? Those three guys weren't Nasties—they were just punks.

It was at this point that my math-in-public brain finally caught up with the rest of me. Not three guys. Four guys.

Dang it.

I hadn't even gotten my sword back in my hand when I was kicked so hard that I actually left my feet. I landed in almost the exact same spot where Mrs. Brown got jumped.

Smaaack!

I hit my head against the wall and crumpled to the ground. I managed to stay conscious, but just barely. I was on my back but twisted my neck so I could look up. What I saw made me wish I had never gotten up that morning.

A small group of Malum lookalikes stared back at me. Their faces were slightly different, but they all carried smug, harsh smiles and the same eyes of darkness. And swords.

Oh, come on! How did they . . . ?

The fourth guy. Not a spectator. He was an actual Malum. Let me guess . . . he went and got reinforcements.

Jamie, you seriously need to work on your observation skills, bro.

It was now painfully obvious that we weren't the only visitors in town. Because I had seen the fourth guy with the other three, I assumed that he was just like them. That assumption might have just gotten me killed.

Too many to take on myself. Maybe I can fly—

The thought was squelched as another goon appeared at the top of the stairs. Four low and one high . . . and he was in a perfect blocking position.

Man, this was just not my day.

Using the wall as a crutch, I gradually climbed to my feet. My cranium was pounding, but I didn't feel any blood.

The Nasties formed a semicircle around me and glared.

Newbies, maybe? Getting their feet wet with muggings before hittin' the big time? Hmm, if they're new, maybe I can use that. "So, how's it goin'?"

No response. The four low guys slowly contracted the semicircle and pointed their swords at my chest.

Come on, Jamie. You got this.

A trickle of sweat crept down my back. My sword jumped abruptly into my hand. They slowed at the sight of my blade, but continued their walk. Their faces were focused and full of hate. A couple of them even had their teeth bared.

My mind raced and my eyes darted, looking for anything that could help me escape. I was backed against a bare wall. There was nothing to stop them.

As one, the four guys raised their swords above their heads. I threw myself into the corner of the building, but there was nowhere to go.

I heard myself cry out with an "Aaaaahhhhhh!"

Hold on. That doesn't *even* sound like me. That sounds like—

The fifth goon landed at my feet in a lump. His scream stopped as abruptly as his body. To be fair, he did bounce a little . . . before exploding in a plume of dark ash.

Cool.

The disintegrating body of their buddy was a bit of a distraction to the other Malum. They stopped in mid-swing. The only movement was the wave of Nasty dust as it flowed down the sidewalk.

A long, dark shadow fell over us. As one, we looked up.

A guy stood at the railing. Though his features were difficult to make out, his silhouette was huge against the afternoon sun. Most importantly, it was clear that the sword in his hand was not black. It was silver, with a gold handle.

That was all I needed to see.

I screamed and charged the Malum. It was a crazy gamble, but it was all I had. I really think it was the one thing they weren't expecting . . . other than the whole buddy falling from the railing surprise, I suppose.

They panicked.

Zaaap! I cut down one of them before he could take two steps, his body exploding in a gust of dust. The other three ran for the end of the alley in a desperate and wild melee. One of them fell to the ground. I was on him in a second.

Swack! I dispatched him as he sought to regain his feet.

The bad news was that the last two were getting away. I ran for them as hard as I could. They both disappeared around the corner of the building and vanished from sight.

Two seconds later I careened around the corner . . . and almost ran smack into a silver blade that was arcing at neck level. I let my feet fly from underneath me and threw my body into a horizontal position. The blade passed in front of, but not into, my body with a smooth swooshing sound.

Yay, right? Except for the whole hitting the ground on my back part. "Ooof!"

I instinctively rolled away. I brought my sword up to brace for the next attack. Everything was suddenly still.

I gazed up from a kneeling position and saw an older man standing above me. He was still holding that silver sword. He had white hair, a grey beard, and intense eyes.

"Is that all of 'em?" he said gruffly.

"Uh-huh." I grunted through heaving, pained breaths.

"You okay?"

"Meh." I shrugged.

For some reason that really seemed to tickle him. His lips pursed as he tried to stifle a smile, and then he visibly relaxed and stowed his sword.

I slowly regained my feet. I glanced around one more time, then stowed my sword as well. I bent over to knock the Malum dust off of my trousers. When I looked up, he was staring at me.

"I guess I owe you a thanks for saving me back there." I offered my hand, and he took it with a strong grip. "Can I ask where you came from?"

"I live here." He shoved his hands in his pockets. "Well, not like this all the time, but in this town, on the other side."

"Are you part of our group?"

As soon as I said that, his demeanor changed. There was a sudden sadness in his eyes. His shoulders dropped a bit and he stared at the ground for a moment before saying, "I'd better go. I think I see your buddy looking for ya."

I stepped past him and looked under the tree where Gunny had left me. There was Gunny, spinning this way and that, full of agitation and concern. I heard a quick "whoosh" and turned back to my new friend.

He was gone.

* * *

"You did *what?*"

Gunny and I were standing in front of Boogie and Al back at the camp, and things were not going well.

"Jamie needed to understand why we are doing what we're doing, and this was the best way," Gunny said matter-of-factly.

Boogie's cheeks flushed red and his foot tapped the ground. For a moment, no one spoke. Boogie took a deep breath and slowly exhaled.

Al was much calmer about the whole thing. "Well, how'd it go? Did you see yo'self? Oh, that's freaky, dude! This one time I walked into town an' . . . " He trailed off when he saw the look in Boogie's eyes. "Well, that's a story for another day, mayun."

"I would have preferred to just tell him," Boogie said in a strained voice.

Gunny shrugged.

I thought Boogie was going to blow a gasket before a new voice said, "What did you learn?"

We all turned at the sound. R.B. was smiling like he didn't have a care in the world. The atmosphere changed immediately as he strode over.

"Well," I began, "as best I can tell, we're physically near town, but the local folks can't see us."

"Um-hm," R.B. said. "What else?"

"My guess is Gunny was looking for Malum. Maybe they hang around the town, doing bad things?"

"You're getting pretty warm with your guesses, Jamie," he said. "Understand this; the Malum do go into towns and cities and affect people for the worse. They not only hang around 'bad' people, but somehow they bring out the worst in just about everyone. And the longer they're in an area, the more their influence grows."

Boogie chimed in. "They turn good cities into terrible ones. Their influence is insidious, and it grows like a cancer."

"Why don't we just go into town and guard it, then?" I asked.

Gunny spoke up. "For the same reason that they do not hang around in population centers until they're cleared of people like us. It's hard to tell who is who. They would prefer to wait until groups like us are wiped out, and then they have the town to themselves."

"So, we fight each other away from the cities and then the winner has control?" I said.

"Not always, but the reality isn't too far from it," R.B. said.

"But . . . why?"

"You might as well ask why they're Hitlers in the world, mayun," Al said. "They just are, and they want the whole world, one city at a time. And right now, they want this one."

I said, "Well, at least there are other good guys out there. If it hadn't been for ol' grey beard I would have been toast."

You could have heard a pin drop.

Oh, yeah. I forgot I hadn't told anyone about my Malum and grey beard experience. Gunny was in a rush to get back, so I never had a chance to explain what went down.

My bad.

Boogie looked as scary upset as I'd ever seen, but he very calmly said, "Jamie, would you please explain what you mean by that?"

So I did.

When I was done there was more silence. I could see Boogie's temples throbbing. Gunny was staring at a point on the ground that must have been very interesting, because he wouldn't look up. Al kept looking from Boogie to Gunny, apparently wondering if there was going to be bloodshed.

R.B. cleared his throat. "It would seem that you got to see, first-hand, what they can do. I would like to tell you that it is all they can do, but that's just the tip of the iceberg."

"Do you know the guy I saw? He was about your age, I think."

A troubled look crossed R.B.'s face, but he didn't answer. Instead, he said, "I'm glad he was there to help, but you can't count on that kind of assistance in the future. You must be very careful, Jamie."

I nodded and got a hollow feeling in my stomach. It wasn't the near-death experience that bothered me as much as the realization that I almost messed things up. Haunted memories threatened to bubble to the surface, but R.B. saved me from my thoughts.

"Now," he said, "Jamie, please excuse us for a few minutes, I need to talk with these fellas for a second."

I turned and walked away wondering, not for the first time, what I had gotten myself into.

CHAPTER 11

Time to act normal, Jamie. Whatever that means.

I pulled up to the curb in front of Boogie's modest home. It was one of those red brick, single story homes so common to the area. Boogie or his wife must have had a really green thumb, because the lawn looked manicured and the flowers were beautiful. Two guys entered the house whom I knew only as members of Alpha Platoon. They looked a lot different without swords in their hands and sky between their toes. In fact, they seemed quite ordinary.

See? Nothing to it. Fake it till you make it.

I stepped out of my car and slid around to the passenger side to retrieve my dish. I was relieved to see the dessert had survived the drive to the cookout in one piece. A couple of large potholes and a distracted driver had put everything at risk.

Score one for the home team!

I was proud of myself. I slaved in my kitchen and made a yummy, fresh cheesecake. I admit that Betty Crocker helped a bit, but I did mix the ingredients, so I considered it homemade.

I ambled up to the house with the dessert in my hands and reached to ring the doorbell. Before I could push the button, the door opened of its own accord. A young lady emerged, looking and talking over her shoulder. She wasn't paying attention to where she was going.

Great, a distracted walker.

If it weren't for my catlike reflexes, we both would have immediately worn my latest creation. Lucky for her, I was on my game.

I deftly moved the dessert from my left hand in front of my body, to my right hand beside and above my body. I now held the cheesecake aloft, much like a waiter.

Nice move, bro!

The bad news was that she wasn't stopping.

She was too close to avoid and was closing in rapidly. I did the only thing I could think of. I absorbed the impact of her body against my chest and tried to spin with her. I thought it might hurt less that way.

It seemed like a really good idea at the time.

At first, it went beautifully. We avoided a harsh collision, I still had the cheesecake sort of under control and I found myself with my arm wrapped around the young lady, spinning in slow motion. Her face was inches from mine.

It was going to be one of those awesome moments, I just knew it.

You know, like in the movies when time stands still and the couple twirls in slow motion. The handsome man confidently holds the surprised lady as the wind softly caresses her beautiful features. They both smile and bask in the sweet irony of the moment, their eyes twinkling as soft music plays . . .

Yeah, I'm delusional. It was nothing like that.

It's okay though, I get it. You don't get mugged by a man holding a cheesecake very often. I can imagine that's a little traumatic. Then again, I didn't plan to go swing-dancing with the manager from the café, either.

To be fair, I did actually have a short moment where time stood still. Everything was frozen in time. Sort of like a car wreck.

I can still see it. The young lady's eyes were wild with fear and her lips were curled into something between a shout for help and a "Noooooooo . . . " Even the veins in her neck were bulging, so it was the complete package. She was not smiling and there was no irony, sweet or otherwise.

Time sped back up, and it wasn't kind.

My twirl turned into a stumble, which progressed instantly into a fall. I realized I was going to land on her. Panic set in.

Don't squish her, dude!

I twisted one more time, effectively placing myself between the concrete sidewalk and the falling female.

Success! Kind of.

"Ooof!"

My back, and then my head, hit the concrete. She bounced as she landed on me. Her elbow happened to land just below my sternum, which knocked the wind out of me.

You know that irony that was missing a minute ago? It came back like a jilted girlfriend.

My cheesecake *splooshed* on the sidewalk, and, with perfect timing, flung bits right into the middle of her face. Would you believe me if I said there was a no-kiddin' cherry on her nose for like a nanosecond?

All I could do was stare at her in pain and embarrassment. I couldn't breathe either, so that didn't help.

To her credit, her face transformed from terror, to bewilderment, to recognition in just a few seconds. She even managed to smile, despite dessert sliding down her cheek.

Impressive.

Normally, that would have been great, right? Except for the whole agony and lack of oxygen thing. Whoever she had been speaking with a moment ago was now helping her up.

Through my misery I heard her say, "I'm okay, just a little cheesecake up the nose. Him, I'm not so sure."

By now the tears in my eyes were fading. I saw my victim and another lady standing over me. They had genuine concern in their eyes.

"I'm. Okay. Breath. Knocked. Out."

They nodded in understanding and waited for me to move again. I eventually found my breath and rolled over to my stomach. It took only a few more seconds to push up to my feet and stand. Cheesecake oozed down my arms.

The lady who had come to our assistance said, "Well now, you must be Jamie! My name is Lorraine, but you can call me Lori. I'm Boogie's wife."

How did she know my name?

I smiled weakly, "That's me!"

My pants and shoes had made it through the ordeal relatively untouched, but the front of my shirt was wrecked. "Lori, I'm really sorry about the mess. Let me go home and change, and then I'll come back and clean up the damage."

She paused and took a breath to respond but my fellow casualty interjected. "Oh no! It was my fault. I wasn't paying attention to where I was going and ran into you. I will grab something to clean up this mess." She paused for a second as cake slid down her cheek. "And my face, too."

Before Lori or I could say I word, she walked back into the house.

Lori looked at me. "Well, Boogie told me you had a way of making an entrance. I had no idea how accurate that would be! Let me go get you one of Boogie's shirts. There's no need for you to go all the way home and back for that." She turned to walk away.

"Lori? Who's that girl I just bumped into? I've seen her . . . um, somewhere before."

Lori's eyebrows rose suspiciously, and her countenance changed. She slowly walked over and stared at me, her eyes searching mine.

My heart stopped for a beat before Lori's smile returned.

"Her name is Kate." She walked away.

* * *

"She's a sweetie," Lori added a minute later when she handed me one of Boogie's gently used T-shirts. I must have had that *I think she's cute* look on my face, because I saw Lori's eyes twinkle. It was at this point that I remembered my encounter with Kate in the café, and my spirits fell.

You were shot down already, Jamie. Remember?

Lori must have noticed the change. "What's wrong?"

So much for my poker face.

I'm not much for lying. "Well, I just remembered where I met her before, and . . . " I paused. "I'm not sure she thought that much of me then. And now"—I gestured toward the destroyed cheesecake, half of which was in the bushes—"I'm pretty sure she has formed a certain opinion of me."

"Well, Jamie," she said quietly, "looks can be deceiving."

Say what?

Just then, Kate exited the house with a spatula, a rag, and a trash can, sans cheesecake on her face. Lori grinned and stepped toward the door.

Oh, come on! Don't leave me hanging! That's just mean.

Lori said loudly, "Jamie, you can change your shirt out here so you don't get cheesecake on anything. I'll run it through the wash while we're cooking out. Kate and I will avert our eyes so we don't stare."

I wasn't sure who she was messing with more, me or Kate. While I did try to stay in shape, I couldn't help thinking that neither of them was going to have a case of the ogles when it came to me. However, like my own, Kate's cheeks flushed bright red.

What have they been talking about?

I gently lifted the cake-encrusted shirt over my head, careful not to get any in my hair. Thankfully, my pullover took the brunt of the attack and I had very little on my hands. I slid Boogie's T-shirt on. "All done."

I thought about adding, *The temptation has passed!* but I figured I would get the same reaction from Kate as I did in the café.

Lori turned and took the cheese-caked shirt from me. "I'll be back in a couple of minutes. If you guys are done before then, I'll meet you out back in a few." With that she was inside the house and on her way to the washing machine.

Kate squatted in silence and began to clean the mess. She used the spatula to gather as much goo as she could. I wasn't sure what else to do, so I grabbed the trash can and tilted it so she could put the bits and pieces in more easily.

She said, "Thanks," and kept working.

Come on, Jamie. Talk to her.

As hard as I tried, I couldn't come up with anything to say. Nothing at all. So I held the trash can in silence, wishing I were someone much cooler than me.

Way to go, Jamie. You put the "awk" in awkward, bro. What a doofus.

I sighed and flicked a random piece of cheesecake-slime off my arm.

Kate looked at me. "I'm sorry."

"Oh! That's not what I meant . . . "

Nice work, dude.

I tried to smooth my gaffe. "Anyhow, it's just cheesecake. Besides, you didn't escape unscathed, either."

"No, not the cheesecake. I mean . . . I'm sorry about that, too. But what I really meant was the other night at the café."

What did she have to be sorry about? I was Mr. Lame Personality.

"Oh, no. I don't blame you a bit." I knelt beside her so I could look her in the eye. "I'm sure lots of guys try to small talk you while you're on the job. I don't blame you for not sticking around, but no kiddin', I wouldn't have wisecracked with you if I knew it was going to weird you out."

"It wasn't the joke that did it, Jamie." She paused. "Okay, I guess maybe it was the joke."

I was so confused.

She looked around, then leaned in close like she was sharing a secret. "When you said something about a black sword, I thought that you might be a Malum. I was scared that maybe they found out who I was. But then I saw the mark on your face," she whispered.

Mark? What mark? I don't have . . .

Dude! Remember Boogie and Al's half-ichthuses?

Oh! *That* mark.

For some reason it never occurred to me that I might have the same imprint as them, much less that it was visible. Since I had seen Kate on the other side, it made sense that she could see it.

As if to make a point, she casually wiped her face. In doing so, she moved the bangs that covered her forehead. Faintly, but distinctly, I saw a line.

Without thinking, I reached out and took Kate's free hand. It was soft, but strong. Her eyes widened and her brows knitted into a questioning crinkle, but she didn't pull against my grasp.

I released the trash can and used that hand to lift the few strands of short brown hair that obscured the front of my noggin. Now she had a clear view of my brow, too. She turned so that we were completely face-to-face, both of us squatting in front of the door.

Supernaturally, another faint line appeared on her forehead and an ichthus appeared. The same thing must have happened to me because her eyes grew wider in wonder. Our gazes met and just like that, we had *a moment*.

Time didn't stand still, but it slowed enough for me to think, *Wow!*

Pretty cheesy, huh?

Our faces were only inches apart and, for the first time, I noticed her lovely perfume. Combine that with her pretty face, which was now smiling at me, and, well, I was about as close to man-swooning as I had ever been in my life.

I know. I'm a dork.

I wasn't sure Kate was all butterflies and hugs or anything, but at least she didn't run away this time.

That's progress, right?

Just then, I heard a familiar voice say, "Well, Jamie. I see you've met my niece."

I cringed.

This one's gonna hurt . . .

There was R.B., standing in the door, his expression somewhere between concern and amusement. Boogie looked over his shoulder at us. He was rolling his eyes and shaking his head.

I was never going to live this one down.

CHAPTER 12

Kate and I dropped our grip on each other's hands and stood. She still held a spatula full of slime speckled with little flecks of grass and I gripped a bucketful of trash. We were quite a pair.

"Lori told me about your little accident, and I wanted to make sure everyone was okay. I can see you're both, um—" He cleared his throat. "—all right. Why don't you both come in the house?"

Right. Moment's over.

I walked inside, but Kate paused by the door.

"I left my cell phone in the car. It's where I was going when we . . . er . . . had our pileup. Be right back." She beamed as she turned and walked down the sidewalk. If she was embarrassed to get caught hand-holding with me, she didn't show it.

"I'll catch up with you in a minute, R.B.," I added. "I don't want to touch anything until I know I'm clean."

"Sounds good. See you in a minute."

I paused in the bathroom to wash my arms. On my way out I glanced in the mirror and found a fleck of cheesecake in my right ear.

Classy, Jamie.

Once I was finally done cleaning, I walked to the backyard. There were quite a few familiar faces, including Al's and Rick's. I realized that word of my incident must have traveled quickly. The guys I knew gave salutes with their soda cans and smiled a little too much.

I waved back.

Hey, at least I'm dressed this time.

The air had a pleasant smell of charcoal and cooked burgers and the breeze carried cheerful voices. The sound meshed well with beach music playing from a small stereo. To me, it was classic southern cookout at its best.

I walked around until I located Boogie. I found him by the grill, where he was chatting with a guy I didn't know. Well, mostly the stranger was talking and Boogie was listening.

Just then, Lori weaved through the crowded patio and brought fresh burgers to burn. In one continuous movement she dropped new patties at Boogie's side and deftly removed those that were ready. It was pretty impressive, actually.

I strode up just as Boogie flipped a burger. He saw me out of the corner of his eye and, without missing a beat said, "Chuck, this is Jamie. We work together on the base."

I shook Chuck's hand and glanced at his forehead for a brief second. Nothing but friendly eyes and a slightly sweaty brow. Apparently, he wasn't one of us.

"So Jamie, Boogie tells me you're a great mechanic. What brands of tools are your favorites?"

Seriously?

That was just the beginning. In the end, it took twenty minutes to get away from Chuck. Not a bad guy, but he could sure use up some oxygen.

I small-talked with some other people for most of the afternoon, albeit on far more interesting subjects. Most of the conversations were about football, family, and fishing. You know, the important stuff. It was quite refreshing to chat about things other than Malum for a few minutes.

I could say that I accidentally found myself talking to Kate . . . but that would be a lie. The truth was that I saw her mingling and schmoozed my way toward her as the evening wore on. It may have been my imagination, but I could swear she did the same thing. We eventually found ourselves face to face again, this time by an empty picnic table.

Due to our cheesecake distraction I hadn't noticed that she was wearing a very pretty sundress. In fact, in more ways than one she looked very different from the girl I saw on the other side. You know, the plain one. This one had her brown hair pulled back in a ponytail, and her eyes glowed.

Dude, you're staring. Stop it.

I blinked and looked away for a second. "Um, so," I began, "R.B. is your uncle."

She nodded. "Yes, but don't let his scary looks shake you. He's just protective of me."

"And for good reason. A guy stalks you from the café to here, you've got to wonder."

"I know to be on my guard with you military types," she said with a mock stern voice. "Okay," she clapped and rubbed her hands together like she was about to dig into something. "What's your story?"

"Story?"

"Yeah. How'd you get here? Where did you come from? You know, your story."

"Well, first there's a Daddy and a Mommy and they love each other very much and then they get married—"

"Okay! Not that much story." She grinned. "Just tell me the big parts."

"Well," I said. "I was born and raised here. Sports-award-winning high schooler and all that. You know . . . big fish, small pond, kind of thing."

"Must have been a really small pond," she deadpanned.

That made me laugh out loud.

"Well, yes, very small pond." I cleared my throat and resumed. "I played football in high school but I wasn't quite big or fast enough to catch anyone's attention. I had good grades and could've gone to college anyway, but after high school I just wanted out of the small pond. I wanted to see what the big pond was like. So, I joined the Air Force and asked for something exciting."

"Was it?"

"Most definitely," I said with a little less enthusiasm than before.

Her eyes narrowed but I charged on before she could say anything.

"Instead of college, I visited some interesting spots around the globe, and now, here I am. I'm back. I work with Boogie at the air base. Well, he flies the jets and I fix them, but that is where we met. In my spare time I take college classes to become a productive member of society."

"Not a chef, I hope!"

"Hey! You didn't even try the cheesecake. You might have liked it."

"I did try it, whether I wanted to or not."

"But—!"

"Yes! I know it's my fault. And . . . it wasn't bad at all."

"What? The cheesecake?"

"No, running into you again."

That, I didn't expect.

I think she surprised herself, too, because her eyes got big and she bit her lip. Then her cheeks flared red again and she stared wide-eyed at the ground.

Hold on. Does she have brain-mouth-disconnect issues, too?

A girl after my own heart.

It wasn't in my nature to be smooth, but I thought I would help her out on this one.

"And what about you? What's your story?"

She visibly relaxed.

You're welcome.

"Oh, you know. Slightly larger pond, but I was never a big fish. Just a quiet one, I guess."

"How about sports, or cheerleading, or playing in the band?"

"I was on the basketball team and I play the flute, so I stayed busy enough in high school, I guess. I'm finishing my degree at the college downtown. To do what, I'm not so sure, but one step at a time."

"You sure you didn't play football, too?"

"Very funny, Mr. Cheesecake. What about your family? I assume you've got a daddy and mommy bear somewhere, right?" She elbowed me in the side.

"Well, yeah. At least a mommy bear. My dad died a year ago. Cancer. It wasn't pretty, but he was a tough old guy. My brother and sister don't live too far away."

"Oh. I'm so sorry, Jamie."

"That's life, you know? What about you?"

"Well, my mom and dad are doing well and live not too far from here. I also have a brother and sister, though they both moved a couple of hours away. I've got good relationships with them, but they, um, aren't in the same 'club' as us."

"Club?"

She raised her eyebrows at me.

"Oh, right! The club. My bad."

She continued. "My parents and siblings are great but I've really connected with my uncle over the years. He's always been there for me. I'm so thankful we 'work' together."

Fighting Malum with a family member? Sounded scary to me.

Out of nowhere, she asked me a doozy of a question.

"So Mr. Big Fish, why are you limping tonight?"

Before I could respond she put her hand to her mouth in sudden realization. "Oh, no! I didn't do that to you did I? I didn't think I hit you that hard! I'm so sorry!"

I held up my hands.

"No, Kate. You didn't do that to me. The bump on the head and bruised back? Umm, maaaaybe."

She punched me playfully on the arm.

"Are you sure about the limp? I crashed into you pretty hard."

My limp had nothing to do with our run-in and everything to do with a memory that was infinitely worse.

Play it off, dude. Don't go there.

"It's your standard war wound. I fell on the way to the bathroom one night in Iraq. I got the purple toilet medal and everything."

I smiled, but I'm afraid she could see the truth in my eyes.

"You know," she said in a soft voice, "I'm a pretty good listener and it might help to talk. We've shared a lot, you and me."

"Shared? Like what?" I said, with a hint of a smile on my face.

"You know, we've had coffee together, we've taken trips, I mean *falls* together . . . "

How could she be so corny and cute at the same time?

" . . . you've scared the tar out of me *and* given me cheesecake. You see, we've shared all kinds of things!" she concluded with a triumphant smile.

She doesn't know what she's asking, dude. Don't do it.

"Kate, it's a war story, and in the real world those usually don't have happy endings. This one sure doesn't. I don't think you really want to know what happened."

Her countenance turned solemn, but she looked me in the eyes. "I think I really do. Trust me. It might be good for both of us."

And just like that, she convinced me to relive the worst day of my life.

* * *

Fallujah, Iraq.

"You PJ's are all the same," he whispered in the darkness.

I could hear the grin in his voice, though his form was mottled by shades of green, scintillating in my night vision goggles. "You wanna play hero with us but still sleep on real beds at night. Stinkin' Air Farce."

I thanked the Lord for Ralph. I didn't know anyone else who could keep things relaxed at a time like this.

"It's a good deal if you can get it, bro," I whispered back. "You do have to know how to spell your own name and crayon consumption is against the rules, so that knocks most of you Special Forces guys out of the running."

Out of the corner of my eye I saw his green smile in the little light reflected from his binocular NVGs. He never stopped scanning over and through the sight on his rifle, though. He was a pro.

Behind the levity we both felt the weight of the mission. One Specialist Mack Spencer, United States Army, got separated from his squad during a firefight the previous day. He had been taken by insurgents who were going to do who-knows-what to him. As far as we knew, he was alive. At least for now.

We were going to get him back.

We paused about fifty meters from our objective, a dimly lit pit of a building. Our Intel shop told us that's where Spencer was. Based on everything we knew, I had come up with the framework for this mission. I was officially leading it, and it was a doozy.

I quietly keyed my microphone and whispered, "Chip Shot," the code word that we were in position to begin our raid. Though we saw the building empty of fighters about five minutes prior, I needed confirmation that the other part of our raid was going according to plan.

"Tiger" would let us know that our unmanned aircraft showed the building minimally manned. The idea was that the rest of the bad guys would be tied up with our distraction. That is, if you call a platoon-sized raiding force raising all sorts of Cain about two kilometers away a distraction.

"Gilmore" meant we had problems and should consider aborting the grab. Either way, the final call to execute or abort was mine.

"Standby," was all the disembodied voice said through my earpiece.

Seconds ticked by. The only sounds I heard were the soft static of my radio and my pounding heart.

Ralph had my back and I his, but we both knew we were pushing our luck that night. You didn't just waltz into the lion's den and hope for the best. Lots of bad things happened down there, and recent insurgent internet videos left little to the imagination. It was the stuff of nightmares.

My radio crackled to life.

"Tiger. I repeat, Tiger."

I knew Ralph heard the same thing through his earpiece. I saw his body tense and feet shift in preparation to move. Rapidly.

"Roger, Tiger," I said into my mic, much more calmly than I felt.

That was it. No more comms until we were done. Just me and Ralph.

You got this, Jamie. Walk in the park, bro.

I was the leader of the mission, but Ralph was the expert assaulter. I deferred to him for the approach and entry. I gestured to him and made an onward movement, with one finger pointing to the front. He was in the lead now.

He gave one slow nod of his head, and then a thumbs-up. We were ready to roll.

He gave a quiet countdown with his fingers. 3, 2, 1 . . .

Moving.

We held a controlled gait to the outer door of the courtyard. "Slow is smooth, smooth is fast," or so the saying goes. We were quiet as shadows and moved into position.

Ralph was a breacher by trade. He could force his way into just about anything short of a concrete bunker. He had come prepared that night.

We hoped the sound of our entry would be lost in the city's racket. The gate was locked, but he managed to bully through it with minimal noise. No explosives necessary.

Attaboy, Ralph.

He went into the courtyard first, with me on his heels. We remained silent as we cleared the courtyard and moved to the house. Ralph prepared to breach the house's side door while I covered his back. Everything was still.

I heard a *click, click* sound in my earpiece.

Ralph had briefly double-keyed his mic. He was trying to get my attention.

I glanced over and saw a confused look on his partially-illuminated face.

The door was open.

Ralph shrugged in an *I don't know why* motion.

No time to worry about it. We're here.

I gave Ralph a *continue* motion with my left hand.

From our position we could see into the main hallway. It was dark and there were no signs of life. Ralph shouldered his weapon and tapped his head.

We were going in.

The smell hit me as we moved down the hallway. Roiling odors of unwashed bodies and spoiled food enveloped us. I almost choked.

Shake it off, Jamie. Check left, check right, look up.

Clear. Moving.

Just then, my danger sense began to tingle. I realized there was something more than sweat and decay in the air. There was a foulness that was difficult to describe but impossible to forget.

The smell of death.

Oh, man.

One glance at Ralph told me he smelled it, too. He cut his eyes toward me in acknowledgement.

A tap to his helmet and we moved on.

We secured each space, in order, and then moved to the next. In fact, we cleared the entire first floor of the house and found no one. However, it was clear that people had recently vacated the premises, and in a hurry. I found a still-steaming cup of hot tea on the floor of what passed for a bathroom.

We crept up the stairs to the second floor, well aware we were running out of time. The bad guys wouldn't stay gone forever.

Ralph was in the lead when we reached the top of the worn stairs. The upper floor was covered in tattered rugs, which helped muffle our movements. Ralph approached the room to our left and I peeled for the door on the right. I heard him whisper "clear" from a few feet behind me just as I entered my assigned room.

I froze.

I had found Specialist Spencer.

He was barely more than a kid, and his slender frame shook. His mouth was taped shut and his hands and feet were bound. Blood oozed from a head wound. He knelt in front of me and stared back with wide eyes that seemed to hold the horror of our worst nightmares.

A man stood beside him. He couldn't have been much older than Spencer, but his dark, full beard made it difficult to tell for sure. He held a pistol in one hand and a live grenade in the other. He smiled a fanatic's grin.

Stay cool, bro.

I gently said, *"Hudu'."* Relax.

I held up an open palm in a calming motion.

Come on, buddy. We can all walk away from this one.

Then I saw his eyes.

Oh, no . . .

He let go of the explosive and rolled it toward my feet.

I heard someone yell "Grenade!" I automatically brought my rife to bear and pulled the trigger. The insurgent went down, a hateful smirk still on his face.

It didn't matter.

The grenade was resting against my right foot. It would detonate before I could save anyone. Even myself.

In slow motion, I looked at Specialist Spencer, who stared at me with helpless eyes.

I'm sor—

I shot backward from the room.

What the . . . ?

Ralph.

He literally yanked me off my feet and back into the hall. It was a superhuman display of strength.

It was futile, but as a last gasp I reached for Spencer. I might as well have been reaching from the moon.

My last image was that of Specialist Spencer, unmoved, still staring into my eyes.

Just as I cleared the doorway, there was a blinding light and a deafening *crack!*

"Oof!" I landed in a heap on top of Ralph.

Ears ringing, I tried to get up and run into the room. That's when my right leg collapsed. It poured blood from a half-dozen shrapnel holes. I was out of the fight.

Ralph hopped over me. "Stay put!"

He disappeared into the smoke-filled room. I waited with sickening dread, trying not to acknowledge the obvious. Nothing to do but try not to bleed to death.

I stanched my bleeding with bandages and gauze.

The seconds passed in silence.

Ralph came out of the room, expressionless. He knelt beside me. "He's gone."

* * *

I was lost in the past.

A gentle, warm hand on my arm brought me to the present.

Whoa. Welcome back, dude.

I was mildly disoriented as the sounds and smells of the cookout returned. It felt like I had teleported from my pit of nightmares to Boogie's back yard. My brain struggled to make sense of the change.

Nice job, bright one. You traumatized Kate and then faded out on her. Class act.

I felt my face flush in embarrassment.

"Kate, I'm sorry for dumping this—"

In a quiet voice, she interrupted me, "And that's why you sometimes walk with a limp."

I turned and looked at her. She had sad eyes and one runaway tear. I gently brushed it away. I took her hand in mine.

She squeezed back and held on.

"Ralph saved my life. But there was too much damage to my knee to run with the teams. Before I knew what was happening, the Air Force decided I was 'unfit for duty.' Just like that"—I snapped my fingers—"they pushed me out."

"I'm so sorry, Jamie."

"Well, it just felt like the whole insult to injury thing. My reward for almost losing my life was losing my career. But I came out better than Spencer, right?" I said with a suddenly hoarse voice.

I didn't trust myself to speak anymore, so I just sat in silence.

Kate was quiet, too. She didn't try to tell me that everything was going to be okay, or tell me what I should do or think. She just sat with me.

It was touching beyond words.

She never let go of my hand. She did scoot a little closer to me, though, so our shoulders touched. We sat like that for a long time, just watching the sun set and listening to the soothing sounds of the afternoon.

I hadn't felt that peaceful in years.

We probably would've sat like that until nightfall if it hadn't been for Lori. I noticed that she was looking for someone. That someone turned out to be Kate.

Once Lori caught sight of Kate, she walked toward us with purposeful strides. We discretely ceased our hand-holding and scooted apart a bit.

Like no one would notice.

As Lori approached, Kate's features jolted in realization. She looked, big-eyed, at her watch. She hopped down from the table.

"Oh my word! Is it already seven o'clock? I feel like I just got here. Jamie, I told Lori I'd help with a project tonight. I'm sorry to run away, but I've got to go!"

She spun around in a circle, looking for her things.

I stood up and glanced around.

"No worries. Um, where did everyone go?"

Apparently, most of the other guests had already said their good-byes. Somehow Kate and I missed all that. I guess we had been in our own little world.

Lori walked up, a crooked smile on her face.

Kate said, "I'm so sorry! I lost track of the time. It is time, right?"

Lori said, "Yep, we've got to leave in about two minutes." She looked at me. "Sorry I have to steal her away, Jamie. Maybe we can get everyone together again sometime soon."

"That sounds great!" I said, a little too enthusiastically.

Mr. Cool strikes again.

Lori just grinned. "Your shirt is clean and is sitting by the front door." Without taking her eyes off of me, she said, "Chop-chop, Kate!" and then strode back toward the house.

Kate quickly gathered her things and turned to face me.

"Um, thanks for listening to me, Kate. It meant a lot."

"I enjoyed talking to you." She leaned a little closer. "Maybe you should come by the café from time to time. For the coffee, of course." She gave me a quick hug and a wink before she turned and walked away.

I couldn't believe my good fortune. Things were definitely looking up!

CHAPTER 13

The following days, on both sides of the veil, blurred together. Training progressed and my earthly job was going just fine, too. Well, except for one thing.

Despite my protests, Peggy fussed over me like a mother hen. She claimed that I "looked tired and needed some rest." I honestly didn't know what had gotten into her.

Being the strong person that I am, I did what any fiercely independent guy would do. I humored her. Seriously, you didn't want that woman mad at you.

In my off time, I made a few trips to see Kate at the café. We chatted on her breaks, and one night I even helped her clean up at closing time. However, I tried not to bother her there too often.

It was funny, in a weird sort of way. We enjoyed seeing each other but weren't officially dating. No idea why. Couldn't have been that I was scared or anything.

Lucky for me I got glimpses of her across the veil, too. That was not to say that I wasn't spending most of my time with my Charlie buddies. I was. In fact, I spent so much time with them that I learned a great deal of important things about them.

For instance, I found out that Tiny liked hamburgers and Harleys. No shocker there. I also found out the Js were about to graduate from high school and both of our newcomers, Mike and Kevin, were deathly scared of flying.

The way I figured it, the newbies both looked like prime candidates for Bravo Platoon. Tiny wasn't scared of flying, but he wasn't too keen on it either. So, my guess was that he would be a Bravo guy, too.

Only the Js and I had a strong desire to join Alpha Platoon, and we talked about it constantly. The idea of flying was like a habit-forming drug to me. The Js were the same way. Maybe too much.

You could say it led to little distractions, here and there. So much so that Gunny constantly warned them to not only search the skies for bad guys, but *look where you're going!* More than once the Js had gone head over feet because they were watching the flights of the "zoomies."

The moment we prayed for finally arrived.

One day Gunny met us as we arrived from our doorways. He got right to it. "Tiny, Mike, Kevin, you are with me today. Jamie, Jacob, Jared . . . you are with Boogie."

Boogie? No, he can't be serious!

I spun around and sure enough, there was Boogie, about to touch down. He deftly landed and jogged to a stop. The Js and I broke into broad grins.

"Now, before you flyer wannabes get too excited," Gunny said, "understand that this is just a test. We are going to see if you have a knack for flying and"—staring at the three of us—"can accept instruction in a timely manner."

In other words, listen to Boogie or stay stuck on the ground with me.

You didn't have to tell me twice.

"Ooh-rah!" we shouted.

I could tell Gunny wanted to grin. Even the ends of his mouth turned upward, but he managed to keep his stony demeanor. "Non-suicidal fighters, follow me."

Gunny and the non-J part of Charlie ran off at a decent pace and disappeared into the forest. The three of us turned and looked at Boogie as one. He grinned. "Follow me and try to keep up."

He then dashed down an unfamiliar trail. I followed immediately behind him, and the Js traced my footsteps. We ran for quite a while.

I thought we were getting flying lessons, not running ones.

My dismay turned to understanding when we approached another section of the training area. It was a sector that had small hills, little valleys, and lots of places from which to run and jump. I soon realized it was the perfect place for fledgling aviators.

Boogie began by leaping off the tops of some small hills, albeit at a quick pace. He would then allow gravity pull him back to earth normally. It other words he would run, jump, and land. Then he would run some more.

The Js and I matched his leaps and jumps almost exactly.

After a couple of laps, Boogie looked back at us. "We're gonna stretch out our jumps. Try to force your body to follow in the exact same path as mine, okay?" We nodded nervously.

The time has come, dude. Stay with him!

When we reached the next hill, Boogie jumped. But this time he leaned forward a little as he leapt. I watched what he did and tried my best to mimic it.

When I left the ground, I leaned forward. It felt different already. The best way I could describe it was a combination of roller-coaster weightlessness and a gravitational pull from the front. It felt like I was pulled onward by a magnetic force. The more I leaned into it, the more the force propelled me forward.

I think we did pretty well for first attempts. By pretty well, I mean we were all over the place. I sort of wish I had filmed it for America's Funniest Veil Videos, or something.

I was able to match Boogie's leap and gentle letdown, though I did stumble a bit upon contact with the ground. Okay, I fell on my face. However, I did manage to end the crash with a tucked-shoulder roll, so that was sort of cool.

The Js were a mixed bag. Jared leapt very high, and came down pretty hard, just short of the intended set-down zone. I could tell the landing jarred him pretty good. I heard his teeth clack on impact. He shook it off like a champ and caught up with Boogie and me.

Jacob did just the opposite. He leaned too far forward and accelerated like a bullet. He shot by me on my right side, clearly out of control. His foot caught on the top of our landing hill and he cartwheeled into the bushes. He, too, hopped up like nothing happened and rejoined our train.

As best I could tell, there was a balance to be had between forward motion and control. I tried to find the happy spot.

Boogie yelled over his shoulder. "Jamie, good! Keep mimicking my movements. Jared, trust yourself to lean forward a little. Jacob, not quite so much. You're doing great!"

We ran the same circuit a few times. By the third lap, all of us could match Boogie's short flights and touch down without knocking any of our teeth loose. I looked back and saw huge grins on the twins' faces. I gave them a thumbs-up and they responded in kind.

Without breaking stride, Boogie turned and took us down another path. He yelled over his shoulder. "Remember, just do what I do and follow me. Don't look around and don't look down. Look only where you want to go."

We rounded a corner by a big oak tree at a full sprint. I suddenly realized that the path ended in about five steps . . . at what looked to be the edge of a small cliff. Well, I guess I assumed it was a small cliff because I was certain that Boogie surely wouldn't drag us off the edge of a trainee killer.

Without warning and without further coaching, Boogie hit the edge of the cliff and launched himself. To his credit, it was the same profile we had seen over and over during the last hour. So, out of now well-drilled habit, we blindly followed him over the edge.

Sort of like lemmings.

It suddenly became very quiet. The only thing I saw was Boogie, and he seemed to hover in the sky.

If we're hovering, why is my shirt rippling?

No, he wouldn't have.

I stole a glance downward. The ground was still there . . . fifty feet below! It glided by and slowly, very slowly rose to meet us.

No. Way.

I heard screaming from behind me. Thankfully, it was the good kind.

"Woo-hoo!" The twins were ecstatic. I could tell from the location of their voices that they managed to stay in position.

Shortly thereafter, we approached a grass-covered hill and touched down at a trot. Somehow, we all made it in one piece. It was quite impressive.

The twins cheered and gave each other high fives. I joined them and even fist-bumped Boogie, who tried in vain to keep a straight face. I felt like a captive released on Christmas Day. I didn't think I could feel any freer or happier than I did then. Our cheers echoed through the countryside.

Boogie held up his arms in a quieting motion. "So, what do you think of flying so far?" In response, he got more yelling and high fives from his overstimulated pupils.

Boogie chewed his lip and stared at us. "If you guys can concentrate really hard on following me and not looking around, I think we might be able to go to Level Two today."

Level Two? Whatever. If was anything like what we just did, sign me up!

"Absolutely."

"Yeah!"

"Whoo-hoo!"

He said, "There is a slight difference. Instead of leaning forward off a jump, we're going to push mostly upward and jump off level ground. If we can't get airborne like that, then we're not ready for Level Two, all right?"

The three of us looked at each other and then nodded at Boogie.

"Okay then, follow me. And one more thing. When you fly, use your eyes to look around, not your head."

How was I supposed to use my eyes and not my head? How else would I look around?

It didn't make sense at the moment, but it did a few minutes later.

Boogie began running, and we followed closely behind. He pointed toward a tall hill in the distance. Then, with exaggerated movements, Boogie leaned forward and, in mid-stride, pushed himself away from the ground.

He lifted off in one smooth, practiced motion. He went into a gentle climb in the afternoon sky. The resulting vector was a straight line to the hill.

It was picture perfect.

Okay, Jamie. Do it just like you did against the flyer. Except for the fall through the tree part. Ready . . . go!

I leapt forward and upward . . . and silently lifted off the ground on the same vector as Boogie.

Yeah, boy! Like that!

The weightlessness already felt familiar, as did the "magnetic" force that pulled me onward. I turned my head to take a quick glance backward at the Js . . . and almost went end over end. I managed to straighten out before I tumbled.

Whoa! Boogie wasn't kidding about the only-move-your-eyes thing.

"Watch it, Jamie!" Boogie said.

That's crazy, dude. How does he fly in front and still keep track of us? It's like he's Super-Boogie or something.

"Do what I do, guys!" Boogie yelled. "When you move your head, it changes your flight path." He held his arms at his side and kept his head fairly still.

All right. Be like Super-Boogie. It's the only way to fly.

I think the Js listened to Boogie's instruction, too. After bonking into each other a couple of times, that is. They started with a couple of "oofs," followed by a "Use your eyes, not your head!" After that, things quieted behind me until there was only the whistle of wind in my ears.

We flew toward the hill, some of us a little wobblier than others. Nonetheless, we all aviated our way to the green, grassy hill and managed to set down in one piece. There was a moment of silence while we looked at each other.

Yep. That just happened.

"Yeaaaah! Whoo-hoo!"

You'd have thought we won the Super Bowl. I'd say we danced but it was too spasmodic for that. The Js celebrated like hyperactive puppies and I wasn't that different.

"Settle down!" He was trying to be stern, but Boogie looked like a proud papa. "You have to prove to me that wasn't a fluke. Show me you can fly back."

Seriously? Let's go!

Off we went. This time, we flew back to where we started. As soon as we got there, we flew back up again. Back and forth we went.

Flying was getting easier by the minute. This rocks!

After a last trip to the big hill, Boogie stopped and stared at us. He chewed his lip and put his chin in his hand. He stood like that for a full minute while we whooped and hollered.

Finally he said, "Guys, I have to admit you're doing extremely well. So well, in fact, that I'm considering Level Three. Free flight."

Could this day get any better?

"You'll still follow me like before, but we'll add maneuvering. It normally takes weeks for guys to get to this level, but for some reason you three"—he pointed at us—"seem to have a real knack for this."

I said, "Maneuvering? As in we turn in the air and follow you around?"

"Yep. We'll play follow the leader. Are you up for one more flight?"

It was like waving a red flag in front of a bull or a Whopper in front of Tiny. All three of us nodded.

"Yep."

"Yes."

"Absolutely!"

That decision almost cost us our lives.

CHAPTER 14

"One more time. Wherever your head goes, that's where you go. Use your eyes if you don't want to change your flight path."

Thumbs-up all around.

Poor Boogie. He looked like a bit like a dad letting his teenage sons drive on the interstate for the first time. Proud but very apprehensive.

After a last glance our way, he took a few steps and confidently leapt into the sky.

Like last time, I flew behind Boogie and Jacob and Jared brought up the rear. At first, Boogie flew directly toward a dark tree line. But slowly, he turned his head to take us down a wide valley.

Now use your head, dude.

I turned my noggin like he did . . . and followed him through a swooping turn.

I can't believe this is really happening. So awesome cool.

He flew much faster this time, but we kept up. It didn't take long to figure out that the more we leaned in a particular direction, the faster we would go. Our little formation stayed about twenty feet off the ground, which turned the rocks and bushes into a blur.

After a few minutes of low-level flight, he tilted his head upward and began to climb. The trees shrunk until they resembled small bushes. The only sounds were the wind and the occasional "Cool!" from one of the Js.

I caught Boogie grinning as he kept an eye on us.

As if that wasn't enough, we then did something I had only dreamed of. We flew around the clouds. At one point, we even skimmed through the top of them. I felt the cool dampness of white, billowy fluff.

I was in heaven.

Next, we flew over a big lake. It was so calm we could see our reflections in the water. I just couldn't imagine walking anywhere, ever again.

This was the Best. Day. Ever.

That is . . . right up until Boogie spun around and threw his sword at my head.

To be fair, he wasn't aiming at me. I just didn't know it at the time. All I knew was that in a microsecond's time he stopped in midair and heaved his sword at what seemed to be my left ear.

"Whaaa—"

On pure instinct, I twisted violently in the air. My maneuver put me out of control. But it also caused his sword to pass my left cheek instead of penetrating it.

The heat of its passing left a mild scorching sensation, like instant razor burn.

I followed the sword's path as it flew by my head and continued toward the twins. Things were suddenly clear.

Malum.

Three of them. And they were about to kill Jared and Jacob.

The twins didn't see the Nasties. All of their concentration was on flying. Jacob now wore the same blank look as I had worn just a moment earlier.

Things were happening way too fast.

The closest Malum reached for Jacob. Boogie's sword hit him just as his fingers grabbed Jacob's shirt. He exploded in a ball of dust.

That's when I saw Jared tumble from the sky in a dazed ball.

Oh, no. The sword! It must have clipped Jared on the way by.

"Dive!" Boogie yelled. He flew by me in a rage.

With a look of utter panic and confusion, Jacob dove after his brother.

I struggled to regain my balance as carnage blossomed in front of me. Boogie crashed into the remaining Malum. The sky filled with shouts and sparks. The two Malum cursed Boogie and renewed their attack from opposite directions. Boogie moved so quickly he looked like a streak of silver and gold.

For a moment, I was frozen in the air, but my mind raced.

Boogie's in trouble. Jared is falling. Who do you save?

"Move, Jamie!" I shouted.

I tucked my shoulder and shot toward Jared. He was halfway to the ground and falling like a wounded duck. Half-conscious, he spun and flailed and fought to regain his senses.

Jacob caught up to him first. He grabbed Jared's arm and pulled upward with all his might. His eyes bulged and his face turned blood red, but the pair screamed toward the surface of the lake.

The wind howled in my ears and tears cascaded from my eyes. My gut clenched.

I won't make it in time. They're going to crash.

I think Jacob knew it, too, but he wouldn't let go. The pair slammed into the water with a sickening *smack!* Water erupted like a meteor strike.

Slow down, Jamie! Going too fas—

I hit the water. Hard. The sky disappeared in murky brown water. Ungh!

Stay calm. Follow the bubbles, swim to the surface . . .

My feet touched mud.

Just stand up, dude!

I sloshed to my feet, clothes soaked with lake water.

Where are they? There! Oh, no.

They were in deeper water. Jacob struggled to stay above the surface. I couldn't see Jared at all.

I dove and swam as hard as I could. I reached Jacob and grabbed him by his shirt. He coughed and sputtered and tried to pull away from me.

"Jare—" was all he managed to sputter before swallowing more water and retching. He was in no shape to save himself, much less his brother.

I swam backward, using my body to buoy Jacob.

Come on, Jamie. Get to the shallows. Move!

In my heart, I knew the last seconds of Jared's life were ticking by.

Out of the corner of my eye I saw a figure with a bright sword, high in the sky. He swirled against two forms with dark blades. Boogie was still alive, if only for the moment.

I felt a surge of hope.

Suddenly, a large form's shadow covered Jacob and me.

Without thought, I whipped my sword out with my right hand . . . and immediately sank beneath the surface. The water covered everything except my sword hand. I could see a water-distorted form hovering over us.

Swim and die or fight and drown. It wasn't lookin' good for the home team.

I suddenly felt a vise grip on my right wrist, which froze my sword arm. Jacob was torn from my grasp. I couldn't process what was happening.

No!

I erupted from the water in a spray of confusion and fear.

Grey Beard yelled, "I got him! Find the other one before he drowns, boy!"

He didn't look anything like a guardian angel, but I couldn't think of a prettier sight.

"I'm on it!"

He had Jacob by the arm. With little evident strain he managed to fly above the surface of the water while towing Jacob to the bank. He was so fast he made a wake.

I swam furiously to where I found Jacob. Jared had to be nearby. I dove deep and searched the muddy water.

The sunlight faded quickly in the murkiness. I could barely see a foot in front of me. I kept searching until I was almost out of air.

Come on, Jared. Where are you, buddy? Help me out here.

I felt something bump against my foot and looked down.

Blond hair. Jared.

I grabbed him by the only thing I could reach, and swam for the surface with all of my might. Blood pounded in my ears and I got tunnel vision. My brain was running out of oxygen.

Almost there. Kick, dude, kick!

My tunnel vision became darker and the surface of the lake faded to a point of light.

I heard my father's voice screaming, *Come on, Jamie! You got this!*

I kicked with everything I had left. My strength faltered.

The world faded silent and dark.

* * *

The next moment exploded in noise and light.

I coughed and gasped for air. One second I was above the surface of the lake, the next I was submerged. I fought for breath and control of Jared's body.

I couldn't keep us both above the waterline in my weakened state.

I managed to yell a strangled "Help!" before I swallowed more water.

Come on, Grey Beard, I could use some help, man!

The next thing I know I'm flying backward, still dragging Jared by the hair on his head. I feel Grey Beard's vise grip on my other hand. He was pulling us both to safety.

As I tried with all my might to hold on to Jared, I got an idea.

I used my legs to pull Jared closer to me so I could get a better grip on him. Then I latched my arm across his chest. I hugged him as tightly as I could against the water rushing around us in churning white waves.

Not gonna lose you now, buddy.

My heart sank. What I didn't feel told me more than I wanted to know.

Jared wasn't breathing.

I couldn't see his face, but his head rolled limply with our movements.

All right, Jamie. The clock is ticking. If you don't get him breathing again, quickly, he's gone for good.

It was strange. I could hear myself gasping and retching and wheezing, but it was like I was hearing someone else. Though my body was wracked, my mind was clear.

You know what to do.

Thump. The world jarred as we hit the bank.

I rolled out from under Jared and looked at his face. His eyes were unfocused and his skin an unnatural shade of white. He was halfway to heaven.

I looked up at Grey Beard and, for the first time, saw panic on his face. He stared at Jared with an open mouth and glassy eyes. He wasn't moving.

"Hey!" I croaked as loudly as I could.

Grey Beard jumped and looked at me with wide eyes.

"I've got this. Go help Boogie!"

I saw confusion on his face. I glanced up, hoping Boogie was still alive. He was, but he was fighting for his life. His motions had slowed and he was caught between the Malum. He barely got his blade around to meet the attacks. He wouldn't last long.

"That guy! Right there! You know, the one fighting the Malum!"

The trance was broken. With a start, he glanced up. He eyes narrowed to slits and his jaw locked.

Boom!

He exploded from the ground in a shower of dust like a Fourth of July rocket. I was in awe, but I had other problems.

Jared's lifeless eyes stared back at me. For a moment, I froze. Then my training kicked in.

ABCs, Jamie. Airway. Breathing. Circulation. Go!

I cleared Jared's mouth of water and began CPR.

One-and-two-and-three-and—

"Nooooo!" came Jacob's strangled cry. He knelt beside us. He was shaking and crying.

My heart broke for him, but I needed his help.

"Jacob! Listen to me. We can save him! Do this . . . " I began chest compressions.

He stared blankly at me.

"Hey! Right now! Do it!" I screamed.

It worked. He did chest compressions and I did mouth-to-mouth. Jacob's tear-stained face now had a look of fierce determination.

There was nothing else for it. Either we saved him or we didn't. I hoped Boogie and Grey Beard were okay.

Well, if they can't save themselves, we're dead anyway.

Keep goin', bro. One thing at a time.

I kept a rhythm with the air. Jacob did compressions like a fiend. I could hear him muttering under his breath, "Come on, Jared, come on!"

Please Lord. Not today. Just not today.

Please.

Jared suddenly convulsed.

We both froze. Jared's body shook.

I shoved him onto his side. He heaved what seemed a gallon of lake water all over the ground. He coughed and wheezed . . . and breathed.

Jacob yelled, "Yeah! That's it! Breathe!" He half-cheered, half-cried for his brother. Tears ran down his face, but he grinned from ear to ear.

I was still worried about Jared. Was he gone too long? Would he really come back to us?

The first words out of his mouth settled it. "Why did Boogie hit me with his sword, and why does my scalp hurt so bad? Ow!"

He looked at Jacob, who was laughing hysterically in relief, and began to laugh, too. He didn't know what happened, but the twins' connection carried the day. He was going to be fine.

I staggered to my feet.

Wait. What about Boogie?

I looked into the bright sky. There were only two figures left, and they screamed toward us at an unbelievable speed.

Don't get caught napping. Not now.

I pulled my sword and braced as I squinted into the sun.

The glimpse of grey gave it away. It wasn't Malum.

Thank you, Lord.

Boogie hit the ground at a run and skidded to a stop by the twins. He was breathing hard and covered in Malum dust. They barely noticed him.

The twins were too busy telling each other stories of how awesome they were. This despite the fact that Jared's laughter was sporadically interrupted by another round of retching, which only made the twins laugh more. I was amazed by their resilience.

The older members of the team were a little worse for the wear.

Boogie thumped down on the ground and put his head in his hands. His shoulders slumped and he kept rubbing his eyes. I heard him muttering something that I couldn't really make out.

Grey Beard stared at the twins. Relief was written all over his face. There was also a faraway look in his eyes that seemed sad.

I walked over to him and said with a hoarse voice, "Thanks. Again. If it hadn't been for you, we would have been toast."

He shook my offered hand with a strong grip and steady eyes, but just nodded.

Boogie looked up, "Yes. Thank you." He got unsteadily to his feet and took a few deep breaths. He slowly walked over to Grey Beard.

"What's your name?" I said.

His eyes narrowed slightly at the question and his mouth turned into a frown. For a second, I thought he would turn and leave. But finally, he took a deep breath and squared his shoulders, like a man preparing to confront something unpleasant.

"You can call me Sam."

"Well Sam, I'm quite pleased to make your acquaintance. You have a habit of pulling my bacon out of the fire, and I thank you for that. I gotta admit, though, I hope I don't need your services so much in the future."

He smiled a small, embarrassed grin, but his eyes sparkled sadly.

"Sam," Boogie began, "it looks like you know how to handle yourself."

Sam nodded slightly, but didn't reply.

"Any chance I can talk you into joining us? I mean, not just in emergency situations. You'd be great to have on our team."

I said, "He may not know what you're talking about, Boogie."

I turned to Sam and began to speak but he held up his hand in a "stop" gesture. He shook his head at me. Boogie and Sam stared at each other, unsaid words passing between them.

Suddenly, Sam spoke. "Jamie, right? Well Jamie, I know all about your little team and what you're tryin' to do. I admire your spirit but it's a foolish thing. Keep this up and you'll all die."

He turned to leave.

By now the twins were watching with wide eyes. Boogie had a look of mournful understanding on his face.

"But . . . but . . . hey, wait! Why do you say that?"

He paused and turned to look at me.

"Jamie, a long time ago there was another group. They were doing the same thing you are, and they're all dead. Almost all of 'em massacred by the Malum."

"What? How do you know that?"

"How? Because I'm the only one left."

With that, he pivoted and flew away.

CHAPTER 15

It was a long walk back to camp that day. No one said a word. My fun meter was pegged and I just wanted to go home. I didn't even stick around to hear what Boogie said to the others. I stepped through the nearest door and tried to put the day behind me.

Boogie must have told R.B., at the very least. The next time I saw him he mutely nodded at me and slapped my back in encouragement. I nodded back. I didn't know what to say to him, either.

I had to wonder: was I the only one who hadn't known that our "ancestors" had gotten wiped out? Boogie didn't act worried that I would tell anyone, so I guess it wasn't a secret. They sure didn't advertise it, though.

For the sake of public relations, it might have been a good note to add to their recruiting spiel . . . "And if you join us today you and your friends may get wiped out by really ugly dudes with bad haircuts and black swords. Act now!" Sheesh. What else weren't they telling me?

Despite whatever questions continued to swirl in my brain, in the end, I guess it didn't bother me too much. I still kept showing up, as did everyone else. I didn't know if we were brave or stupid. Or both.

Over the following days the twins seemed outwardly none worse for the wear, though I wasn't so sure about the inside. A mild chill settled over their normally carefree attitudes. Whether from the fall, or our fight with the Malum, or from Sam's warning, something had changed them.

If anything, they stuck together more closely than before, neither venturing too far away from the other's sight. I couldn't imagine what it would be like to lose a brother like that. A shiver ran down my spine at the thought of it.

I didn't want to dwell on how things could have turned out, but Sam's words kept replaying in my mind. Why was he the only one left? What happened? What was really going on?

The more I thought about it the more I knew there was only one way to find out.

* * *

I sat on the park bench at the courthouse for almost a whole weekend before he showed. The weather was nice enough, but the hard bench got a little old. I only hoped I looked innocent enough to not have the cops called on me for loitering. Thankfully, he eventually ambled up and casually sat down on the other end of the bench. He looked the same as he always had. Grey beard, white hair . . . sad eyes.

For a while, neither of us spoke.

Then he broke the silence. "You know, Jamie. This probably isn't a very smart thing to do."

"You mean talking? In public?"

"Yeah. Somethin' like that."

"Well, I figured you would check the area before you showed. Make sure everything is okay."

He gave a thin smile and a mild nod of his head. "Not bad, son."

"How do you do that? I mean, you seem to be able to visit at will."

"Old tricks of the trade, son. Best not to say anything more right now."

Okay, new tack. Keep it light to get him talking.

"So, what's new in your life? Seen any cool movies?"

He looked over at me and raised his eyebrows like, *Really?*

Oka-a-ay. Fail.

Let's try the direct approach.

"For someone who wants no part of our little endeavor, you seem to show up a lot."

No reaction, except for a deep breath.

"I just don't get you, Sam."

Suddenly he flashed anger. "There's a lot you don't get, Jamie."

Whoa. "Uh, sorry, Sam. I'm not so good at this."

He put his head on his chest and sighed. "No, I'm sorry. I guess I'm just a little sensitive about some things." He turned and looked at me. "Why are you here, son? Is there somethin' you need?"

Great question, actually.

"I don't really know, Sam. I mean, we would love to have you with us, but that's not why I came looking for you. I guess . . . I feel like there is more going on here than I know, and you have the key."

Another long silence.

"You know the basics. Bad beings are doing bad things. Your group is trying to stop them. That's pretty much the story."

"Then what am I missing? And why do you seem to be my guardian angel? I mean, no-kiddin' thank you, but something doesn't add up. Why me?"

He rubbed his eyes and then stared at the sky, as if looking for a good answer. All at once, he seemed to deflate. Without turning his head he said, "You look just like him, you know."

Huh? "I look just like who?"

"Your father."

I was speechless. My heart pounded as my head tried to make sense of what my ears just heard.

No, he couldn't really mean—

"Your dad was a good man. I wasn't lying the other day when I said I was the only one left. I am. But the complete truth is that your dad and I were the only survivors from . . . before."

My thoughts were too jumbled and coming too fast to make any sense. All I could get out was, "My dad . . . was . . . one of us?"

"Oh yeah, and he was good at it. Really good. I can tell you got your skills from him. And his recklessness." He smiled as he said the last part.

It couldn't be true, could it? Then again . . . why not? It made sense, really.

The factualness of it calmed me. My dad was one of us. How awesome-cool is that?

"But . . . what happened?!"

He did a calming motion with his hands. "Jamie. I probably should not have told you that right now. I can't get into it here. I am sorry."

My head was still spinning. "But . . . "

"Jamie, I'm here because your dad was a dear, dear friend of mine. He was a good man, and I don't want to see his son die an early death for no good reason."

Sometimes my mouth could outrun my brain. "No good reason? It seems like a great reason! We're protecting our families."

The anger flashed again. "Really? Well, *they* are back again, aren't they? And all of my 'family' are still dead! Lots of good that did! It don't seem like a very good reason to me!" He stood to leave.

"Sam, wait!" I jumped up.

He spun and stuck his finger in my chest, pushing me back to the bench. "Jamie, you think long and hard about what you're doin'. I showed up 'cause your dad saved me more times than I can count, but I can't always be there to protect you. Save yourself and stay home." He walked away.

My emotions got the best of me. I followed him, shouting, "Is that what my dad would say? 'Abandon your friends. Stay home. Save yourself.'"

That stopped him in his tracks, and he glared at me. The pain on his face told me he was miserably trapped between outrage and heartbreak. After a couple of seconds he shook his head and walked away.

Nice job, Jamie. Insult the man who's saved you multiple times.

I stood there and watched him until he was out of sight. I plopped back down on the bench and stared at nothing in particular. The conversation replayed in my head. *Is that what my dad would say?* I was such a hypocrite.

The irony of my words to Sam was not lost on me. I realized I'd been wrestling with the same questions. We really weren't so different, he and I. He had merely chosen one of the answers, and it was one I found entirely rational.

In the end, my own words haunted me. What *would* my dad say? I thought I knew, but could I follow through?

* * *

I chose to keep the meeting with Sam to myself. Given everything that had happened, I didn't feel like explaining things to anyone. I'd probably get another lecture or "training" session about not wandering around on my own.

Whatever. It was worth it.

I still couldn't get over what Sam told me. My dad was one of us! If it were possible, it made me wish he were still around even more. I wished he could have seen me fly.

Speaking of that, I advanced rapidly through the flying training program. Despite the trauma from our previous session, the twins also continued to do extremely well in our flying lessons. They began to shake off some of the lingering hangover, with their irrepressible, youthful enthusiasm carrying the day. Their laughter eventually returned, as did their confidence.

Though some of the other instructors helped out, Boogie continued to meet us and teach us, albeit at a slower pace. We did stay a little closer to our base but nothing was ever said about Sam or the events at the lake. I figured I had said enough for the time being, so I kept my mouth shut.

Boogie did mention that we would spend some more time with Gunny before our final platoon assignments were made. He did not want our ground-fighting skills to atrophy and even hinted that we would soon begin learning how to sword fight airborne. The three of us appeared to be destined for Alpha Platoon, assuming nothing went too badly.

In a quiet moment, I asked Boogie about Kate. I had seen her a few more times at our meeting site, but she was always quietly talking to R.B. Before I could ever get her attention, she would leave. I couldn't quite figure out what was going on.

Boogie was evasive. He just mumbled something about her "helping us with a few things." I could tell that he really didn't want to talk about it, so I dropped the subject. I still wondered though, what was she doing there?

After only a few more training sessions, the Js and I were rocketing around the sky. Everyone was a little bit more cautious than before, but we relished the increasingly difficult game of follow-the-leader. We even got to lead from time to time.

We became very adept at quickly changing altitudes and airspeed. However, hovering was still extremely difficult. It took a great amount of concentration but it was attainable, if only for a few moments.

I wasn't sure if there were limits on how high we could fly, but at some point it was increasingly difficult to climb. We became familiar with our limits, physical or otherwise, and worked on maneuverability and stamina. Flying took a good deal of mental and physical effort, so it was easy to get fatigued if you were out of shape.

Gunny took us back for a couple of training sessions and grudgingly admitted that our fighting skills had not eroded too far. He worked us over, gave us some pointers, and then sent us back to

Boogie for more air training. All three of us made it through without getting stun-gunned, so I called it a win!

The next day we returned to Boogie for more flight training, but things were already different. He met us with his sword in his hand. "Same object of the game as before, but now you keep up holding onto this." With no further words, he lifted off from the ground in a blur.

We brandished our swords and dutifully zoomed through the sky in his wake. It was not quite so easy to fly with a sword, but with a little practice it became doable. The balance was the toughest thing, especially if you tried to swing it and maneuver at the same time.

We roared and soared through the bright sky, chasing each other and the occasional hawk with increasing delight. My heart pounded and my eyes teared as we dove and climbed all afternoon. I kept getting bugs in my teeth from grinning.

When I was flying, everything just felt right.

My first indication that something was wrong wasn't something I saw, but instead it was something I felt. Out of nowhere, a harsh fear jolted my heart. I literally spun around twice like a corkscrew looking for Malum. It was like nothing I had experienced before. But all I saw was sleepy, sunny countryside, apparently devoid of anything sinister.

What's going on, dude? Panic attack?

No. Too real.

Then what?

It was like I was feeling someone else's emotions. Terror. Fear. Anger. Everything all at once.

Boogie didn't notice my flailing but the twins sure did. Their eyes grew large as they saw me twisting and turning, surely with a look of alarm on my face. Without knowing why they, in turn, began to look for danger.

What Boogie did notice was people streaming back to camp. Uncharacteristically, a crowd was gathering in the clearing. I could see others running and flying to join them there. The furrows on Boogie's brow and his pursed lips told me he was worried. Without a word, he spun and dove directly for camp, the twins and I on his tail. The wind howled in our ears as we struggled to keep up.

Boogie was the first one there. He touched down and ran straight to where Al and Gunny were speaking with R.B. Our leader's expression was a mask of worry and fear. He repeatedly waved his hands and gestured at the forest.

He paused when he saw me, a peculiar expression settling on his face. The others stared at me for a moment, too. Then they resumed their animated discussion.

What's that about?

I and the rest of Charlie stood apart from the others, waiting and watching. For reasons I didn't understand, my heart jackhammered and my palms began to sweat.

Stop freaking out, Mr. Combat Vet. Everything is gonna be fine.

I had just gotten my heart rate under control when Tiny walked up. I hadn't noticed before, but he had eased close to R.B. to hear what was going on. The look on his face told me he wish he hadn't.

"Well?" I said as everyone edged closer. "What's going on?"

Tiny repeatedly tried to speak, but stopped before he could say anything.

I was getting impatient.

"Come on, Tiny. Spit it out!"

His next words froze me.

"Kate's been taken."

PART III
BEHIND THE LINES

CHAPTER 16

I flinched like I'd been punched in the gut. *"What?* Who took Kate?"

"The Nasties, Jamie," Tiny said, in a deep, anguished voice.

My breathing came in shallow gulps. "Malum? Why?"

Nothing made sense. What's Kate got to do with anything? My head was spinning.

Tiny leaned in. "Kate wuz spyin' on the Nasties. She been sneakin' near their place and reportin' back. R.B. let 'er scout for us so we can prepare for whatever's comin'."

"R.B. let her . . . "

Oh, man.

Everything fell into place. Sweet little Kate, sneaking through the woods to spy on the Malum. R.B. had let her do it, and now she was . . .

"Do we know for sure that's who's got her?" Mike asked.

"Yeah. Weasel wuz flyin' cover for 'er. He saw the Nasties attack and drag 'er away. There wuz so many and it happened so fast that he didn't have a chance to help 'er. He wuz able to follow 'em long enough to see where they'd taken 'er, though."

I looked at the gathering of Alpha Platoon. There was Weasel, pacing back and forth and anxiously rubbing his shaved head with one hand. The other hand sporadically clenched and unclenched in a fist. His eyes were wide and filled with anguish.

"Can't we just go get her?" I asked.

"That's what they tryin' to figure out," Tiny said. "I overheard 'em sayin' that she been taken to a spot where they are dozens of Nasties. They worried that if we make a frontal assault, the Nasties will kill 'er." He kicked at a rock. "If they haven't already."

I could tell he didn't mean for those last words to come out. He cringed and looked away.

"Can't we mount an airborne assault?" I offered. "Maybe we can swoop in with Alpha and get her before they know what is going on."

"There's one problem with that," Kevin said. "Some of the Malum fly, too. Word is they have some of those guys round here. They'll see us comin' from a mile away."

For a minute, no one said a word.

"Jamie, didn't you use to save people and stuff?" Kevin said. "Maybe you could do some of that rescue magic, y'know?"

I unintentionally visualized Specialist Spencer. I jumped as he morphed into Kate, her eyes pleading with me.

"Jamie, you okay man?" Mike said.

I barely heard him. I was listening to another voice.

My dad's words echoed in my head. *Okay, Jamie. It's game time and it's all or nothin'. What's the call? Are you in, or what?*

Of course. Anything for Kate.

Okay then. Man up.

Without a word, I turned and walked away.

"Jamie! Where you goin'?" Kevin yelled.

I wasn't invited, but I walked up to R.B. and the others anyways. If anything, their conversation was more animated, and desperate, than before. R.B. was as close to a meltdown as I had ever seen him.

Boogie gave me a grim look. He said quietly, "Jamie, we're a little busy. Please give us a minute, okay?"

I cleared my throat and spoke in a loud voice that sounded bolder than I felt. "I think I know how we can get Kate back."

As one, they turned and stared at me.

Most of them were a bit hard to read, but I knew I was pushing it. Their practiced, military stares were like hardened shells over reservoirs of intensity. I was intruding at a stressful time.

Then there was Al. He was easy to read. For reasons unknown, he looked like he was ready to throttle me.

Whatever, man. I want Kate back.

Surprisingly, R.B. gave me a nod and motioned for me to continue.

"Do we know where Kate is?" I asked.

"Yes," Boogie said.

"Can we reach it by foot and get out of the target area before dark?"

Gunny considered the question for a moment, and then he nodded. "It would take some fast movement through Malum country, but it's doable."

"Would it be fair to say that we believe she is still alive?" Again, my voice sounded much better than my heart.

"Yes." R.B. seemed to struggle to keep his emotions in check. "We have reason to believe she'll be kept alive until tonight, when their local bigwig commander will visit them. After that . . . " He let the sentence fade in the afternoon breeze.

"Can someone show me a rough draft of what the target area looks like? Significant features, terrain?"

R.B. nodded and quickly sketched a coarse diagram in the dirt based on what Weasel had told him. Everyone gathered around while I stared at the drawing and ran some basic computations in my head. I didn't really like what I came up with.

"A few years back I was a pararescue specialist in the Air Force. We're called para-jumpers, or PJs." They didn't look surprised. I guess they knew more about me than I thought. "We worked a similar problem for one of our troops that had been captured. Based on that, I think I know what we have to do."

"Please explain." R.B. gave me an intense stare.

It felt like I was cracking open the door to a room I swore would remain locked forever. A wave of fear rolled through me. I took a deep breath. "In simplest terms, Alpha and Bravo will act as diversions so we can sneak a two-man team in and snatch Kate from under their noses. The timing of the diversion and the arrival of our two-man team have to be synched to make it work."

"Show us," Boogie said.

I drew in the dirt, sketching the movement of Alpha and Bravo platoons and the approach route of the two-person team. "Boogie, Al, I need Bravo to approach from the east-northeast with Alpha overhead. We need to make it appear like we're looking for Kate, but we're not quite sure where she is. The small team will simultaneously approach from the southwest."

Boogie nodded and Al grunted his assent.

I continued. "I need you to start a fight with the Malum, but do not get bogged down. I just want you to take their attention for a few minutes, and then withdraw. You'll be way too deep in their territory to get anchored there. Think hit-and-run tactics, especially the run part."

I could see their wheels spinning. Boogie was the first with a question. "If Al and I are leading our platoons, who is on the grab team?"

Great question. Here goes nothin' . . .

"I think Gunny and I are the best candidates."

Al stiffened.

I kept talking anyway. "I've got rescue and medical expertise, and Gunny is well suited to cover ground quietly. We can get out quickly, even if we have to carry someone."

I saw the doubt in their eyes, especially Al's. They weren't sure if I was up to the task. They also knew that I was uniquely qualified for this sort of mission. So they were sort of stuck between a rock and a hard place.

Welcome to my life, guys.

"Anything else we should consider?" R.B. asked.

"Yes. The grab team will be in a dangerous place. If something bad happens, no one will be able to come to their rescue. Even if things go fairly well, the chances of everyone making it out unscathed aren't great."

Al said dryly, "So, in your *expert* 'pinion, this is gonna be dangerous."

What is his problem?

Boogie jumped in. "Al, come on. He's trying to—"

"In other words, this could be suicide for the grab team." My eyes locked onto his. "The one I'm volunteering for. With my *expert* opinion."

Al growled. "Boy, I'll—"

"That's enough!" R.B. glared at both of us.

Al crossed his arms and looked away.

"Sorry, R.B.," I said. "But just give me a chance. I won't let you down."

R.B. searched my eyes. "Jamie, I hear you. Give us a minute to discuss this."

"Okay." I turned and began to walk away.

Before I got very far, R.B. added, "Jamie, what happened with your rescue mission? Was it successful?"

I faced him and answered without pause.

"No."

*　*　*

I reviewed the plan in my head in case they decided to listen to me.

We need stealth, hence, a small snatch team. Check. The plan requires a ton of audacity. Yep, bringin' it. We need the entire team's full support. To be determined.

We need to get going!

A few minutes after I had walked away, I was summoned back.

"Hey, Jamie," Boogie called out. "Come here for a minute."

I jogged to where the leaders were still conferring.

"We're in agreement," R.B. began, "that your plan is our best shot at getting Kate back."

Really? If they all thought this was our best shot, they didn't look very happy about it. What was I missing?

Gunny was stone-faced, as always, but Al looked ready to hurt someone. He had his fists clenched and fidgeted in place, all the while silently shaking his head. Boogie was as upset as I'd ever seen him, too. He had his arms crossed on his chest and stood motionless, staring into the distance, but his chest heaved like a thoroughbred getting ready to charge.

"However," R.B. said, "there's a change to the makeup of the snatch team. I'm going with you."

Oh. That's not strange at all.

Actually, I was stunned. I wasn't sure R.B. was up for something like this.

I think R.B. read the skepticism in my eyes. "Don't worry, Jamie, I won't slow you down, and I can hold my own against the Malum."

Al spoke up forcefully. "For the record, I'm against you goin', R.B.! This ain't very smart. I realize we gotta take some risks with personnel, but you're way too important to send on this one."

Why did he look at me when he said that?

Oh, I get it. Risks *from* personnel, not *to* personnel. He's really got it in for me.

Al's voice softened a bit. "Look, I know Kate's your niece. But all that does is tell me that you'll take risks. We can't lose you, especially with everything that's goin' on."

His argument did make perfect sense. So much so that I expected Boogie to support him. But Boogie remained silent and only stood nearby with a dreadful look on his face. Boogie wouldn't even meet Al's gaze.

Al threw his arms up in frustration and looked around angrily at the small group.

R.B. said calmly, "Al, what you said is wise, but I need you to trust me on this one. I know what I'm doing. Jamie, let's get ready to go."

I nodded. "So, we're set with the other players in this rescue?" Meaning the support of Alpha and Bravo platoons.

Boogie broke from his stare. "Yes. We'll execute your plan. You just get in and get Kate, then get out as fast as you can. I don't know how long you'll have."

"Wilco," I said. "Al, any questions on the plan?"

I braced, expecting a torrent.

"No," he said with a pained but resigned expression. "You better get goin' if we're gonna make this work, mayun."

Oka-a-y.

He was right, though. We were wasting valuable time. I looked at R.B. "How much time do you need to be ready to roll?"

R.B. glanced at the guys. "I only need a minute. I'll be right with you."

"Okay. I'll be right back."

I walked back to the members of Charlie Platoon. I told them what was going on. "I need you guys to be ready to fight. If the Nasties manage to follow us back here, we'll need you. Ooh-rah?"

"Ooh-rah," they replied in unison. No questions, no objections.

I stared at them for a second. There was something they weren't telling me.

Dude, we don't have time for this. Let's go!

I walked back to R.B., who was shaking hands with the three other leaders. We grabbed the few things that we needed and began to walk away. Before he got to the tree line, R.B. turned and said to Boogie, "Remember what I told you and do exactly as I said."

Boogie looked crestfallen. "Okay, R.B." Without a backward glance, we quickly strode into the woods, a silent, pleading prayer on my lips.

God, I know You don't owe me anything, but please bring Kate back to us.

It turned out R.B. was in pretty decent shape. Despite the rolling terrain and thick foliage, I don't think he even broke a sweat. He whispered directions and I led the way. With R.B. mimicking my movements, we moved noiselessly from place to place. Well-traveled paths narrowed to game trails and then no trail at all. We picked our way through the thickening underbrush. My brain registered that the sweet smells of honeysuckle and pine began to give way to an unnatural scent of decay.

We traveled as quickly as we could. However, we intentionally took a roundabout route to the Malum outpost. The idea was to avoid any sentries posted along the obvious avenues of approach.

The farther we ventured into our route, the more the hair on the back of my neck stood up. I couldn't visibly see any differences on the ground or in the air, but I could sure feel it. I felt edgy, and I could tell R.B. was affected as well. His normally unflappable demeanor gave way to a mild jumpiness that manifested in subtle starts and stops.

Chill, R.B. We can do this.

I had an old habit when operating behind enemy lines. I stopped periodically, knelt down, and just listened for a couple of minutes. I knew R.B. was anxious to proceed but he waited patiently with me when I stopped.

We were just about to resume our trek after one such pause, when I heard something unnatural. I almost missed it. At first it was just low, muffled tones and soft *thump, thumps* on the ground.

What is that? It's . . . getting closer!

I covertly motioned for R.B. to hide under vegetation. I slid under some low-hanging vines, adjacent to a large bush. He mimicked my moves. By the time I looked at his position again, he had effectively disappeared from sight.

Good job, R.B.

The murmur evolved into a combination of soft footfalls and quiet conversation. Seconds later, two twenty-something-year-olds walked into sight. They were both males, both of average height, and both had black hair and black, almost pupil-less eyes.

Malum.

Their appearance was human. But the giveaway was that each held a black sword. They walked carefully, quietly, and were alert. I took this as a sign that we were about to breach their perimeter.

Their path took them within steps of our position. They were vigilant and swept their gazes from side to side, but did not seem particularly alarmed. If they were aware of a presence in their neck of the woods, they hid it well.

I waited five minutes after the last sound of their passing before slowly extricating myself from under the vines. I made a small motion in front of my face, but visible from R.B.'s last position, in a "let's go" movement. R.B. appeared silently from under the foliage and quietly made his way to me.

R.B. held up two fingers and mouthed "two hundred meters" to indicate that we were approaching the Malum outpost. I knew he had all the region's information, and more, inside his head. That could be a big help for this mission.

It also meant it was quite dangerous for us if he got captured.

Not awesome. Once again, what was he thinking?

There wasn't much to do about it at this point, though it nagged at me. We approached from the west and encountered only one other patrol. The Nasties were similarly clothed, and they had the same dark hair and dark eyes.

We arrived at our planned observation post in one piece. It was nothing more than a small hill a hundred meters away from the Malum outpost. We hid ourselves behind some small bushes.

Though it was cramped, the position gave us an unobstructed view of the enemy. I looked at the encampment and slowly exhaled.

Okay, it's about what we expected. That's a good first step.

The Malum had congregated in a small clearing, not unlike the one we used as our meeting place. I was relieved that the intelligence from Weasel had been accurate. If we had gotten that part wrong, Kate was doomed.

How did Weasel manage to follow them this far without being seen? That dude had some serious skills.

There were about fifty Malum scattered around the clearing. If we added in the patrols that we knew were in the area, we were clearly outnumbered. That was even if we managed to bring every member of our group to the fight.

I felt R.B. suddenly stiffen. I followed his gaze.

Kate.

She was tied to a tree in the middle of the clearing.

Stay cool, Jamie. Stick with the plan.

Her hat was gone and her sunglasses, too. She slumped against the ropes that held her fast to a large oak. She had small patches of blood on her arms and hands and a scary-looking cut on her face.

First things first. Is she breathing?

I held mine as I checked for hers.

Her chest was moving.

Oh, thank you, Lord.

It was great news that she appeared to be breathing, albeit in small, shallow breaths. Of course, I couldn't tell if her breathing was due to the way the Malum had tied her against the tree or if her injuries were worse than we could see. Either way, she looked to be in no shape to travel on her own.

You planned for this possibility, Jamie. No surprises so far.

I sat back and took a deep breath. This wasn't going to be easy.

Hold on, Kate. I'm comin' for ya.

R.B. and I looked at each other one last time. We both knew our jobs. It was time to get it done.

I said a another quick prayer, took a calming breath, and then slid from our hiding place on my belly. I was careful to stay hidden from the Malums' line of sight. R.B. followed the same path.

We made our way toward the edge of the clearing, barely moving more than a foot or two at a time. Our low crawl was painful, but necessary. We repeatedly paused under cover to let the ebb and flow of nature mask our approach.

In my mind, the seconds were ticking by. I could only hope that Boogie and Al were on schedule. Kate's life, as well as ours, depended on it.

We were past the point of no return.

CHAPTER 17

We crept as close as we dared, stopping about ten yards from the edge of the clearing. There wasn't much cover, but we hoped there was enough brush and shadows to hide us from the casual observer. That was, as long as no one came within a few feet of us. If that happened, there would be no missing us.

From this vantage point we could see Kate more clearly. She had not stirred during our silent trek down the hillside. Except for the steady rise and fall of her chest, she gave no other signs of life.

I slowly turned my head and glanced at R.B. His eyes were wide and I could see his pulse pounding at his temple. Not only that, his jaw trembled and his breathing was ragged.

Come on, R.B. Hold it together, man.

I watched him carefully. He caught me scrutinizing him and slowly nodded his head. Over a full minute, he methodically calmed himself down. He closed his eyes and began to take slow, deliberate breaths. I saw his shoulders relax and the tension leave his face.

That's what I'm talking about. We gotta stay cool if we're gonna pull this off.

All at once, there was a commotion among the Malum.

A few of them ran back and forth, shouting at each other about an approaching enemy. It was only a few seconds before another Malum, larger than the others and bearing a scar across his forehead, entered the clearing. He bellowed orders to the others and got them organized.

The similarities of their group with ours were startling. They were much better organized than I would have thought. As I watched, I realized they were actually quite efficient.

I suppose I had confused "evil" with "stupid." I wondered for a moment what my dad would say.

Probably something like, *Stop daydreaming and pay attention.*

Right.

The Malum promptly split into two groups. The first one immediately took flight to the east. The second, a larger force than the first, ran through the underbrush toward the northeast. By all accounts, they were frantically preparing for an invasion.

Which was exactly what we hoped they would do.

All we had to do then was sneak past, or kill, the few Malum that were left behind and rescue Kate. Easy day. As long as there weren't too many of them.

At first, the plan worked brilliantly. We were left with only four Malum in the clearing. These guys did not look or act like they were the sharpest tacks in the drawer.

Then something unexpected happened. The four remaining Malum began talking, rather loudly, and an argument ensued. I couldn't quite pick up what they were saying.

I was about to signal to R.B. for us to move forward when he grabbed my arm. He leaned in close and whispered, "They are scared, so they are gonna move Kate. If they get the jump on us, she is gone."

This can't be happening.

The Malum were already cutting Kate's ropes and gathering their things. This was getting complicated quickly. My head spun. Panicking would not help, but I struggled against the rising fear in my throat.

R.B. paused for a moment, his eyes darting back and forth. He whispered, "Reposition so you can intercept them as they leave the clearing. I'll create a diversion from here and push them to you. Go!"

I wasn't leaving my battle buddy.

"No!" I whispered back. "We don't split up."

He pleaded, "It's the only way. If they think I'm the lead of an attack, they'll leave everyone except the one or two carrying Kate. Don't worry about me. I've got a plan."

He was right. We had to divide them to get our hands on Kate.

If the Malum got Kate mobile and into the woods, she was gone. I didn't like it, though.

"Go!" he whispered again, his eyes now imploring me.

I felt like I had no choice. I slid from our hiding place and low-crawled away as quickly as I could. I traversed the edge of the perimeter and re-approached the clearing from the north.

I gradually rose from the ground behind the cover of a large pine tree. I waited, my hammering heart threatening to drown out all other sound. I could barely see R.B., but I gave a discreet thumbs-up.

That was the moment two Malum grabbed Kate and began dragging her toward me.

R.B. erupted from the undergrowth and charged the Malum. A couple of them were so startled that they flashed from human faces to Malum ones, and then back again. They were well trained, though, and began to fight. Two of them brandished their swords and split up to encircle R.B. The surprise of the attack had them off-balance.

R.B. cut down one of the Malum before he could even raise his sword. The two that had Kate suddenly sprinted like scalded dogs. Lucky for me, they ran directly toward where I was standing, still hiding behind a large brown tree trunk.

Come on, R.B. Keep 'em looking that way.

I would get only once chance at this, and if I got it wrong it would cost Kate her life.

The pair of Nasties carrying Kate were completely focused on getting her out of the clearing. In fact, the two Malum moved Kate so fast that her feet barely touched the ground. They each had her by an arm, but it took both pairs of hands to hold her up.

That meant I was the only one holding a sword. At least for now.

Her rebounding tennis shoes left small troughs in the soft ground at regular intervals. And her drooping, bouncing head was aligned with the Malums' chests.

That gave me a clear shot at their noggins.

Timing is everything in life . . .

I took a calming breath and smoothly brandished my sword, careful to keep it hidden behind the tree. I waited until the last moment to do so, which turned out to be a good decision. You know, the whole glowing sword in a dark forest thing.

As the Malum tore by my position I swung hard and fast at head level. I was hoping for a two-fer. One of the Nasties never saw it coming.

My swing cleanly decapitated, and thereby dusted, one of the two Malum. His disintegrating head flew by me with a look of utter surprise on its face. So funny, but inappropriate. What was left of his body flew into the brush like an emptying sack of ashes.

Unfortunately, the other Malum must have seen the glow of my sword. He leaned away from the strike in the half-second it took for my blade to get there. He managed to turn my swing into a glancing blow against his Malum forehead.

The force of the hit sent the Nasty sprawling. The Malum slammed against a tree on the other side of the path. He fell on his face in a patch of pine needles and kudzu.

My resurgent ADD made me wonder if he landed in poison ivy, too. Honestly, it could only help his complexion.

Kate went down hard but rolled toward me in a semiconscious state. Her body came to rest about two feet from where I stood. She did not stir.

I hit the Malum but he didn't dust. Which meant he was down but not out.

I bent to try to help Kate up.

Come on, Malum dude. Stay down.

I heard him before I saw him. He screamed in rage and emerged from the brush, covered in leaves. He staggered toward me and brandished his black sword.

Wonderful. Angry Malum. Just what I need.

I would have preferred to keep my distance. But Kate was lying directly between us and she was in no shape to defend herself. Not a great battlefield.

I had to finish this guy and get Kate out of there.

It's been said that if all you have is a hammer, everything looks like a nail. So, I grabbed my hammer and did what came naturally. I threw myself into a frontal attack.

I leapt over Kate and rushed the enraged Nasty. He came at me with an aggressive swing and, without warning, threw a handful of dirt in my face. I have to admit, that was not something we had practiced. I wasn't completely unprepared for it, though.

I squinted as best I could through the dust and swung in an arc. The spray of sparks gave away his location, if even for a moment, and kept him away. My vision quickly cleared.

I regained focus. The Malum and I faced off once more, each on opposite sides of the wide path. Unfortunately, Kate was again between us.

The clock was ticking and we needed to go! R.B. was waiting.

The Nasty glanced at me, and then at Kate, and then back at me. I didn't think it was possible, but he got an even more evil look in his coal-black eyes. All at once, the Malum ran forward, raised his sword, and began to swing.

I numbly registered the truth . . . he was going to kill Kate. Right in front of me.

My brain told me I couldn't stop him.

I told my brain to shut it.

In pure reaction mode, I reversed my grip on my sword, raised it above my right shoulder, and then launched it as hard as I could toward the Malum's chest like a javelin.

The Malum's face had a look of victory . . .

. . . right up until the moment the tip of my blade penetrated his torso. My saber was a blur as it disappeared into, and then through, his body. It firmly lodged itself in a nearby oak tree with a solid *thok*.

The Nasty exploded in a shower of black particles. The dark sword disintegrated mere inches from Kate's side. The Malum was no more.

The black dust had barely settled when I retrieved my sword and, in a habit born of years of training, lifted Kate onto my shoulders in a fireman's carry. Without pausing, I began to double-time toward our rejoin point.

We were now running for our lives.

* * *

I dashed to the prearranged rejoin point. I was slower than if alone, but Kate didn't weigh very much, so I was able to move at a decent clip. She was still out of it and didn't make any noise.

I scampered around the perimeter of the clearing and then ran away from it. The sounds of fighting echoed through the woods. It was time for R.B. to disengage.

I glanced over my left shoulder as I reached the hill. I expected to see R.B. running to join us on our departure. He knew that by now I would either have Kate or I wouldn't. Either way, it was time for him to leave.

He wasn't. Something was wrong.

R.B. was where I had last seen him, and he was fighting. As I watched, he cleanly dispatched one Malum and charged through the dissipating dust at another. He was fearless and attacked with fury. This despite the fact that other Malum had joined the fight. Neither thing was terribly surprising. What was surprising was that he wasn't moving to leave.

What's he doing? He knows it's time to go!

But he didn't appear to be trying to escape. In fact, instead of attempting to get away, he looked intent on staying right there. He was going to fight the Malum to the death.

I looked back and forth between R.B. and Kate.

This can't be happening.

The Malum's numbers had quickly increased since our initial engagement. I watched as others raced into the clearing to join the battle. The noise and commotion emanating from the fighting in their camp had likely gained the attention of the roaming patrols.

It was R.B. versus everyone.

Man, he was something to behold. Though his mind was clearly tense in concentration, an almost glowing aura emanated from his face. If I didn't know better, I would have said he was happy.

R.B. alertly noticed us out of the corner of us eye but didn't look in our direction. Instead, he just yelled, "Go!" and continued to fight. Fearsome fighter or no, he was outnumbered and wouldn't last very long. The only way to save him was to join him.

I'm not gonna leave him behind. Not now, not ever.

I gently placed Kate on the ground and grabbed my sword. As I started down the hill, R.B. dispatched three more Malum and was down to the last four. That was when the fifth, who had hidden and waited for the fight to reach his position, stepped forward and stabbed R.B. violently in the back.

He did so with such force that the sword tip emerged from the front of R.B.'s shirt, its ugly blackness violating his body.

I froze in place as I watched the horror scene play out.

R.B. gave a surprised grimace from the pain and surreptitiously looked in our direction one last time. He managed to mouth the word *Go.*

Then he disappeared in a brilliant, but sorrowful, shower of sparks.

CHAPTER 18

No. That didn't just happen. R.B. was just there, now he's . . .

Snap out of it, Jamie!

I shook my head and looked at Kate, who was lying helpless on the ground.

Right. Lock it down, dude. Let's go.

Five Malum remained, and they were coming for us. I could hear their frantic shouts.

I knew it wouldn't be long before they figured out that I had Kate and which way we'd gone. We had to move.

Kate was waking. She groaned softly and stirred.

She's in no shape to walk bro, much less run. It's on you.

I again lifted her onto my shoulders and moved out. Stealth was outweighed by the odds of discovery, so I sprinted. I dashed as fast as my tiring legs would take me. My thighs began to burn and my knees ached, but I raced toward our rally point. We were supposed to meet R.B. there and continue together . . .

Later, Jamie. Never give up, never stop, no matter what.

I dashed through the trees. Poor Kate bounced on my shoulders as I ran. I had one hand on her lower leg to hold her steady and the other carried my softly glowing sword.

Halfway to the rally point, I heard a shrieking scream. They were only a hundred yards away. They were on our trail and gaining fast.

I glanced over my shoulder. Bad call. I could actually see them running and gaining on us. Their black swords were visible and seemed to dim the light from the afternoon air.

Focus on the front. Move!

My motivation was high, but still we involuntarily slowed. My breathing was raspy from overexertion, and my legs felt like jelly. My body was done, and I knew it.

We weren't gonna make it.

I stumbled into the next clearing I could find and fell face-first. Kate bounced off me and sprawled in the grass. She was semi-coherent but still incapable of defending herself. I slowly got to my feet and stood by for the inevitable.

I didn't have to wait long.

Seconds later, the Malum barreled into the clearing. Instead of attacking, they enveloped Kate and me. The two of us were in the center of their circle.

What are they waiting for? Oh. They want to savor the kill.

Like vultures circling their prey, they paced and glared at us through angry, empty eyes. I got a familiar, sickening feeling in my gut. It was the feeling you got when you knew you're probably going to die. Worse, I was taking Kate with me.

I'm so sorry, Kate.

Enough whining, Jamie. You'll have the rest of your life for that.

I smiled in spite of myself.

I've got nothing else on my calendar today. Let's do this.

One of them spoke up in a raspy voice. "You were foolish to come here, boy. I'm going to hurt you. And then I'm going to send you to see your dead daddy. How does that sound?"

I guess I was supposed to be frightened. Yeah, he knew about my dad. So what? He'd have to do better than that.

I shook my head. "Seriously? That's the best scary-voice-thing you've got? You've got to work on your delivery, dude. You sound like a wheezy robot."

The look on his face was priceless. It was like I had de-pantsed him in public.

I would have laughed, but I was mad.

To think, I'll die at the hands of these ugly idiots. After everything I've been through, these guys take me out? That's just embarrassing. Maybe Gunny was right.

That triggered something.

Gunny taught me . . . right . . .

I yelled at the one who had spoken. "You sure talk a lot for someone who was left behind by the real warriors. What's the matter, couldn't cut it?"

His buddies stared at me, then him, in surprise.

Work it, Jamie. You're on a roll.

I closed in. "We all know you're scared to face me on your own. You're nothing without your buddies. So, why don't you let someone else do the talking, Mr. Weenie, chain-smoker-dude!"

I couldn't handle them all at once, but maybe I could buy some time. That assumed I could provoke this guy. It was hard to know what made Malum click.

I shouldn't have worried. He reacted like most egocentric young men who were called out in public.

I guess it took one to know one.

He shook with fury and looked at his buddies, who stared back at him.

Put up or shut up time, dude.

He rushed me in a rage.

He was all sound and fury, but clearly lacking in sword-fighting skills. Much like young humans, his friends goaded him on. We clashed violently for a few seconds, but I fended off his initial attack. He started with a broad crisscross swing and followed with a vertical strike. Even in my fatigued state, I easily deflected them.

He kept attacking and became more aggressive. At first, he would strike and then jump back to safety, but he got bolder with each charge. Before long, he rarely got out of sword's reach of me.

The other Malum were enjoying the show. They yelled and whistled for their buddy to kill me. They probably thought their leader would send me out in my own shower of sparks.

It didn't go quite like that.

He brought lots of emotion and reckless energy, which wasn't necessarily a good thing. For him, that is. It was exactly what I was hoping for.

I remained calm and dodged his wild slices and hungry jabs. I looked for any opening I could exploit. It didn't take long before I found one.

He was so angry that he left himself vulnerable to a counterattack. He took a wild swing at my head. Instead of backing away, I ducked and ignored the black blade's freezing breeze above my hairline. The momentum of his swing left his torso unguarded. His eyes widened in recognition, and he tried to spin away. I jumped forward and shoved my sword below where his rib cage should be.

Now, I had no idea if they had rib cages or not. I did aim a little low, just in case, though. My sword entered cleanly and the fight ended without further ado. His dust billowed up in a dark cloud, then descended straight down in the windless afternoon, leaving little black Malum dots on my shoes.

Seriously?

I stomped around for a few seconds to get the dust off my shoes then swatted at my pants leg at a particularly dirty, Malum-y patch.

Oh, come on. These are new britches!

My clean-my-pants-and-shoes dance must have taken everyone by surprise. No one made a move until I was finished. When I was finally satisfied that I didn't have any more Nasty-dust on my clothes, I looked up.

After the trauma of losing their leader wore off, well, let me just say they were not impressed. They didn't say a word. What they did do was simultaneously raise their swords and begin a coordinated assault.

Well, Jamie. You knew it might come to this.

They stepped slowly but deliberately toward me. The air became very still.

Honestly, I was sort of relieved the whole thing was over. I was tired of being scared and tired of running. But then I felt a pang of sorrow for Kate.

I'm so sorry, Kate. It'll be over soon. I'll see you on the other side, hon.

I looked back up at the approaching Malum and squared my shoulders.

I had always been a warrior. It was time to die like one.

Their circle contracted. Only seconds to go.

I gritted my teeth as the four Malum advanced. My sword hummed in my hand.

Who's first?

They held their swords high. Crescendos of snarls escaped their lips.

Wait for it . . . now!

They were only steps away. I launched myself into the middle of their formation like a crazed linebacker. I had my head down, teeth bared and sword swinging.

The world exploded in dust and screams.

I swung my sword at a Malum . . . and he exploded into black fertilizer just before my sword got to him.

Wha— Keep fighting, Jamie!

I looked right and saw was another large cauldron of dust. But . . .

Go left! I started a left backhand but was abruptly knocked to the ground. I hit hard but rolled.

Move!

I twisted to a crouch with my sword in front of me, ready for the end.

What I saw made me want to cry.

My Charlie buddies.

Tiny, who had unintentionally upended me, rushed the two remaining Malum. Mike and Kevin were right with him.

The Nasties apparently realized they were no longer in the majority. They tried to run for the tree line to save their slimy skins. They never had a chance.

Kevin went crazy and charged them like a buzz saw. Mike bracketed the creatures from the other side, swinging his sword in a large figure-eight pattern. Tiny took two of his large steps and swung his sword like a slugger going for the home run record.

The panicked Malum simultaneously caught all three blades. They screeched and exploded in terror. Their ashes combined into a dust storm that engulfed my three friends.

The boys found themselves covered in cinders, with no Malum in sight.

I breathed in gasps and lowered my sword by my side. I was happily confused.

"How did . . . you know . . . the first two?"

I abruptly became aware of a presence. Two presences actually, one on each side of me. I spun and saw a grinning Jacob on my left and a smirking Jared on my right.

Oh, those sneaky boys.

"So, you two flew in and . . . they never saw you."

The triumphant looks on their faces said it all.

I was impressed, I was relieved, and I was spent. I slowly turned and moved to Kate.

As I did, I smiled a thankful grin at my rogue compatriots.

They weren't supposed to be here, they were supposed to be guarding our base. My gut told me they had disobeyed orders and risked their lives, and the wrath of Gunny, to check on us. We'd have been dead if they hadn't.

I held Kate in my arms. She was still incoherent. For a brief moment there was silence.

Tiny said, "We need to keep movin'. It's not safe here."

I nodded.

"Tiny, will you carry Kate? I'm a little smoked."

"No problem."

He gently lifted her from the ground, like a big papa bear. She looked as light as air to him.

We were about to move out when Tiny suddenly swung around. He looked like he had remembered something important. "Where's R.B.? Is he bringin' up the rear?"

I thought I was going to be sick. I slowly shook my head.

The mood of our crew went from jubilant to speechless in only a moment.

I didn't want to, but I spoke up.

"Guys, this may sound harsh, but we'll have time for mourning later. I didn't know you would be here to save us, but you did and I'm very thankful. But now we've got a mission to finish. We need to go."

The Js wiped away a few tears while Mike and Kevin patted them on the backs.

"Tiny, lead the way. I'll be the rear guard and ensure we don't get jumped. We gotta move fast to get back by dark."

We bounded away, each of us trying to outrun what pursued us.

* * *

"Keep moving guys. We're almost there."

Everyone was exhausted and the sun was almost down. But we were essentially home. Only a little further to go.

That's when Tiny abruptly stopped. We all froze, panting from exertion. The only sound was the soft chirp of forest creatures and the quiet hum of our glowing swords.

He suddenly shouted, "It's aaight, we're clear!" He turned and looked at the rest of us with a relieved gaze. "It's Bravo."

Sure enough, Bravo Platoon emerged from the tree line like a silent line of ghosts, swords at the ready. Al motioned us forward with hurried waves and a shushing motion. His serious gaze brightened at the sight of Kate.

As we walked up, I saw him count us. A distraught look settled on his features. He counted us again. Then he looked at me, anger hardening his face. His eyes were slits and his sword arm flexed.

Are we gonna do this here? Seriously?

He stared at me, hard, for a few seconds. Then he turned his back.

I can't believe this is really happening.

With all quiet again, Al took the lead of Charlie platoon. The rest of Bravo fell in behind us to escort us back to safety. We arrived just as the sun began to touch the distant horizon.

As soon as we made it through the wood line into the clearing, Al spun on me. "Jamie, where's R.B.?"

I was on the verge of losing it. My thoughts raced and my breaths were ragged. Charlie platoon stared at me in concern.

All I could do was point in the direction we had come from.

"What? You left him behind? We don't leave anyone behind, mayun! I knew it, I knew it. Bravo platoon! Come on! We gotta—"

I screamed, "He's dead!"

The whole camp froze in place.

My breaths now came in heaves and my eyes watered. Still, I shouted at Al, "The Malum killed him, okay? They killed him right in front of me. They . . . "

I realized my fists were clenched and my sword had jumped into my hand.

Al's mouth was open in shock. He stood rock still.

I shook from head to toe. "What do you want from me, huh? You want me to admit I wasn't good enough? Is that what you want to hear? Fine! I wasn't good enough to bring him home alive. It's. My. Fault. He's. Dead!"

A calm, sad voice behind me said, "No, Jamie. That's not true at all."

I spun around. There was Boogie, surrounded by the rest of Alpha.

They were breathing hard and sporting fresh wounds. Boogie had a thin streak of blood down his left arm. His hands were open in a plaintive pose.

He spoke softly, but still loud enough for the rest to hear. "Jamie, listen to me. R.B. was way ahead of you on this one."

I numbly regarded him through foggy eyes and swayed on exhausted legs.

"Don't ask me how he knew, but he was pretty sure he wasn't coming out of this one alive. He had a gut feeling it was his time, and he wasn't going to let anyone else take his place."

I pursed my lips and began to shake my head—

"Don't believe me? Then let me read you something." He unfolded a small piece of paper from his pants pocket.

"My dearest friends and brothers, if you are reading this note then I have finally made it home. Do not cry for me, for I have lived a wonderful life. I know I shouldn't be, but I am actually excited to go on this mission today. I will not needlessly give my life away, but if I don't return, then know that I am with my beloved wife, and I am happy."

His chin trembled as he continued. "As a few of you know, I'm a fan of old cowboy movies. So just remember this: if I go out today, I go out with my boots on, and that's more than I could have ever hoped for. I pray an expectant prayer that my sweet Kate is safe and sound by now. I'm quite sure I picked the right man for the job. I'll see you all again one day.—R.B."

Great. A suicide note. Is that supposed to make everything okay?

Boogie quietly folded the piece of paper and put it back in his pocket. He looked away for a second and then back at me. The whole camp held their breaths.

He said, "Jamie, this was a horrible, no-win spot we put you in today. I'm terribly sorry. But you got the mission done when none of us even knew where to begin."

He sent a sharp glance across the clearing. "Right, Al?"

The Bravo commander exhaled deeply and stared at the ground. "Right."

"R.B. told me to tell you he was proud of you. He believed in you. And he hoped you would still believe, no matter what happened."

He took a step toward me and held out his hand.

I felt everyone's stares. My mind spun and I couldn't form a rational thought.

"No kiddin', Jamie."

I didn't know what to say and I didn't know what to do. I just wanted to leave. Right then.

I walked away. I was halfway to the nearest door before I heard my name.

"Jamie," was all the voice said, but it stopped me in my tracks.

Kate.

I slowly turned and looked at her.

Tears mingled with the blood from the cut on her cheek. Her face was bruised and filled with anguish. She stared at me with shell-shocked eyes.

I almost sobbed. She turned blurry as I spun and jogged toward the door.

"Jamie! Wait!"

I dove through the door, wishing it would swallow me forever.

CHAPTER 19

It was the hardest funeral I never attended.

At that moment, across town, Kate was burying her uncle. My heart ached for her. I wanted to be with her so badly but . . . well, everything. I'm not sure things could've been any more complicated.

Let's see. I "saved" her but led her uncle to his death. Yep, that's pretty messed up.

I felt like I needed counseling from just thinking it. I had an idea of what she was going through, too. Except for the whole significant-other involved in the death of a loved one part . . .

I recalled burying my dad. It was just another on the increasingly long list of things I wish I had never had to experience. This new one had to be somewhere near the top, though.

Despite wearing a large jacket, I shivered.

Officially, I wasn't at the funeral because we weren't allowed. Unless you were close friends with R.B. on the "normal" side, you weren't supposed to go to the funeral. Why? Malum this, Malum that, they could be watching . . . blah, blah, blah.

Works for me this time, I guess.

Anyway, what would I say to his family and friends? "Hi, I'm Jamie and I watched him die, but it's all cool because he sparkled and had his boots on!"

I rubbed my eyes and dug my hands into my jacket pockets. Fall had fallen, even in Columbus, and it was a damp, dreary, misty morning. It fit my mood perfectly. It had been days since I lost R.B. and I felt adrift.

Where do I go from here?

Good question, Jamie. Good question.

The hairs on my neck suddenly stood up and my pulse quickened. It felt like somebody was watching me.

Oh, come on, you're just getting paranoid.

Honor the threat, Jamie, my inner voice whispered.

Okay. Fine.

I made like I was stretching and casually looked over my right shoulder. Nothing. All right, act natural. Slow twist . . . left shoulder . . . nothing. Quick glance behind, nothing.

I was all alone in the park.

You are so losing it, dude. This junk's gone to your head.

It was like someone was watching me that I couldn't see . . .

No, it can't be.

Well, why not?

If I was going crazy anyway, there was no harm in giving it a shot.

"Sam! Come on out. I'll wait for you here."

There was no answer, just a slight wind and the muted rustling of leaves. I felt as silly as I looked, speaking to invisible friends. Funny Farm calling Jamie, answer the phone . . .

I waited for ten minutes and nothing happened.

I decided to give it five more.

I sat. My mind wandered back to where it was before. Decisions, decisions . . .

"Hey, boy."

I jumped clear off of the bench. Sam chuckled and sat down. He crossed his legs at the ankles and cozied into his end.

"Dude! Seriously, you're going to give me a heart attack. A real one!"

"Aw, come on, Jamie. You knew I was here, what's there to be surprised 'bout? I'm impressed you figured it out, though. I'm usually pretty covert."

I sat back down and tried to get my heart rate under control. "Well, you are pretty sneaky, Sam. I didn't even hear you walk up. You did walk, right?"

He raised his eyebrows in a *maybe I did, maybe I didn't* expression. He clearly enjoyed messing with me. Yet . . . his eyes held a different story.

His smile faded a little. "Old tricks of the trade, son. Maybe you'll learn 'em one day . . . if you keep trainin'." He cut his eyes at me when he said it.

"Oh. So you heard, huh? I guess word travels fast, even to the 'retired' side."

My needling didn't seem to bother him.

"Well, yeah, I've heard a few things, Jamie. For example, I heard you did somethin' pretty amazin'. I also heard that you took a loss hard. Real hard."

I fired back. "Wouldn't you have? Or should I say, didn't you?"

He looked almost serene.

Man, this guy is on some serious happy pills or something.

"Jamie, you are pretty hard on me for someone who stormed off on his friends in their time of need. What's the matter? Afraid you'll end up like me? Or is it that you already see too much of me . . . in you?"

That one shut me up.

I took a deep breath and slowly let it out, my cheeks bulging as I did so. The telling of truths had begun, and it was going to hurt.

My voice went monotone. "Yeah, Sam. Something like that."

After a few seconds he said, "Let's take a walk, Jamie."

"A walk? In this weather?"

"Why not? It'll help keep us warm."

I shrugged. "Sure. Why not."

He was pretty fast for an older guy. I didn't know what he did when he wasn't skulking behind the veil, but it must have kept him in shape. The only sounds were the *swish, swish* of shoes through wet grass and the occasional *crunch* of boots on gravel.

We walked until we topped a vaguely familiar hill. I stopped short.

"The cemetery, Sam? Really? Is the day not quite dreary enough for you?"

He kept walking and yelled over his shoulder, "Don't worry, I won't leave you here!"

Hilarious. What is up with this guy today? He's awfully chipper for the Sam I know.

I jogged to catch up and we resumed our march into the garden of stone. The grass was freshly cut, and the dew made it stick to our shoes. It muffled our steps such that it turned us into silent apparitions.

Sam kept walking toward a corner of the graveyard.

"Sam, what are we doing? I'm getting a little—" I bumped into his back as he came to an abrupt stop. "Hey! Warn me before you . . . "

I jumped when I saw it. The stone hadn't changed in the year since I last peered at it, but it startled me just the same.

My dad's grave.

At first, I stared blankly. I didn't really feel sorrow or joy, only a profound sense of loss. I was rooted to the spot. A lifetime of memories tore through my mind in seconds. My dad's smiling face was the last thing I saw before I caught movement out of the corner of my eye.

I turned my head and looked at Sam. He had bent over and was picking leaves off of the headstone. He finished by straightening a little American flag that was situated at the front. He finally rose and moved by my side.

We stood for a while, neither saying a word. I stared across the tops of the markers, watching the wind bend the grass in the field.

After a couple of minutes I said, "You know, this isn't exactly a pick-me-up today. Why are we here?"

He exhaled deeply. "Well, you may think it weird, but I've come by here a good bit lately. It helps me think things through."

"A graveyard helps you think things through? Please don't tell me that you're hearing voices or anything, Sam. I don't think I can handle that today."

He chuckled. "Voices? Naw. These folks are gone, son. Including your dad. This is just a place to remember. And to think . . . " He faded off.

I scratched my head impatiently and shoved my hands in my pants pockets.

Okay, I'll bite.

"Well Sam, what have you been thinking about?"

Silence.

Whatever Sam. I've got nowhere else to be.

We settled into the comfortable stillness. The only movements were our clouds of breath in the chilly air.

Eventually, my eyes refocused on the stone. It made my heart ache. We must have stood that way for twenty minutes.

All at once Sam spoke up. "Did you know that your dad and I played football together when we were in high school?"

That one made me turn in surprise.

"I didn't know you went that far back."

"Yeah, well, your dad was a handful, son, at least back when we were in school. Now, he was a good guy, but he hated losing. At anything."

That sounded familiar.

He continued. "So, you can imagine what he was like on the football field. He was a buck-seventy-five of hard-nosed country boy, and he brought every bit of it, every time."

I smiled at the thought. Yeah, I could see that.

"So, anyhow. This one time we were playin' a team from near the capital. They were bigger than us, faster than us, and just plain better than us. They were beatin' our butts. By the end of the third quarter, we had bloody noses, bruised bodies, and crumblin' pride. We all just wanted to quit. Everyone except your dad."

Despite myself, I chuckled out loud. "That sounds just like him. He'd fight you till the end of the world and make you glad it was over."

By then Sam was leaning over and getting into the story. "Okay, so we're in the huddle before the fourth quarter begins and you know what your dad does?"

I shake my head, but I'm smiling regardless.

"He starts telling a joke! A joke about a pig, a monkey, and a farmer. I'm sure you know it, if you're his son!"

Of course I did, but I couldn't stop him. And I didn't want to, anyway.

He told the joke, just like my dad used to, with the arm motions and everything. By then, I was laughing so hard tears were coming down my face. That was my dad. He could always make me laugh. Even now.

"Now then, everyone on the team is laughing hysterically. One guy even had to lie down he was wheezing so hard. And you know what he did then?"

I shook my head. I realized I was holding my breath.

"He said, 'Boys, we've been through way too much to quit now. What you say we make sure those goons from the capital know we were here? I'll lead the way.' And you know what we did?"

"You came back and beat 'em, right?"

"Heck no, son. They still won, by a lot."

"What?"

"What we did do was whoop on them so much they couldn't wait to leave our field. We laid into 'em with everything we had. Their backs started running out of bounds so we wouldn't hit 'em, and the coach even tried to run the clock out. They didn't want any of us no more."

I could see it clearly, in my mind. That was definitely something my dad would do. Fight to the very end, no matter what.

"They may have won on the scoreboard but we beat them at the end. I've never been so proud after a loss in my life."

Sam turned back to the grave and smiled, a distant look on his face. "Maybe there's somethin' we can learn from your dad, even now. The both of us. What do you think?"

I stared at him. No, he couldn't be . . .

He turned and looked at me, waiting for an answer.

"Sam, if I didn't know better I'd say you were re-considering your hiatus. But that can't be true, because we're 'all gonna die,' right?" I gestured to the sea of gravestones.

He did the same raised eyebrow thing, but his eyes twinkled.

* * *

We were standing together. I didn't know who was more nervous. I did feel a little like I was returning to the scene of a crime, though.

Well Jamie, time to face up and stop running.

I looked at Sam and he nodded, though for the first time he looked a little unsure of himself.

"Remember the monkey, Sam."

He laughed gently. "All right, Jamie. Lead on."

We walked into the clearing and tried to act natural. It was a little difficult with everyone staring and all, but we kept walking until we approached Charlie platoon. Sam kept pace with me and looked straight ahead.

We approached within a dozen paces of Charlie before the twins noticed us. They excitedly nudged Tiny and Mike, while Kevin remained oblivious to everything except Gunny's briefing. We had walked right up to them before Gunny realized we were there.

"And now we will discuss—" He froze in midsentence. He eye-balled Sam with a neutral gaze, before turning his glare on me. He tucked his clipboard under his arm and walked within reach of me, pointing a knife hand in my face.

"Mis-ter Jamie! You do not belong here. You are no longer one of us."

My heart dropped. I felt Sam tighten with anger.

"But, but . . . "

"Out-standing comeback. Perhaps your new platoon will take as much pleasure from your oratory skills as we did!"

"My new platoon?"

"That is co-rrect! You and the twins are now Alpha platoon's prob-lem! Now, go away!" The smirk on his face was classic.

The twins erupted in yells and high-fives.

"And you three!" Mike and Kevin stood at attention. Tiny just stared. "You three are now Bravo property, so be gone!"

It was like we had just won a big game. Everyone began shaking hands and congratulating each other. Tiny slapped me so hard on the back I couldn't talk. It was like I had never left.

Gunny's voice softened a little when he said, "Mister Sam, it is good to make your acquaintance, as well. I am quite sure that our little group can make use of your experience and skills."

Sam nodded and exhaled, the ends of his mouth turning up a bit.

Gunny looked at the three newest Bravo recruits. "You three! Why are you still standing here? Your new platoon is awaiting its fresh meat! Go find them."

In a blur, Tiny, Kevin, and Mike took off to join up with Bravo. We watched them run away until it got quiet again.

"You two," Gunny said, pointing at the Js, "Your platoon knows you will likely get confused if left to your own devices. You will wait here until further notice."

"Ooh-rah, Gunny!" they shouted.

I looked at the twins, who were now staring at Sam. "Oh, right. Jacob, Jared, you remember Sam, don't you?"

"We do," Jared said.

In unison, they walked up to him and offered their hands.

Jacob said, "Thanks for saving us, Mister Sam. My momma would want to meet you . . . if we could tell her, I mean."

Sam smiled uncomfortably. "You're welcome, boys. Glad I could help. So, how's your trainin' goin'?"

They lit up like Christmas trees. They both began rambling to Sam, telling him every little thing they were learning, almost like he was their granddad. I would swear Sam was enjoying it, too. He grinned and began to quiz them on their maneuvers.

I said quietly, "Welcome home, Sam."

"I guess I should say the same to you."

I spun and automatically spat out, "Hey, Boogie."

He was standing alone, a friendly countenance on his face.

I decided to get right to it. "I . . . ah . . . I'm sorry about the other day. All of it. I—"

"It's all good, Jamie." Boogie walked closer. "It was a hard day for everyone, and none of us were at our best." He lowered his voice a notch. "I hope you know I meant what I said. R.B. made the right choice to pick you. It may not feel like it, but what you did was nothing short of miraculous."

"I really appreciate that. Thanks, Boogie."

He smiled back. "Now that we got that out of the way, I really need to discuss some business with you." He looked up. "And since he's here, Sam, too."

At the sound of his name, Sam turned around. He saw Boogie's nod and began parting from the twins.

Boogie pointed to the edge of the forest. "Jacob, Jared, go find Rick. He's waiting at the start of route four. He'll get you going on your new training program."

The boys looked at each other for a second and grinned from ear to ear. They took off like shots.

"Take it easy on him, okay?" Gunny yelled after them.

Boogie waved us on. "Guys, follow me. I've got something I'd like to show you."

* * *

It was a map of the area.

"Okay, here's where we are." Boogie pointed to a spot on the map, but didn't mark it. "And here's where we think they are." He pointed to another place on the map, but this one was circled.

"Whoa," I said, "how do we know for sure?"

"We don't, but this is our best estimate . . . from Kate. For a while, she pretended to be hurt a little worse than she was and she heard them talking. But it's all based on what she thought she heard and where we know she was being held. It's sort of thin, but it's all we got."

"Did she have a guess on how many fighters they have. And flyers?"

"Well, that's the rub. She thought she had a decent idea on their numbers, but then she heard them talk about reinforcements that just arrived. Now we're not really sure what we're up against."

"Why don't we do a recon? It'd help to confirm their location and numbers, right?"

Boogie nodded thoughtfully. "Reconnaissance mission. Hmm. Might be tricky at that distance. Sam, what do you think?"

At first the only indication he had heard Boogie was narrowed eyes. A few seconds passed. Finally, he said, "Yeah. You prob'ly need to get eyes on to be sure. That's what happened last time. They had a lot more than we thought, and it cost us. I wouldn't want that to happen again."

I stared at the map a little more. "Boogie, that's awfully far away. I don't think our ground-pounders could get there and back very easily. Plus, they'd be too far away from any help. This has Alpha written all over it."

"Yeah, that's what I was thinking, too," he said. "Let me think on that a little. Sam, I wouldn't mind if you did the same. Two heads and all that."

Sam nodded. "Yep. I can do that."

I didn't want to bring it up, but . . . "Boogie, um . . . how's everybody coping with, you know . . . R.B.? I know there was a funeral . . ."

"Everybody's coping in their own way, Jamie. We'll have our own memorial service after everything calms down, but you know how it is with a group of guys like this. Most of 'em internalize everything until they can come to grips with it. But they're strong. They'll be okay."

"Yeah. Okay. I guess what I mean is . . . should I stay out of the way? I really—"

"Jamie, no one blames you for R.B.'s death. In fact, now that everyone knows what happened, you're sorta famous. Well, infamous, actually." He grinned.

Whew.

"Cool. Well, what about . . . you know, Kate? How is she holding up?

"Why don't you ask her yourself? She is right over there." He pointed a mere fifty feet away.

My breath caught in my throat. There she was, staring at me. I involuntarily took a step back as my pulse raced. I couldn't meet her gaze.

I looked at Boogie for support, but he shook his head. "No, dude. You gotta face this one on your own."

Sam did a paternal nod.

Okay. I guess I am on my own. Really, how bad could it be?

I don't know, you got her uncle killed so, yeah, pretty bad.

Right.

Deep breath. Go.

I started walking.

She was in jeans and a light jacket. Her hair swayed in the breeze, and she clasped her hands in front of her. The closer I got, the more I could see the wound on her face. It was healing, but still angry looking.

I sauntered over and stopped in front of her.

Take it like a man, dude.

"Hi, Kate."

"Hi." She stared at the ground, a mournful look on her face.

Wow. This is going well. Why don't I just punch myself and get it over with?

"How're you holding up?"

She shrugged. "About as good as can be expected, you know?"

"Yeah."

Another long silence.

"Why did you leave the other night?"

Right to it, huh?

I kicked at the ground with the toe of my shoe. "I'm not really sure I know. I was . . ."

"You were what?" Her insistent eyes searched me.

Ugh. Just get it over with.

Now I stared at the ground. "I was ashamed. I felt like I failed you and got R.B. killed. It was all just a bit too much at once."

"You know that's not true, right?"

I looked up. "What's not true?"

"You didn't get my uncle killed. No offense, Jamie, but he's been at this a lot longer than you. He knew what he was doing."

"Well . . . maybe. I just feel responsible."

She took a half-step towards me. "Well . . . don't."

"Easier said than done."

"What about me?"

"I . . . I don't understand."

"I know what you did. You risked your life to save me," she said in a soft voice.

I looked her in the eye. Something in my heart strained to get out. "And I'd do it all over again."

"Why?"

I felt like I was talking to a lawyer.

"Why? What do you mean, 'why'?"

"Jamie, you saved me. And then . . ."

"And then, what?"

It came out like a flood. "Then you walked away. I haven't heard from you in days. I thought, you know, we were . . . oh, I'm being ridiculous." She looked away and wiped at a runaway tear.

I stepped within arm's reach. "No, you're not ridiculous. It's a lot to take in."

"I just . . . " She hung her head on her chest. "It's so childish. When you left, I . . . felt like you didn't like me anymore. How lame is that? Given everything that's happened, and I'm acting like a crushing teen?"

"Yeah, that's pretty embarrassing."

"Jamie!"

"Just kidding! Come here."

She slowly stepped up to me, still looking down. I wiped away the remnants of her tear.

"For the record, I still like you. A lot."

I had no idea how she could smile so beautifully at a time like that, but she did. "Really? And please don't say yes just to be nice. I want the truth. I'm not as fragile as I may look right now."

"You may be many things, Kate, but fragile is not one of them."

She stared at me. "So, you and me. We're good?"

"Of course we're good. Other than the fact that you're hanging out with a jerk."

She actually laughed out loud. "Well, I happen to like this big jerk."

"There is one serious thing I need to ask you though. There's no getting around it."

She leaned back, her smile fading. She appeared to brace herself. "Okay. What's that?"

"Would you go out with me? Like on a real date?"

There it was. That smile again. "Hmm. Let me think. Maybe I should get back to you on that."

"I'll make it worth your while. You get to choose the restaurant."

She spread her arms. "That's it? That's the big reward?"

"What if I threw in ice cream? Would that clinch the deal?"

"Cookies and cream?"

"Of course."

"Done! You've got yourself a date, Mr. Big Jerk."

I smiled and grasped her hand.

She put her forehead against mine and said quietly, "I'm glad you're here, Jamie. I missed you. Now, don't you dare stand me up again!" she said with a faux angry face.

Never again, Kate.

"Go play with your buddies and"—she leaned up and kissed me on the cheek—"stay safe."

"For you, Katie, anything."

"Katie, huh? I sorta like it." She smiled and waved me away. "Now go!"

I jogged back over to where Sam and Boogie stood. They acted like they hadn't seen or heard a thing. Fakers.

"So, how'd it go?" Boogie smirked.

"Seriously, man? You're gonna do that right now?"

Sam chuckled.

Boogie slapped me on the back. "Well, Jamie, she's been through a lot. It's good to see her smile again. But, enough of that. Since the gang's all here, let's get to work."

* * *

For some reason, I was one of the first to arrive on the next training day. I meandered into the clearing and caught a glimpse of Boogie and Sam walking toward the perimeter of the woods. At the edge of those trees was a person I had not seen before.

Our visitor had the rugged, wind-burned look of someone who spent a great deal of time outside. I saw them shake hands and, even from that distance, saw the ichthys form on his face.

He's one of us but not in our group? Interesting.

Boogie glanced up and saw me staring.

Uh-oh. Busted.

He waved me over as if he knew I had been there the whole time. Knowing him, he probably did. I jogged over and walked to a halt as I approached the trio. They were standing under the deep shade of a large pine tree.

"Jamie, I'd like you to meet Flash. He's from . . . " Boogie paused for a moment as he searched for the right words. "West of here."

Flash had black hair and a weight lifter's upper body, but the legs of a runner. We shook hands. "Nice to meet you, Jamie."

"Flash has been helping us prepare for the Malum," Boogie said. "He's had some experience fighting these things, not too far from here. He thinks he's got some ideas that might help."

Flash nodded. "I've heard a lot about you, Jamie, and your mission the other day. I know it feels rough right now, but just hang in there."

The reminder made me flinch. I could suddenly see R.B.'s sparkle show in my mind. I guess it made me frown.

"Hey, bud," Flash said, "Boogie told me everything. I'm sorry you feel the way you do, but you saved Kate. That's a lot to be proud of."

I looked him in the eye. "Thanks."

He had to be ex-military. He was way too honest and direct.

I immediately took a liking to Flash.

I noticed Sam had a dour expression on his face. Even Boogie seemed a little agitated. If I didn't know better, I'd say there was some tension among these three.

Nah, couldn't be.

"Jamie," Boogie said, "why don't you head back up to the clearing? Sam and I need to chat with Flash for a minute, and then we'll be up to get everyone going."

On second thought . . .

"Sure thing," I said.

"Nice to meet you," Flash called out.

I yelled over my shoulder. "You too, Flash."

As I slowly trekked up the hill, I "accidentally" overheard some of their conversation.

Flash said, "Look, you gotta know we're with you, okay? But you're asking a lot from us. You should reconsider and just get outta the way until you're stronger."

"Flash, there's nowhere for us to go," came Boogie's calm voice. "We really need your help."

"Boogie, I'm responsible for my guys and I'm not gonna lead them into a slaughter. There are just too many unknowns. Sam, you get what I'm talkin' about."

Sam's baritone voice answered. "'Course I do. No one knows better than me. But . . . who do you think showed up when your dad needed help?"

What?

Flash sighed. "I know, and we haven't forgotten what you did. But look, even if we wanna help, we may not be able to make it in time. You'll get virtually no warning and you know how long it takes for us to get here. It's not like it used to be."

"Well, we're workin' on that . . . "

That was the last thing I heard before I got out of earshot.

As others arrived in the clearing the level of chatter increased exponentially. I stole another glance. From all appearances, they had agreed to disagree.

Flash walked into the woods and Boogie and Sam just watched him go. The somber looks on their faces told the story. They weren't very happy.

I struggled to process what I'd just heard.

We were trying to get some help from another group like ours.

That made sense.

But Flash didn't seem to think it was a good idea. He didn't like the odds.

Yeah, well, if the Nasties were bringing reinforcements, I couldn't blame him.

So, where did that leave us?

As the two caught up to me I asked, "Is everything okay?"

Sam paused and took a breath to answer, then thought better of it. He shook his head and walked on by.

Boogie walked up to me and put his hand on my shoulder. He said confidently, "We'll be fine."

PART IV
FIGHT TO THE FINISH

CHAPTER 20

The day's training was one of the most focused and productive we'd had to date. The teamwork between the platoons was really coming together. I guess we were peaking at the right time.

At the end of the day, we gathered back in the clearing.

"Jamie, come over here!" Boogie waved me over to where he and Al and Gunny were standing. I jogged over.

Whoa. There are some seriously stressful vibes with these dudes.

Gunny stood at parade rest, stiff as a board. I guess that was sort of normal for him, but his knitted eyebrows and pursed lips told me something was off. It was a small thing, but it was a tell that something wasn't quite right.

Al had his muscular arms crossed. He stared daggers at Boogie and kept swaying from side to side. His tell was lip biting. He looked like he was about to break the skin.

Sheesh. What's Boogie done to make them so upset?

Boogie looked at me and said, "Jamie, I'd like for you to accompany me on a mission tonight."

Tonight? Oh. That'll do it.

I was stunned.

"Um, not to put too fine a point on it, but I thought there was a reason we didn't do much in the evenings. Especially at night. Don't the Malum have the upper hand? I mean, I heard they can see better at night than we can."

Al pointed at me. "See! Even Jamie gets it." He caught himself. "No offense, mayun."

None taken.

Boogie smiled and said, "Old WOMs and unverified folklore."

"WOMs?" I asked.

Gunny gruffly replied, "Words of Mouth, hero. Consider it urban legend until verified."

Al pounced. "Yeah, but what if it's true, Boogie? Are you willin' to sacrifice you two to find out? Gunny and me ain't ready to lead this group by ourselves, so you can't be gettin' killed or nothin'."

Aw. That was a pretty touching sentiment, especially for Al.

"What does Sam say?" I asked.

"He's not here right now," Boogie replied.

"What? Is he okay?"

"He's fine and he's still with us. He's just busy with . . . some stuff right now. He'll be back soon."

I couldn't fathom why Sam would run off like that.

Al turned to me. "Listen, Jamie, you don't have to go." He glanced at Boogie. "And neither do you, for that matter. We got a good idea of when they'll attack and about how many they are. That should be enough."

Boogie sighed. "Al, I completely understand what you're saying, and you may be right. But something tells me we need to get eyes on these guys before they show up. If our new sources are correct, they're in place now, preparing to attack. We gotta know what we're up against."

New sources?

Boogie quickly added, "And yes, I know it might be extremely dangerous to be out at night. We know they don't have many fly-ers, but I acknowledge that the ones they do have may have the upper hand."

I was glad to know they didn't have many flyers and all, but if the ones that could fly were not affected by the dark, we could be in for a rough night. I thought flying and fighting during the day were tough. If we got jumped at night, it could be a blood bath. Not Malum blood, either.

But Boogie wanted me to go. That was all I needed to hear.

"I'm with you, Boogie. No worries."

Al clenched his jaw but Gunny didn't move a muscle. Boogie looked at them apologetically. Boogie said to Al, "Remember, if we're not back by dawn, then we're not coming back. You will be in charge."

Say again? I thought it was supposed to be a recon mission, not a kamikaze run.

I took a breath to say, well, *something.* I quickly realized it didn't matter. The three of them were too busy talking to even pay me any attention.

Nope, don't mind me. I'll just update my will or something.

Oh, what have I done? Again.

At last, Al and Gunny shook hands with Boogie. Then they both shook mine. Al said, "God be with you," and they both turned and walked away.

* * *

We waited until the very end.

As usual, Boogie debriefed the crowd at the conclusion of the day. "Remember everyone, we probably have only one or two more days before game time. Focus on your job and everything will fall into place. Keep your heads in the game and we'll see you soon."

Or lose your heads, I thought darkly.

People began filing out through the nearest doors. It took only a few minutes for the last of the team to disappear in shimmers of light. When it was said and done, the only people left in the clearing were Boogie, me, Gunny, Al, and Kate.

Kate put on a brave face and stayed by my side. She reminded me of the wives I used to see sending their men off to war. So strong and courageous, yet left waiting alone.

I gave her hand a squeeze. She smiled and pressed her side against mine. My stomach felt hollow, like I was staring into a murky abyss, but Kate's warmth was reassuring. She was great for me, but I wasn't the only reason she was there.

She had a keen mind to go along with the pretty face. Somehow, she had managed to effectively catalogue everything we knew about the Malum. During the next few minutes, she reminded us of what we might expect.

"Guys, they will likely have all of their troops together by now. That means you can expect a group larger than ours. Whereas we number in the dozens we think they, with the addition of their reserves, will have over a hundred."

I glanced at Boogie. He had his chin in his hand, but showed no emotion.

She continued. "They'll likely have some airborne troops, but we're more concerned about their ground soldiers. Depending on how badly they outnumber us, it might change how we fight. For example, if we have to prepare some of Alpha to help with a big ground battle, we need to know that now."

Last minute cross-training? Great.

She waved into the evening air. "They don't normally encounter us at night, so you should have the advantage of surprise. Bottom line, if you can, find out where they are, how many there are, and anything else that could help. But don't linger. Or do anything else silly."

She looked my way when she said that last bit.

What? Me silly?

Al said, "Kate, did you remind 'em about the leader?"

"Oh, right," Kate said. "There's a rumor that their higher-tier leader is with them. That's unconfirmed at this point, and we're not sure how to tell him from the others. You may be able to figure it out if you look closely enough. But not too closely."

Another glance my way.

Seriously? Am I that bad?

"Got it, Kate. Thanks for being here for us," Boogie said.

She smiled. "I'll be waiting on you when you return." She then walked over to me and said softly, "Remember. You and I have a date. Don't let me down."

"Aye-aye, Katie." I gave her a quick hug.

At long last, it was time.

Gunny, Al, and Kate stood together and watched as Boogie and I prepared to depart. We put on jackets for the cool night air, but otherwise were dressed as during the day. I took a last swallow of water before pronouncing myself ready to go.

The twilight had faded and the last dark blues of the evening sky were replaced with a deep black. The only light in our camp came from the fire that burned in the center. I supposed Malum scouts could find us by it, but the odds were long for that on this one night.

Boogie said, "Gunny? Anything to add?"

Gunny shook his head.

"And Al?" Boogie asked.

"Nothin' I haven't already said. Get in, get your intel, and then get out. That's it, flyboys," Al said with a forced smile.

"Wilco, brother Al." Boogie smiled back. "Let's roll."

Without another word, the two of us took a couple of accelerating steps away from the trio. We quietly left the ground into the starry night.

* * *

It was a good thing we were flying, otherwise we would never have made it there and back in time. It didn't look that bad on the map, but now that we were flying it, at night? It made me second-guess my decision to come along.

We are *way* beyond the lines here, bro. If you're not careful, your eagerness to please is gonna get costly.

Seeing as how Boogie didn't have any lights on him like an airplane does, I stuck close to him. I didn't want to lose track of him in the dark night sky. There was no moon and no clouds, but lots of stars.

The stars were a saving grace, just not in the way you'd think.

I quickly learned that when it was hard to see Boogie, an absence of stars in a small area of the sky was an indicator of his location. His body blocked the light of the stars. Or, I thought cynically, it could be an indicator of something that we didn't want to run into.

Either way, I figured it probably wasn't a good idea to lose him.

Yep, let's just snuggle in.

I flew only a few feet away from him, since he was easier to see that way. He was a good flight leader. He kept his turns gentle and predictable through the somber night.

I was glad we had dressed more warmly than normal. Not only did it cool down when the sun disappeared, but we also flew higher than usual. The higher we went the colder it became.

After flying for about thirty minutes, I recognized a large point on the ground that indicated we were close to the Malum encampment. It was a large split in a river, barely recognizable without moonlight. The river was fed by three tributaries, which curved and eventually melded into one river. The resulting design, as seen from the air, had an eerie resemblance to a pitchfork.

I decided to just think of it as a cactus.

Shortly after passing the rivers' intersection, I noticed a light in the distance. I pointed to it and said, "Hey Boogie, look—"

He grabbed my arm and shook his head. He put his finger to his mouth in a *quiet* gesture. He then pointed downward, directly underneath us.

Huh? Farmland? What's that have to do—

Then I saw them. Dozens of small shadows, moving silently.

Malum. Good call on the whole shush thing.

I wasn't sure how sharp their hearing was, but that probably wasn't the time to ops test it. We flew steadily onward for another couple of minutes. The light in the distance grew larger and brighter by the second.

I chanced another glance down.

What I saw made my skin crawl. It was like we were getting closer to a disturbed ant bed or something. The number of Nasties was increasing. They were everywhere . . .

Wha—!

Without warning, Boogie grabbed me by the arm and yanked us down in a dive. We descended so fast it made my ears pop and my eyes water. Boogie leveled us off at about half of our previous altitude.

Boogie's eyes were wide and his head swiveled from side to side. He was afraid. I had never seen him like this.

Abruptly, he pointed at a tall stand of trees. They were full and tall and had strong, broad branches. We tore through the air until we arrived at the tree line. I mimicked his movements and alighted on a large branch of a tree that was filled with foliage.

What was going on?

We sat as still as stones for a few minutes. The only movement was Boogie's eyes. They were in constant motion, scanning the sky. My heart was pounding from the surprise. Something scared Boogie, and that wasn't easy to do.

Apparently satisfied that it was safe to speak for a moment, Boogie whispered to me, "Did you see them?"

See who? I shook my head.

He whispered again. "Their flyers. We almost ran right into them."

That sent a chill down my spine. "What? Where?"

"Right before we descended, I noticed black spots blocking the stars. It took me a second to recognize it. Lucky for us, they were crossing our flight path and probably not looking in our direction."

Praise the Lord for Boogie's fighter pilot eyes. I never knew we had even gotten close.

Boogie looked shaken.

He leaned even closer to me. "Okay, we're going to stay close to the trees. We've got to go slower than normal. If I suddenly fly away from the target area, get home as fast as you can and do not wait for me."

No. Just . . . no. I wasn't having that again.

I was glad he couldn't see my face. He might have turned and gone home if he could.

We crept along, through the air. It took more effort and concentration than just flying at a normal pace. It took ten minutes more to reach the edge of the Malum encampment. We had to stop twice to let Malum go by. We passed one group on the ground and one in the air.

The whole thing just didn't seem right. Where were are all of these Nasties comin' from?

Forget it. You're here. It's too late to turn back.

We eased among the tall trees. Finally, we got as close as we dared to the large fire the Malum had burning in their camp. Shadows danced like sinister puppets.

We concealed ourselves among the tree's branches and carefully peered out from the cover. Eventually, my eyes adjusted to the brightness of their fire. I was finally able to make out its inhabitants. What we saw made my blood run cold.

The sight of the Malum was as we expected. They looked some-what human, had dark hair, dark eyes, and poor fashion sense.

No, that wasn't the problem.

The problem was that there weren't just a hundred or so Malum, as we had thought. Nope, there had to be over two hundred of them. And the most frightening thing about them was that almost every last one of them . . . was flying.

CHAPTER 21

Oh, no.

I slowly turned and looked at Boogie. I could see his shocked face, even in the dark shadows of the trees.

Great. Score one for the Nasties, huh?

We barely had time to register the sight when, all at once, the Malum stopped flying. They landed and quickly formed ranks near the large fire. There were rows and rows, extending into the darkness.

Oh, man. There're so many.

We kept watching. What came into sight next caught me off guard. It was a Malum, but it didn't look like a normal Malum, at least none that I'd ever seen.

One obvious distinction was that he was huge.

If the other Malum were of average height, this one was a good two feet taller. Not only that, but he was big. I mean Tiny big. And yet, somehow he looked nimble as he flew into the clearing.

Did I mention he was hideous?

I guess that was the other thing. This dude didn't even attempt to hide his Malum face. His mug was a cross between Freddy Krueger of horror movie fame and a zombie.

I thought I might throw up in my mouth.

Everything went silent when he appeared. Then, he began to speak to his troops. I couldn't make out all that he was saying, but my guess was it was akin to "kill silver swords, take over the world," or something like that.

I'd seen enough. I wanted to go home.

I looked at Boogie but he held a hand up in a "wait" signal. He had his eyes closed and his left ear cocked in their direction. He seemed to be straining to hear what Freddy said.

Right. We're supposed to gather intel. The whole scary army of flying Nasties must have thrown me off my game.

I focused on their leader and listened as intently as possible. I could make out only a few words here and there. I picked up what I thought were the words "two days," then "kill," then "victory."

They're going to kill us all in two days. Lovely.

I looked around at the gathered army. They were quite worked up.

I bet they outnumber us at least three to one. Where'd they get so many flyers? Man, this is so not cool.

I glanced back at Boogie. He nodded at me and began to twist in place. Suddenly, he stopped in mid-motion. He cocked his ear toward the clearing again. Something important was happening.

I strained to hear what was going on. That's when I heard, "after the slaughter, then we move westward," then something about "solidifying control of regions." That was all I heard before they all started cheering and screaming and flickering.

Boogie looked at me and mouthed, *Let's go. Quietly.*

Amen to that.

I nodded slowly, just as the Malum gave a great cheer of approval to whatever else Freddy had said. We lifted silently off the branch and began making our way back through the Malum-infested forest. We moved carefully through the trees, trying to keep cover above us.

The first few minutes were silent and uneventful, so I began to relax. By my own estimation, we were near the outer limits of the Malum's encampment. Still, we flew through the trees, thinning though they may be, careful so as not to disturb any branches.

We had just passed an open spot in the forest's canopy when it happened.

There was a large crash! It sounded like splintering tree branches. Then, from just a few feet behind us, there arose the unmistakable screech of Malum.

We both spun in midair.

There were two Nasties fighting to get through the branches. Their ambush was almost perfect. Their timing was off by only a couple of seconds.

"Go!" Boogie shouted. "Make for camp as fast as you can. Split up!"

He was right. I knew I couldn't keep track of him during a night fight free-for-all.

"Move, Jamie!"

I tore off as fast as I could, flying as low as I knew how. I could still hear the screech of the Malum, but it was fading. They were moving parallel to my path.

They were ganging up on Boogie. Two of 'em versus Boogie, at night? He was a goner if I left him.

As if to emphasize that point, I heard an "Arrgh!" that could only have come from Boogie. Then the crashing noises continued. In my mind I could visualize it. They were nipping at his heels and probably scored a hit on him, but not enough to take him down.

I tried to be responsible and do the mature thing. I considered racing for camp to report on what we saw and heard . . . for a second or two.

Really? Are you gonna watch another friend die?

I went straight up like a rocket. I cleared the tops of the trees in a moment, which made me a big target to any passing Malum. But all was quiet on high.

Well, I guess if they had any friends nearby they would already be here. Two versus two, then. Good enough odds for me.

Okay, Boogie, where are you? Come on, show me somethin', man.

I heard a large branch snap and saw a quick flash of sparks.

Gotcha. Hang in there buddy, I'm on the way.

I lowered my head and flew in a rush toward the sparks. I didn't know what I was going to do, but I couldn't leave him like this. My ability to hover and fight was not great.

Come on, think! I need to . . . Weasel. Do a Weasel.

Yeah, that might just work.

I briefly leveled off until I was sure I knew exactly where they were fighting. Two more showers of sparks did the trick. I flew as fast as I could toward a spot directly above their fight. As I approached, I took in the scene.

Dang it. The Malum had Boogie trapped in the trees. He couldn't maneuver . . . and he was wounded.

Boogie's jacket was torn and blood ran from his side. If he tried to run the Malum would make quick work of him. It was only a matter of time.

It was now or never.

As soon as I reached the spot above them, I flipped over on my back. I then led with my head, pointing my body straight at the ground. I quickly accelerated toward the fight.

I waited until the last possible moment to pull my sword. I didn't want to give them any warning. I hoped the Malum were so intent on finishing Boogie that they would never see me approach.

Boogie did, and he played it masterfully. At the last possible moment, he pulled his arms and legs into a ball. He wisely moved out of the way of the runaway Jamie.

I pulled my sword and literally flew through the middle of one of the Nasties. He disintegrated into a million pieces of gross soot. I guess I had my mouth open, 'cause it was suddenly like I had licked an ash tray. I almost hurled.

My momentum carried me right by Boogie and out of the bottom of the tree. I could barely stop my descent and slammed into the ground. Luckily, I bounced more than splatted and I ricocheted back into the air. I stayed low until I cleared the tree.

I gagged and retched and tried to clear my mouth. "Urkkk, yackkk." I would have laughed at me if I'd had the time. Through the throes of heaves, I had a thought.

Boogie may need help with the last one. Like now.

If I were suddenly on the losing side of a fight with Boogie, what would I do? Hmm . . .

I flew as fast as I could away from the tree and back in the direction of the Malums' base camp. As soon as I cleared the grove of trees, I flew upward.

This should be a good spot.

I pitched back toward where I had last seen Boogie. It was like a sideways U. I couldn't really see much. It was just so dark.

Nothing . . . nothing . . . blank spot in the stars . . . that's moving right at me! Swing, Jamie!

At the last possible moment, I swung at the dark spot. At first, I thought I'd missed him. Then I started gagging and retching again.

Oh, come on! Keep your mouth closed, dude!

Whether by blind luck or a shrewd guess, I'd timed it perfectly. My sword had met him in mid-flight. I'm glad there weren't other Malum around, though, because I sounded like a frat boy after an all-nighter.

"Huuuunnhhr. Aaaarrrhhhgh!"

So embarrassing.

After what seemed an eternity, I stopped dry heaving. I did a final spit and wiped my mouth on my sleeve.

That's so gross. Wait. Where's Boogie?

I flew to where I'd last seen him. I kept my sword out so he wouldn't mistake me for one of the bad guys. He wasn't there.

Come on, Boogie. I can't handle this today, man.

After a second, I heard a softly spoken "up here." Boogie had apparently risen to give chase to the Malum before he saw our midair meeting. He was in pain, but he was still grinning and gave me a big thumbs-up.

Oh, thank you, Lord.

Without further words, he motioned me to follow. We flew as fast as we could toward our camp, and we arrived just as the first light of dawn showed in the sky.

* * *

Kate was relieved to see me alive. Beyond that, our reception wasn't so great. Something about the blood and Nasty dust, I guess.

"You were supposed to avoid contact!" Al yelled at Boogie. The veins on his neck bulged and he paced back and forth.

The anger management thing was gettin' old. Fast.

But he was just getting started. "You said this was a simple recon mission. Nothin' more. But what'd you do?"

Boogie grimaced while Kate bandaged his arm with the supplies Fudd always kept on hand. "Al, I—"

"I'll tell ya what ya did! You tried to play hero. Did you listen to me? Uh-uh."

"Al, sincerely, we did our best to—"

"Did yo' best? Really? If that's yo' best then it's not very good."

I'd had enough.

"Hey!" the sound of my voice was like a gunshot.

Kate froze in mid-wrap. Al spun on me, wild-eyed.

Enough bullying. I was done with it.

"What is your problem, Al? First, you go all combative on me when it's time to save Kate. Now, you come unglued on Boogie. On Boogie! After a successful mission. What is your malfunction?"

"My malfunction. *My* malfunction?" He started walking toward me.

"Al, wait!" Boogie yelled.

Poor Kate. She could only stare at the in-progress train wreck.

"You heard me! What's eating at you?"

Gunny strode on an intercept course for us.

I held my ground. This had to end.

Al and Gunny arrived at the same time.

Al pointed his finger in my face. "Boy, I'll stomp you into the ground."

"Really? Then do it, Al," I said calmly.

Al bit his lip and balled his fists.

Gunny tensed.

The standoff stretched for what felt like forever.

I didn't know where it came from, but then I said, "Who are you actually upset with? It could be me, but it's definitely not Boogie. Al, no kiddin', what's goin' on?"

I stared at him and, for the first time, I saw something unexpected in his eyes.

Fear.

Huh? I knew he wasn't scared of me or anyone else. What gave?

His chin trembled and his eyes watered, but he kept his fists clenched. Abruptly, he turned and walked to the other side of the meeting area.

Okaay. Not stressful at all.

I let out a long breath and glanced around. Kate had her hand over her mouth and Boogie stood nearby, his bandage hanging loosely from his arm. Boogie scratched his head and blinked his eyes in a "oh, my" manner.

Everyone took a few minutes to calm down. At least, that's what I tried to do. I put my hands on my head and watched the clouds go by.

Happy thoughts, bro. Think happy thoughts.

Kate finished her work on Boogie's wound and pronounced him none the worse for the wear. Eventually, Boogie called out, "Everyone! Come over here so we can discuss what Jamie and I found out."

Everyone walked over, including Al. Gunny smoothly placed himself between Al and me. Just in case, I guess.

Al studiously avoided eye contact with me. Which was fine. I was fresh out of argue juice, anyway.

Boogie said, "Jamie and I learned a lot on our mission and we need to talk about it. Now."

The others perked up as Boogie relayed the events of the evening. Al and Gunny were shocked at the news of the airborne Nasties. I guess none of us saw that one coming.

Kate became animated when we mentioned Freddy. "Wait a minute. Describe him again."

So Boogie did.

Kate said, "Well, I guess that makes sense."

"Um, what makes sense?" I asked.

"Consider our location, strategically. If we fall, the Malum have a clear shot at attacking Flash's guys." She pointed westward. "They're looking ahead."

Boogie rubbed his wounded arm. "Guys, I didn't say anything before now because I wasn't sure until tonight. I think Kate is correct. We are at an important crossroads. If the Malum can make us run—"

"Or wipe us out . . . " I added.

Boogie nodded. "Then they will control the entire region. They'd have a great place to launch their next operation against Flash and his group, and anyone else, after that."

I said, "So if they wipe us out, they can do the same to Flash's guys and keep marching from there?" Images of wild hordes of Malum marching across the countryside came to mind.

Kate nodded. "Yeah. That must be why they brought in all the extra flyers and the big shot leader. They plan to overwhelm our air support and then overrun our ground forces. Makes perfect sense."

"So, how's it going with getting Flash's guys to help us out?" I asked.

The look on Boogie's face made me feel like a spy.

"Sorry. I overheard you guys talking the other day. Maybe if he understood how important this place is, to them, they would help out."

Gunny, Al, and Boogie looked at each other but didn't say anything.

Kate answered for them. "Jamie, like Sam told you, we're not the first to be here. There was a group before us and, as now, the Malum massed to attack. Flash's dad and his men came to our rescue, but the cost was terrible. For everyone."

"That's the bad part, of course." Boogie loosened his neck. "The good news is that our combined groups beat the Malum. It's taken a long time for the Nasties to regroup."

Kate said, "Last time, Flash's group was brave, but young and inexperienced. We lost lots of guys, but so did they."

"We've asked so much of them in the past," Boogie said, "I'm not sure we can push them for anything more. We've got to prepare to fight on our own."

I understood what that was like. To feel like you couldn't ask, or give, anything more.

"So, where does that leave us?" I asked.

"We prepare to fight, hero," Gunny said.

Boogie added, "And we pray for a miracle."

* * *

Al eyed me as we were walking to the doors. It wasn't quite threatening, but it wasn't friendly either. I didn't think anything about it until hours later, on the other side, when I was leaving work for the day.

That's strange. Somebody's got my car blocked in. Who would do that?

I walked up to the offending vehicle just as its passenger window rolled down. I stopped in mid-step.

"Hi, Al. Somethin' I can do for you?"

I looked around. Not a single witness in sight.

"Get in, mayun."

Oh, come on.

"Look, Al. I'm tired and this probably isn't the place for . . . whatever you have in mind. What do you say we just take a rain check, okay?"

He leaned across the seat and pushed the passenger door open.

"Get in." He paused, a pained look on his face. "Please."

Well, Jamie. You're the one that wanted to know what was up.

"Okay, Al. Just 'cause you asked so nice."

No reaction whatsoever.

This was going to be fun. I could just tell.

I climbed in and slammed the pickup's door shut.

Al pulled away from the curb and accelerated off base. Before I knew it, we were off the main road and going deep into the woods. Al had not uttered a sound since we left.

Might as well just ride it out, dude. He'll talk when he's ready. Or not.

I stared out the window and watched the trees blur by. The setting sun rippled shadows across the country road, and for a while, the only sounds were the tires on the pavement and the wind rushing by.

"It took me a while to figure it out, mayun."

I jumped at the deep sound of his voice.

"Figure what out, Al?"

"You know. I been a little, uh, short tempered lately."

"Really? I hadn't noticed."

He stared at me with a "Are you gonna do that right now?" look.

"Sorry, Al. Old habits. Please, go ahead."

He took a calming breath. "Did you know I was downrange at the same time as you? Same area, too. I was a sergeant back then."

"Rick said something about that. What were you doing?"

"You know. Standard infantry missions. Raids, clear-n-holds, stuff like that. We weren't special ops or nothin', but we were good at our job. Really good."

He pulled down a dirt driveway. I could see a log cabin in an open spot.

I heard the pain in his voice. "We were days from leavin'. I hadn't lost a troop in the eleven months we'd been there. That's when it happened."

He pulled to a stop in front of the cabin.

"What happened?"

He didn't answer, but he reached into the glove box and pulled something out. It was on a ball chain necklace. Dog tags.

"This is what happened." He handed me the tags and stepped out of the truck.

I looked at the name . . . and almost passed out. Blood pounded in my ears and I started to hyperventilate.

No. This isn't real. This can't be.

The dog tags read, Spencer, James Mackintosh, U.S. Army.

CHAPTER 22

I felt like I was in a terrible nightmare. Once again, my past was right in front of me. It was something I could never seem to escape.

Why did Al have these? Was this some sick joke?

Then it hit me.

Al was there at the same time. He lost a guy at the end. He has Spencer's dog tags.

Specialist Spencer was one of his men.

I closed my eyes and saw Spencer's face. He still stared at me.

That explained the hostility. I'd hate me, too.

I looked around at the cabin and woods.

Why were we there? It couldn't be good. Well, only one way to find out.

I don't know why, but I put Spencer's dog tags in my pocket. It didn't feel right to leave them alone in the truck. I steeled myself and opened the door.

I made it halfway to the cabin before Al walked out.

Yeah, I'm dead.

Al carried a M&P 15, a civilian version of the Army's M-4 rifle, and it was crowned with a bayonet.

I fought the impulse to run.

I looked around and saw only a large rock. It was no match for his weapons, but it was all I had, so I picked it up. I hefted it, hoping to reenact the whole David and Goliath thing.

A most peculiar look transfixed Al's face.

"Boy, are you outta your ever-lovin' mind? Come here and help me."

"But . . . aren't you going to shoot me?"

"I wouldn't waste good bullets on you, boy, now come over here!"

I slowly walked toward him, confused and on my guard.

He pointed at the items behind him. A Kevlar helmet and a pair of military boots.

A helmet and boots? What does he . . . ? Oh.

"Come on, mayun. I think we both need to do this."

I dropped the rock. I understood.

I grabbed the helmet and boots and followed him to the back yard.

"Still got the dog tags?" he said over his shoulder.

"In my pocket."

We went to work. It didn't take long. When we were finished, it was almost dark. There was barely enough light to see our creation.

The rifle was real, but it wasn't loaded. It stood upright on its pointy end, the grounded bayonet blade keeping it in place. The helmet sat on the rifle's stock. The boots sat at the base.

Silently, I placed Spencer's dog tags on the grip of the gun.

The effect was one of terrible sadness. It was like the owner had stepped away. But anyone who saw the memorial knew the owner wasn't coming back.

Not in this lifetime, at least.

A wave of sadness nearly made my knees buckle. It felt as fresh as the day I last saw Spencer drawing breath. In my mind, he had never really finished dying. Until now.

"Before we do this, mayun, let's get square. We can't honor him if we've got unfinished business."

"Okay, Al."

Al began, "I didn't know you but I blamed you for Mack's death. I wanted us to go get him, not some hotshot special ops dudes. He died and I went home believin' I coulda saved him."

My gut twisted further in knots.

"I get it, Al. I really do. It was my mission, so if it's anybody's fault, it's mine. I take full responsibility."

"Well, that's what I finally figured out, mayun. No matter how bad we want to, we can't fix everything. Sometimes . . . sometimes bad things just happen."

I looked at him.

"Jamie, listen to me. Somethin' you said earlier got me to thinkin'."

"Yeah? What was that?"

"You asked me, 'who'm I actually upset with'? That hit a nerve. I realized I was upset . . . with me."

"What do you mean?"

"Simple. It was easier to be angry than admit I couldn't save him. I felt helpless. I was even scared. Scared I would lose my friends again."

I felt the old emotions rise. "Yeah, Al. That sounds familiar."

"Exactly, mayun. You and me, we both been feelin' helpless and responsible for stuff we couldn't control. You did everything you could to save my troop. I know that now."

I nodded at him, afraid to say anything right then.

"Jamie, I think it's time we put it down. We both need to drop our chains and say farewell to our brother. I really think that's what Mack would want us to do."

I croaked out, "I think you're right. I think it'd be good for both of us."

Al had started a bonfire, which now blazed and gave light to our service.

I'd attended enough of these to know how they went, but Al led this one. Al prayed for us and then quoted from the Bible, from the sixth chapter of Isaiah. The words sent chills down my spine and brought tears to my eyes.

"Then I heard a voice of the Lord saying, 'Whom shall I send? And who will go for us? And I said, 'Here am I. Send me!'"

Yes, Lord. Thank you for my brothers and sisters who answer the call.

Then Al sang "Amazing Grace." It was beautiful. I didn't know he had it in him.

I would have joined in but I was blubbering like a baby. Yeah, Mr. Cool Dude struck again.

At least Al was crying too, but he was cooler about it. He even managed to sing at the same time. I'd completely underestimated his talents.

By the time we got to the roll call, I was spent.

"Specialist Spencer . . . Specialist Spencer . . . Specialist James Mackintosh Spencer."

Silence greeted the call.

Al sniffed and said, "I don't play the bugle, so we'll have to imagine 'Taps', mayun."

After crying my eyes out, it sounded like I had a cold. "Yeah, Al. I think that's fine."

Al said, "One last time. For Mack. Present . . . arms!"

Al and I both snapped a salute, and held it. The fire stilled and the evening breeze calmed, if only for a moment. It was as if nature wanted to pay its respects.

"Order . . . arms!"

We both stood there, tears easing down our faces. We stared at the memorial to our comrade in arms, each of us saying our good-byes. Both of us, I imagined, letting go.

It was strange. Despite the pain, I felt different. Lighter, even.

It was like some great burden had fallen from my shoulders. A buoyancy made me feel light on my feet. In spite of our circumstance, I smiled.

Minutes passed in silence. Eventually, Al's eyes and mine met. We had reconciled, with Mack and with each other.

We did a one hand clasped, one arm bro-hug to seal the deal.

"Hey, mayun. You want some food?"

"Yeah, Al. That'd be great."

"I hope you like barbecue and sweet tea dude, 'cause that's all I got!"

I laughed. "Of course. I'd love some."

As Al went to get the food, I sat by the fire and watched the stars dance in the night. For the first time in years, I felt completely at peace.

I wonder if I'll feel the same by this time tomorrow?

Of course you will, dude! How could you not?

* * *

It was like the world had taken angry pills.

That's not completely true. Some acted like they were on anxiety-causing meds. I was cut off three time before I got to work, the gate guard was surly, and the local morning radio announcer sounded like he was having a nervous breakdown.

I hoped things would be better when I got to work.

Not so much.

It was like a madhouse in the maintenance area. Our normally friendly superintendent snapped at people and guys who barely knew each other were arguing over silly things. Even Ed, my jet-launching buddy, looked out of sorts.

"Ed, what's going on, dude? Are you okay?"

"Hey, Jamie. I don't know man, I just feel off today. I almost didn't come to work, but I need the paycheck, right?"

"Yeah, dude, I know what you mean. Well, keep your head up. Surely things will turn around."

He shrugged, then walked out the door and onto the flight line.

Good grief. What's going on?

My mind returned to the night mission. Did we kick the hornet's nest? Or was this something else . . . ?

"Hi, Jamie!"

I jumped. "Oh hey, Peggy. Sorry about that, I guess I'm catching a little of what's going around."

"Oh, what's that, hon?"

"I don't know. Whatever's got everyone so uptight today. Maybe something's in the water. Anyway, how are you doing?"

"Oh, I'm fine, dear." She smiled warmly at me, but there was concern in her eyes. It was only then that I noted the deep scratches on the side of her neck. They looked soothed, but I had never noticed them before.

"Peggy, are you okay?" I gestured toward her neck.

"Oh! Of course." She looked embarrassed as she pulled her collar up. "I take care of all kinds of animals, you know. Some of them are a little rougher than others."

"Well Peggy, you should really think about—"

She stepped close to me and whispered. "Jamie, listen to me, honey. It's about to begin. You need to go home."

"I . . . I don't understand. What is—"

"Yes you do, dear." She grasped my hand and stared at me for a moment before casually moving her bangs to the side.

No. Way. All this time . . .

I stood there, in the middle of the chaos, with big eyes and mouth slightly open, watching the ichthus appear on her face.

"Now, Jamie. Do like I told you, honey. Get some food and some rest and get ready for . . . you know. I'll say a special prayer for you." She had tears in her eyes.

I leaned in and told her, "Don't you worry. Thank you."

She smiled a brave smile and nodded toward the door.

I quietly slipped from the bedlam and ran for my car. I had one place to go before I went home.

* * *

I could see Kate through the window, and she looked stressed. I guess the day was wearing on everyone. She must have had a sixth sense because after a few seconds, her head jerked up and she looked my way.

She held up her hand in a "wait there" motion. It took her only a few seconds to join me.

There was a relieved and scared look on her face as she walked outside. We stepped around the corner, out of view of the café, and she immediately grabbed my hand. "I'm on a short break."

I looked at her in amazement. She was quite a combination of vulnerability and strength.

"It's about to begin, isn't it?" she said.

I nodded slowly.

We stared at each other for a moment before she wrapped her arms around my neck and hugged me tightly. I squeezed her back, wishing I could hold on forever.

"I don't know what to say, Katie."

"Say I'll see you later. And mean it."

I smiled my bravest smile. "In that case, I know I'll see you later."

She put her forehead against mine, then kissed me softly on the lips. Her tears mingled with the ones that had escaped from my eyes. "Now, go!" She kissed me one more time and then spun around and walked away.

I barely remember driving home, nor do I remember much else from that afternoon other than staring at an electric door. But one thought was seared into my consciousness; the road back to Kate goes through the leader of the Malum.

"Elm Street or no, I'm coming for you, Freddy."

I stepped through the door.

CHAPTER 23

There was no big ceremony before the fight, no just-in-case good-byes among the men. Everyone just showed up, grim-faced and determined, ready for whatever the day brought.

Boogie was briefing Alpha, whose members were staying limber and ready to fly, when one of their fastest members zoomed into the clearing. He was out of breath and said loudly enough for everyone to hear, "They're coming."

Al barked orders and Bravo, plus the new members of Charlie, tore off at a run toward the enemy. Alpha took a little extra time before lifting off. We wanted to meet the enemy at the same time as the ground forces. It would not take nearly as long for us to arrive in the target area.

I knelt to pray and felt a hand on my shoulder. Boogie knelt beside me and closed his eyes. I prayed for strength, for forgiveness of my wrongs, and for mercy and grace. If I was going to meet God, I was okay with that, but it wasn't going to be because I didn't ask for help.

Boogie and I stood and he turned and looked at me. I don't know how he did it, but he smiled broadly. "Okay, Jamie. You're quarterbacking this thing. You ready?"

"Let's do it, Boogie."

"Fight's on, Jamie!"

* * *

The enemy approached with their airborne troops over their ground forces. That section of the sky was dark with Malum. You could hear their screeches reverberating through the still air for miles. Even with all of Alpha in front of me, it was still an intimidating sight.

I counted Malum as we flew toward them. They had at least a two-to-one advantage against a few dozen or so of us. It was bad, but it could've been worse.

Still, something bothered me.

The lead part of Alpha flew to meet the main force of inbound Malum. Just in time, Alpha arrived overhead of our ground forces, exactly as we had planned. Good so far.

Boogie spurred Alpha on and intentionally shot ahead of the ground forces. The idea was to meet the Malum ahead of where our ground troops waited. It was crucial to the plan.

At that moment Freddy chose to show himself. He looked huge in the bright daylight as he took the lead of their formation. But what got our attention was that their formation appeared to divide and multiply in the air.

Somehow they had managed to cluster together to veil their vastly superior numbers. What initially looked like maybe a two-to-one advantage for the Malum quickly multiplied into a three-to-one. Not cool.

We all saw the numbers multiply in front of us. There was nothing to do but execute the mission. We had to sell our part to make the others work.

Boogie yelled, "Abort!"

As one, Alpha turned around.

Well, almost as one. I took that moment of confusion to split from Alpha and fly toward our ground force. I looked over my shoulder to follow Alpha's progress and make sure no Nasty followed me.

Alpha acted not one bit happy as they twisted and dove away from the approaching horde. They completed a gut-wrenching hundred-and-eighty-degree diving turn and descended rapidly to gain as much velocity as they could. They shot downward and away from the Malum.

I landed in a tall tree, behind our ground guys, to watch their progress. Our ground troops, led by Gunny, saw the flyers zooming away. They also saw the approaching Malum ground troops, now covered by airborne invaders with no opposition.

Gunny yelled, "Fall back!" and screamed at the troops to run.

Our ground troops ran upward and over the small hills that surrounded their position. Their ground path diverged from the airborne retreat of Alpha. Whatever airborne support our guys may have gotten from Alpha was negated by retreating along this path. To the casual observer, it looked suicidal.

With apparent recklessness, they ran themselves into a small dead-end canyon. It was surrounded on three sides by steep banks and overhanging, menacing trees. There was no way out or in, from the side or from above.

The airborne Malum were after Alpha. Good.

Okay, here goes nothing . . .

While the airborne Malum continued onward to give chase to Alpha, our ground force came to a screeching halt at the back of the canyon. The Malum ran gleefully down the canyon in the shadows of the trees, savoring the moment. From where I sat I could see and hear everything.

The Malum slowed to a walk, drew their jet-black swords, and steadily moved in for the kill. The captain of their ground force kept his non-flicker face on and approached Gunny. "Surrender now, and we'll torture you for only a little while," he hissed.

The Malum just laughed, their creepy howls echoing through the ravine. That is, all except one. He frantically tried to get the captain's attention. He was literally yanking on his jacket, but his boss kept swatting him away.

The captain shouted, "I'll tell you what we're going to do! We're going to—What? What is it?" he said to the interrupting Malum.

"There aren't enough of them!"

"Of course there aren't enough of them, that's why we're . . . going . . . to . . . " The captain's words trailed off. His black eyes danced with panic. He stared at Gunny.

Gunny smiled back and said, "That's right, sweetheart. Pucker up."

The tree lines on both sides of the gully erupted with screams. A merciless contingent of Bravo platoon attacked the Malum from both sides.

Al leapt from the top of the hill and dusted three Malum before they could move a muscle.

A few Malum tried to run, but Bravo was ready. They cut off their escape at the back of the gorge. There was nowhere for them to hide. Our guys tore through the panicked invaders like a remorseless buzz saw. They quickly covered the ground in ash.

It was a glorious massacre.

I looked up and smiled at the protective covering of the overlapping trees. Al was tough but pretty dang smart, too. He's the one who'd realized that the Malum's airborne support couldn't help them here.

I got ready to leave.

Charlie and Bravo had played their part to perfection. Now it was up to Alpha and a wild rabbit chase.

I took a shortcut back, hoping that Alpha was hanging on.

* * *

They were, but by the time I caught up with them, the Malum were almost on top of Alpha. There was no time to spare. I took a position where I could monitor this part of the plan.

Our guys were greatly outnumbered and flying hard.

Freddy had moved from the front to the back of his force. Maybe he didn't want to get his hands dirty. One of his captains took the lead of the Malum air attack.

On cue, the men of Alpha flew toward a gap in the nearest tree line. I watched as they progressively flew lower and lower. They flew so low they were almost on the ground by the time they reached it.

At the gap in the tree line, all of Alpha Platoon, every last one of them, banked hard left and immediately maneuvered out of sight of the Malum. Close on their heels, the Nasties flew around the corner at full velocity . . . and screeched to a halt. There was nothing there but a big, tall tree line, thick with heavy trunks and full green branches.

The Malum stood in the clearing at the base of the silent trees, confused. In a weird kind of mash-up derby, their fellow Malum continued to slam into one another as eager Malum aviators rounded the corner at full speed. Alpha had seemingly disappeared into thin air.

The Malum were in a small, confined area bordered by tall oaks and thick pines. Perfect.

Come on Boogie, get there!

One of the Malum shouted "Get out!" He had barely enough time to say those two words before a large portion of Alpha Platoon screamed down from the sky. They attacked from above and behind the confused Malum.

Alpha tore through their ranks and created a dust storm of disintegrating Nasties. The Malum easily lost half of their troops in the initial attack. The remaining Malum tried to fly out of danger, but Alpha attacked once more from above. They dusted most of the remaining Nasties where they stood.

As the literal dust settled from the initial attacks, the Malum remnants attempted to regroup and escape.

At that moment I flew out of the woods from behind the Malum. The air tore at my shirt as I screamed along just inches above the ground. I attacked with a vengeance.

This one's for R.B.! And this one's for Kate!

I would dust one and barely get past him before I swung at another. My arm felt filled with lightning and my heart pounded in joy. It was like a thrilling game of whack-a-Malum, only on fast forward.

I dusted at least a dozen in the process. I even caught the bellowing Malum air captain with a well-placed sword strike just as he was leaving the ground. His ash spouted upward, like black fireworks.

I blew through their formation and then flew up into the sky to reset. One half-loop later I was diving back toward the remaining

Malum, most of which were still struggling to get off the ground. Boogie saw me and rejoined with me as I zoomed by.

A few Malum did manage to get airborne, but they were quickly engaged by the returning members of Alpha. Eventually, most of the fights spiraled to the ground. No one could keep fighting that hard and stay in the air.

Despite our early success we were still outnumbered, and the surviving Malum knew it. We had hoped to have their numbers down to a more manageable size before now. There were still too many of them.

I flinched when I looked up and saw an Alpha guy get wounded. He tumbled down to the ground in a heap. Thankfully, a second later he got up and started fighting again.

I shook my head. Amazing.

I finally had the breath to yell at Boogie. "Where's Bravo and Charlie? They should be here by now!"

"Just keep fighting, Jamie! Have a little faith!"

I'm trying, Boogie.

Boogie and I had just dusted a few more when we heard a commotion. At first all I could see was a storm of flying dust, and then Gunny stepped through it, a huge grin on his face.

Yeah, boy!

The Bravo troops, with Al at the front, screamed into the fray. Gunny's new Charlie guys launched into the fight from the other side.

Oh, thank you, Lord.

I saw Gunny tear into three Malum at once. I think he was laughing. Figures.

I also caught a glance of two blond-headed boys dive-bombing unsuspecting Nasties. They swooped down like angry birds and *schwack'd* Nasties on the head.

It was a savage melee, but we were winning. I couldn't believe it. The plan actually worked!

That what I was thinking, right before I heard Boogie give a terrible shout. At first I thought he had been wounded.

Where is he? Wait, there he is.

He was fine and he was . . . pointing upward.

I gazed in the direction in which he was pointing and froze. My mouth went dry and I stared numbly, vaguely aware that my heart was threatening to bang out of my chest.

Freddy. He was leading a swarm of airborne Malum. A swarm of Malum that he hid.

So he could kill us.

The look of anguish on Boogie's face said it all . . . Freddy had played us for fools.

CHAPTER 24

For all the good it did, my brain kept processing.

Freddy waited until we were beat down and unable to leave. Then he attacks with overwhelming force. Pretty smart, actually.

The panicked look on Boogie's face was not comforting. He glanced at the battlefield, which was full of our guys fighting, oblivious to what was about to happen. Weasel landed beside Boogie. He stared up at the approaching horde with a resigned expression.

Boogie and Weasel's eyes met. They nodded. An unspoken decision passed between the two.

What are they . . . ? No, they can't be serious. They're going to attack.

It was insane. They had zero chance to survive.

Oh well, Jamie. Got *your* boots on?

Of course I do.

I ran and joined them as they left the ground. The three of us were blurs. We shot toward the approaching cloud.

I saw Weasel and Boogie exchange one more glance. They had been friends since they were kids, and now they would die together.

Boogie stared at me with the same sad look on his face. I smiled.

I was done being scared.

Let's do this.

He nodded, and then his features hardened. He eyed the approaching crowd of Malum. He looked at Weasel and me and mouthed the words "Pincer. Freddy."

Attack from multiple directions? Got it.

Freddy continued to lead the Malum. We were close enough now to see the maniacal look on his face. He knew it would be a slaughter.

The other Malum had closed the gap on their leader. There was no way we would escape after the attack.

Boogie shouted, "Action!"

Weasel dove and accelerated to remain underneath Boogie's flight path.

I climbed aggressively, but also stayed parallel to Boogie's path.

In seconds, Weasel and I apexed. Then we aimed for Freddy.

Our three-pronged attack happened too fast for him. We attacked from above, below, and in front.

As we converged, everything went silent and time seemed to slow. I couldn't hear the screeching, or the wind, or my raspy breath, but I saw everything in high-definition detail.

Boogie led with his sword, the gleaming edge lighting his face. His eyes were fierce with determination.

Weasel attacked from underneath. He swiveled his blade upward, using his momentum to create an unstoppable swing.

Freddy's face was frozen in a mix of shock and fear.

I dove at Freddy with only one thought on my mind: Take him with us.

I brought my sword down, swinging with all my might.

In an instant the world exploded in light, sparks, and noise.

No!

Freddy deflected Boogie's attack entirely. Weasel got a glancing blow on Freddy's leg. It drew blood but wasn't enough to bring him down.

In the moment it took for me to swing at Freddy, he twisted and dove away. My swing caught only his lower back. I saw a splattering of inky blood and a small cloud of black flecks erupt from his trunk.

He screamed in pain and spun toward the ground.

Oh wait, I'm probably dead.

There's no way the other Malum couldn't have gotten me. It was strange though . . . I didn't feel any different.

I was so confused.

I looked back. I wanted to see if I was "sparkling" like R.B.

In a glance that lasted perhaps a second, I realized a few things.

One, I wasn't sparkling. That really bothered me until I realized that, two, I wasn't sparkling because I wasn't dying.

Three, I was staring at the most beautiful sight in the world . . . a large group of guys from the west. Flash and his men had torn into the Nasties with perfect timing.

Technically, they were outnumbered by the Malum. Technically. But I'm not sure they would have seen it that way.

They blazed through the center of the Malum formation. It was like one big dust bomb. I'd never seen anything like it.

Then, they split and attacked from every direction. They were swaths of silver bowling through the enemy. The Malum were confused, threats coming at them from every angle.

As soon as a Nasty would spin one way, one of Flash's guys would attack from the other. The west's unbridled aggressiveness was fierce. The Nasties never stood a chance.

I caught a glimpse of Flash. He grinned as he slaughtered one after the other. I also saw a flash of grey tearing through the Malum. Is that Sam?

No time, Jamie. Find Boogie.

There!

He was still alive but tangled up with a wounded Malum.

Boogie screamed at me. "Jamie! Get Freddy!"

I tucked and accelerated, trying to make up lost ground. I could barely see Freddy, who had recovered enough to fly way. He was in full-on escape mode.

Weasel appeared on my right side, slightly bloodied but smiling. He yelled, "Wait for me at the big oak. I'll run him right to ya."

I nodded and Weasel streaked away. I don't know how, but he caught up to Freddy within seconds and went right to work.

Weasel relentlessly feinted, dove, and attacked. *Clang!* Their swords met in a shower of light. He taunted him, "Hey, did you get a free bowl of soup with that face?"

He even called him names and stuck his tongue out at him. He herded Freddy around the sky.

If it wasn't so serious I would have busted out laughing.

I think the taunting finally did it. Freddy started fighting back. His escape attempt turned into a murderous game of tag.

As soon as Freddy turned to fight, Weasel would run. When Weasel ran, he drug Freddy where Weasel wanted him to go. If Freddy tried to disengage, Weasel re-attacked and taunted him to make him fight.

This back-and-forth continued until Weasel got a good strike on Freddy. Weasel's blade tip tore Freddy's skin from his ear to almost the corner of his mouth. Freddy's scream shook the ground as inky blood suddenly ran down his neck. The deadly game shifted gears.

Freddy bellowed and zoomed after Weasel.

Oh, boy. I knew Freddy wouldn't stop now until he caught up with him.

Freddy gained on the normally swift Weasel.

Weasel spun and twisted to evade Freddy's long-armed swings. Then he turned abruptly in my direction.

Perfect. Freddy was completely focused on Weasel.

Okay, Katie. This one's for you.

As they flashed through the opening in the tree line, I leapt from behind my tree and swung for Freddy's head.

He twisted at the last possible moment.

I cringed as my sword missed his head.

But my enthusiastic follow-through tore through his chest and down his left leg. He roared and ash spewed.

Way cool, except for the other thing.

My follow-through caused me to crash into Freddy.

"Ooof!"

I remember seeing my sword flying away from me just before Freddy and I went end-over-end together.

As the world rotated I realized we were flying into the middle of the battlefield. I eventually came to rest, sprawled on my chest and sans sword. I was covered in mud, Nasty dust, and, by the taste of it, some of my own blood.

Come on, Jamie, get up! Get up! Get—

Suddenly, I couldn't breathe and had grown two feet taller. Both things disturbed me.

Then I realized a huge, bloody, monstrous arm was underneath my chin.

I swung my arms and kicked my legs as hard as I could . . . right up to the point I felt the Malum sword against my face. Its tip was ice cold and emanated fear and despair.

I went still.

Oh, come on. This is not happening! That was a perfectly good ambush.

There weren't many Malum left on the battlefield, at least that I could see. My guess was we had massacred most of them. There were just a few stragglers left.

His large, cold voice shouted, "Halt!"

The sight of Freddy caused everyone, friend and foe alike, to stop in their tracks. The only sounds were heavy breathing and groans of the wounded.

Freddy shouted. "You will put your weapons down and let us pass or this worthless creature dies. You have fought well. There is no need to lose another of your warriors."

I pushed and kicked some more.

He continued, "After we depart we will let him go. There has been enough loss today."

Boogie stepped forward.

Good. Get it done, Boogie.

Unexpectedly, I saw indecision in his eyes.

Oh, no . . .

I struggled harder against Freddy's arm, but he dug the soul-sucking sword in my face. The cold tip suddenly felt hot as fire.

I screamed.

"Wait!" Boogie called out. "Everyone, put your swords away!"

I saw disbelief in our troops' eyes. Flash's guys looked to him for guidance. Flash glanced at Boogie and yelled, "You heard him, put your swords away."

Reluctantly, all of our men stowed their weapons.

The surviving Malum clamored together. I heard Freddy tell them, in a quiet voice, "Go! I'll finish this one off after you're gone."

Before I could utter a sound, the remaining Malum flew away. I watched them turn to dots in the sky. Freddy momentarily lowered his sword.

I screamed, "He's going to kill me anyway! Get him!"

Freddy chuckled, "Of course I'm going to kill you, Jamie. You're much too important to leave alive." He brought his sword up to my neck, about to make me all sparkly.

I saw panic in everyone's eyes. It was too late.

Just as Freddy's blade approached my neck, I felt like I grabbed an electric fence.

The muscle-searing pain grew exponentially until I was wide-eyed, openmouthed, and convulsing. Freddy still held me tightly, anchored by his giant forearm under my chin. I was vaguely aware that his right arm had frozen in place, the blade only inches from my neck.

Somehow, I glanced down.

Hey, look. A silver sword sticking from my chest.

All at once, Freddy released his grasp on me. I fell, stunned, to the ground.

Freddy bellowed in agony and stared at the silver sword, now snugly stuck through the middle of his torso.

He twisted to find his attacker. I looked, too. What we saw shocked us both.

There was cute little Kate.

She had both hands on her hips and stared hard at Freddy, even though she came only up to about the middle of his deteriorating chest. As Freddy shook and the dust flew, Kate looked at him serenely. "Boo!"

Freddy exploded in a volcano of dust and screams, knocking Kate backward and covering both of us in Freddy dust.

I slowly sat up and . . . promptly began gagging on Freddy dust. Again.

I gagged and coughed for what felt like the longest time. Eventually, I was down to drooling and spitting. I decided to call it a win.

Kate still stood there, calmly shaking Freddy from her hair. Her clothes were tattered and her face was a mess. She had smudges of dirt and Malum bits on her arms.

I couldn't have imagined a more beautiful sight.

She offered her hand and helped me to my feet.

"Katie? What . . . what are you doing here?"

"Aren't you glad to see me?"

"What I mean is, why did you . . . what did you . . . "

"C'mon, spit it out Jamie." She patted me on the back.

"Ow!"

She cringed. "Ooh! I'm sorry I had to, you know, go through you to get to him. I didn't know what else to do."

I rubbed the sore spot. "Well, as a matter of fact, that was the nicest thing anyone's ever done for me. Promise me you'll never do it again?"

She smiled a beautiful smile. "I promise."

I wrapped my arms around her. "Seriously, how did you know where we would be? I thought you were sitting this one out."

"Well, let's just say I may have had a little help." She looked over her right shoulder.

There was a lady walking up to us. She looked awfully familiar . . . "Peggy?"

"Hey, hon!" She ran over and hugged both of us.

What?

"You two . . . know each other?" I said.

"We're recent acquaintances, dear, but isn't she just so cute?"

Kate blushed. "Peggy!"

I was dumbfounded. "Wow. Okay, I had no idea. So . . . Peggy. How long have you been, you know, one of us?

"Oh, sugar, longer than you've been alive." She laughed. "But I've been on a . . . break."

"A break?"

"Yes, Jamie. Just a break. But now we're back!" She beamed.

"We?" I was so confused.

"She means the two of us, son."

That voice. I'd know it anywhere. I turned slowly . . .

"Sam. Let me guess, Peggy is your bride?"

"Well, who else could put up with me all these years?" Peggy slapped him on the shoulder and leaned into him. He wrapped an arm around her.

I pointed at Peggy. "You little spy! You knew the whole time, didn't you?"

"Well of course I did, hon! Everybody needs someone to keep an eye on 'em, right Sam?"

He nodded. "You're right, Peg. You're absolutely right."

There was a sudden noise.

I jumped back and looked around.

It was our combined groups, Flash's and ours, cheering. Guys were slapping each other on the back and yelling. Flash did a head count to ensure that all of his guys were still there. When he realized that they were, he gave a huge sigh of relief. He grinned broadly at Boogie, who was doing the same.

I saw that my old Charlie buddies were alive and well, too. The twins were doing a victory dance that would make any professional athlete proud. They even tried to teach it to Tiny, Mike, and Kevin. I have to admit, they were actually getting the hang of it.

Gunny stood to the side of it all and watched the troops like a proud father.

Bravo tended to their wounded. Even with that, the platoon was rowdy and excited. Of course, they reverted to good-natured ribbing of the flyboys from Alpha, whom they accused of trying to claim all the glory.

Eventually Boogie, Al, Gunny, and Flash joined us as we surveyed the battlefield. All that was left of the invading horde was some gently blowing black dust that was quickly dissipating in the evening breeze.

Something occurred to me as we stood there in the sunshine. "Flash."

He looked my way and nodded.

"How did you know we were going to be attacked today?"

Flash smiled at me. "Well, Jamie. I guess you're not the only one with spies."

I struggled to make sense of it until I saw him glance at Sam, who was studiously examining the ground.

So that's where Sam had been. He was working with Flash's guys.

"Well, Flash"—I held out my hand—"thank you for saving our bacon. I know you didn't have to come to the rescue, but I'm sure glad you did."

Flash shook my hand firmly. "Believe me, it was an honor and a privilege to get to fight with you." He grinned.

"Well, what now? Are we safe?" I said.

Boogie and Flash shared a look.

Then Boogie said, "Well, I think we've bought some time. I don't think they'll attack here anytime soon."

"Why is that, Boogie?" I asked.

"For one, the Malum usually look for weak spots and attack there. If they run into a tough area, they usually try to go around it and look for other areas to occupy. After today, I don't think they'll be in any shape to come back at us for a while."

"I like the way that sounds," I said.

"But," Boogie added, "they will eventually come back. This area is too important for them to ignore forever. So when they do, we've got to be ready."

Sam said, "Flash, from what I hear things aren't exactly quiet out your way."

We all looked at Flash, who said, "Yep. It's not as bad as things have gotten here. Not yet. But it's only a matter of time before they try to take us out. We'll be ready for them, but it sure wouldn't hurt my feelings to know we can count on y'all."

Boogie nodded.

Al said, "You can count on it, mayun."

Gunny just replied, "Ooh-rah!"

Flash stopped and looked at me, a questioning look on his face. "And you, Jamie? What do you say? Will you stand with us?"

Even Kate was looking at me expectantly, as if I was a leader. I guess I was. And I was humbled and proud to be counted as such.

I looked back at Flash and said to him simply, "Absolutely."

EPILOGUE

It's hard to believe that a few months ago I didn't even know this place existed. I'd never have believed it if I didn't, you know, get thrown into it. And I definitely would never have guessed that I would be shepherding a big group of flyers through the sky.

Why am I leading them? As the commander of Alpha platoon, I'm supposed to.

I know! Me, in charge of a platoon of flyers. How cool is that?

Don't worry, Boogie is safe and sound. He joins us when he can, but he's in charge of our whole outfit now. So, he's a bit busier than he used to be.

I think one of the best parts of leading Alpha is getting to teach the newbies to fly. They're a handful, but it keeps me on my toes. And I guess I get to be a pilot after all. Not a jet pilot, but something better, I think.

My old Charlie buddies are doing just great and are now seasoned veterans. Even the twins have earned the respect of the guys. They're now two of my best Alpha dudes.

Bravo still chides my men for being flyboys instead of being in the dirt with the ground troops. It's mostly good-natured and Al, who continues his command of Bravo Platoon, uses our rivalries to their fullest. He also uses our fights with the Malum as training material for the new guys.

Speaking of new guys, Gunny is still whipping new recruits into shape. I even saw one recruit return from a training run with a burned spot on his shirt and a dejected look on his face.

I feel ya, buddy.

Our numbers are growing by the week, and it won't be long before we will need to stand up another platoon. We're still discussing the makeup of this one, but it will likely be something a little different than Alpha or Bravo. The rescue and night missions showed us that we have to be prepared for anything, so we're giving it serious thought.

It turns out that during our battle, we employed some tactics that hadn't been used before. We're sharing them with Flash's guys, and they are doing the same with us. We're working much more closely together, now that we're traversing the distances more easily. Sam was the first one of us to figure out how to do it, so I guess we all owe him our lives.

I also owe Kate. Well, I probably doubly owe her, even though the whole sword-through-the-stomach thing was pushing it a little bit. I can think of worse people to owe something to, and, at this moment, I owe her dinner and a movie. The food will be pizza, and the movie will be a comedy, because I think we've had about all the drama that we can stand for a while.

Kate is still amazing, and I'm still a dork, so at least that much hasn't changed. We enjoy hanging out together and we speak often of her uncle and my dad. It turns out that they were a lot alike and they, for the better, affected us greatly. We've also decided that they have probably struck up a great friendship in Heaven.

I care a great deal for Kate. She seems to like me a lot, in spite of my lame sense of humor and my trouble with cheesecake. I'm working on the humor, because I don't think I can do cheesecake any better than I already have.

We're not sure where this relationship is going, and at the moment we don't care. We've already shared enough fear, sorrow, and excitement to last us awhile, so we're content just to be together when we can.

The doorways don't happen nearly as often as they used to, but we still get to train at least a few times each month. I know that when we do have our training sessions, it's serious business. But I can't help being happy to be there with the whole crew.

What's the future hold? I don't know. I'm living a day at time, but now I'm trying to live with purpose and hope and love. I love my brothers with whom I fight and I'm learning to love others, too. It's not easy, but I'm giving it a shot.

Speaking of the future, I need you to do something for me. We're always looking for some good recruits, so if you're having weird dreams or someone walks up to you and asks you to shake their hand . . . *run away!*

Just kidding, pal. We're always on the lookout for new talent and could sure use some good dudes, or dudettes, on our side. The pay's not great, but the people are awesome and maybe, just maybe, you'll learn to fly.

One bit of advice, though, if you ever see an electric doorway and you feel an urge to step through it, do me a favor . . . put on some pants.

No kiddin'.

"For our struggle is not against flesh and blood, but against the rulers, against the authorities, against the powers of this dark world and against the spiritual forces of evil in the heavenly realms."

– The Apostle Paul (Ephesians 6:12 NIV)

ACKNOWLEDGMENTS

The vast majority of my earthly gratitude is for my wife Carroll. I can't thank you enough for all that you do and are. You're my sounding board, my confidante, the love of my life and my best friend. God sure broke the mold when He made you.

I also want to thank Kristen Stieffel, editor extraordinaire, who had the temerity to be honest with me! She helped me see the error of my (writing) ways. Her earnest feedback and thoughtful suggestions made all kinds of difference.

To Crimson Rose . . . thank you for being my first beta reader. You suffered through some hideous early copies (I hope you've recovered okay), but gave me valuable insight. Thanks for hanging in there.

I want to specifically say thank you to Dr. Sam Lowry, Publisher and CEO of Ambassador International. Thank you for taking a chance on me and seeing something in EVOCATUS worth sharing with the world.

Last, but certainly not least, I thank God who loves me and whom I strive to please. Thank you for loving rough sheep like me.

Burke Speed

For more information about
Burke Speed
and
Evocatus
please visit:

www.burkespeed.com
www.facebook.com/Burke.Speed.Author
@BurkeSpeed
Instagram: burkespeed_author

For more information about
AMBASSADOR INTERNATIONAL
please visit:

www.ambassador-international.com
@AmbassadorIntl
www.facebook.com/AmbassadorIntl

If you enjoyed this book, please consider leaving us a review on Amazon, Goodreads, or our website.

More from Ambassador International

Ten years after a brutal war, cannibals and humans fight over the pieces of a hardscrabble existence.

Former Navy SEAL Doyle has been prowling the broken remnants of a devastated America for years. He is used to being on his own—with cannibals always a threat, alone is better. Until he has to stop at a city for repairs and provisions. One heroic act and now he's the leader of a small band of Christians determined to spread the gospel to the rumored neighboring cities. It's a task he's qualified for, but he didn't plan on the effect that this little group would have on him as they battle their way through cannibals, a deranged city mayor, and an evil super solider.

Solitary Man
by Eric Landfried

the reluctant
DISCIPLE
A NOVEL

"FAST PACED ... EERILY PROPHETIC."
—AWARD-WINNING AUTHOR D.M. WEBB

JIM O'SHEA

Ryan Kates is the host of a popular cable TV talk show focused on the para-normal, and with the recent worldwide increase in UFO sightings, hauntings, and demonic possessions, he's become one of the biggest names in the global media. When an old flame re-enters his life, she brings her family along for the ride and together they expose a demonic conspiracy of biblical proportions.

The Reluctant Disciple

by Jim O'Shea